To Alma & Bob —
I hope you have a fantastic
time reading this.
Glenn

ONE DEATH TOO MANY

BY
GLENN ICKLER

CYNTOMEDIA CORPORATION

Pittsburgh, PA

ISBN 1-56315-304-1

Paperback Fiction
© Copyright 2003 Glenn Ickler
All Rights Reserved
First Printing—2003
Library of Congress #2002113644

Request for information should be addressed to:

SterlingHouse Publisher, Inc.
7436 Washington Avenue
Pittsburgh, PA 15218
www.sterlinghousepublisher.com

SterlingHouse Publisher, Inc. is a company
of the CyntoMedia Corporation.

Book Design: Kathleen M. Gall
Cover Design: Eric C. Moresea—SterlingHouse Publisher, Inc.

Printed in the United States of America

ONE DEATH TOO MANY

A Mystery Novel

BY
GLENN ICKLER

for Jo

CHAPTER 1

TEN O'CLOCK SCHOLAR

The drop of sweat formed at Warren Mitchell's hairline, rolled slowly down the center of his forehead and gained speed as it moved along the inward-curving bridge of his nose. It hung suspended at the tip of the nose just long enough to create a tickling sensation before it dropped off and landed deep in the suntanned cleavage of the woman lying beneath him on the bed.

Jennifer Tilton giggled and said, "You're trying to drown me again."

"It's your own fault," Mitch said, looking into her twinkling hazel eyes. "You always heat me up way past the boiling point."

"Let's see just how far above boiling I can get you," she said, pulling his head back down to meet hers and planting a warm, wet kiss on his lips.

"Jen, I have to go to work today. I'm already going to be late." It was Monday morning and Mitch had spent Saturday night and all of Sunday in Jennifer's house, bed and arms. Now he needed to be on his way to his job, a reporter at the Daily Dispatch in downtown St. Paul, twenty miles from Jennifer Tilton's bluff-side home in the St. Croix River community of Afton.

"You always say that Monday is a slow news day; they won't miss you for awhile," Jennifer said. He felt her naked body move beneath his as she tried to squirm into a position that would allow him to enter her for the second time that morning.

"They missed me the last time I was late after I spent the night with you and Don wasn't at all happy about it. He needs me there." Don was Don O'Rourke, the Daily Dispatch city editor.

"I need you here."

"I'm not sure I could do it again even if I stayed."

"Getting old?" she asked in a teasing tone. "Body parts wearing out?"

"I'll show you whose parts are wearing out." Like a train gliding into a tunnel, he slipped smoothly into the offered opening and another half hour of exertion, exhilaration and exhaustion went by before he finally disentangled his sweat-slicked body from her demanding legs and arms. He pushed himself up from the bed and was walking toward the shower when the bedside phone rang. Jennifer frowned and answered it.

"Hi, Jennifer, this is Al Jeffrey," said the caller. "Is our ten-o'clock-scholar still there?" Alan Jeffrey was a Daily Dispatch photographer and Mitch's longtime college and Navy buddy. In fact, it was through Alan Jeffrey's efforts that Mitch had found a job at the Daily Dispatch.

"It's for you," she said to Mitch, who was about to turn on the shower water. "Your fellow news hound has tracked you down."

Mitch emerged and took the phone. "What's up?" he said.

"I can imagine one thing that's been up quite a bit," Al said. "But that's not what I'm calling about. The manager of your apartment building just called the office looking for you and she sounded kind of agitated. Haven't you been paying the rent?"

"Mrs. Peterson sounded agitated?"

"Said she needs to talk to you as soon as possible."

"I'll call her right now. And I'll see you in about an hour."

Mrs. Peterson was in her mid-eighties and lived across the hall from Mitch on the ground floor of a two-story brick building on Grand Avenue. He punched in the number and asked what he could do for her.

"I got a favor to ask," she said. Her speech still reflected her northern-Minnesota Scandinavian heritage. "I wonder if you could fill in as manager here for a couple of days while I'm away from home. My older sister died Saturday night and the funeral and burial are going to be in our hometown up near Duluth."

"I'm sorry to hear that you lost your sister," Mitch said. "Of course I'll help out with the building. Had your sister been ill very long?"

"She really hadn't been sick at all. She was eighty-eight and she was startin' to fail, so this spring she moved into one of those places that takes care of older people who can't keep house no more but ain't quite ready for a nursing home."

"So her death was unexpected?"

"Yah. It was awful sudden. She seemed to be doing pretty good."

"Again, I'm sorry. When are you leaving for Duluth?"

"It's Askov, actually, right up near Duluth. And I'm going up first thing tomorrow morning. That's why I needed to talk to you today."

"Okay. I'll drop by your apartment when I get home after work and you can fill me in on anything I need to know."

"What was that all about?" Jennifer asked when Mitch hung up.

"Mrs. Peterson's sister died and she wants me to fill in as building manager while she goes up to Askov to bury her. You've met Mrs. Peterson, haven't you?"

"Yes, the day you showed the kids and me your apartment. It's a shame she lost her sister."

"Yeah. She said it was very unexpected, so I guess it's kind of a double shock. Well, I'm off to the shower."

"Scrub your back?" Jennifer followed him into the shower and pressed the front of her wet body against the back of his. Although she was only five-feet-two-inches tall, her breasts would have done credit to a woman six inches taller and Mitch could feel the stand-up nipples pushing against his skin halfway down his back. It was those breasts that every man (and every woman, but not for the same reason) noticed first when meeting Jennifer Tilton.

"Jen, I really, really, really have to go to work."

She let go of what she had grasped with her right hand, unwrapped her arms from around his hips and backed away. "Okay, if you promise to come back tonight."

"I can't do that, either. I have to talk to Mrs. Peterson and find out what she wants me to do. She's leaving early tomorrow morning."

"You could come late and stay over."

"I'd better not. It's a long commute from here and you never let me get started on time. Don has been putting up with my being late after a night out here, but I don't want to push him too far." Mitch was drying his close-cropped, light brown hair with a fluffy pink bath towel, which was the only color Jennifer provided in the pink-and-purple bathroom adjoining her bedroom. "We put out a newspaper every day, remember?"

"How could I forget? All you want to do is go there." The lower lip of her Cupid's bow mouth was out slightly in a pout as she sat wet and naked on the toilet with the lid down, enjoying the ripple of his muscles as he dried himself. It was only two weeks past Memorial Day but already her body glowed with the early stage of an all-over tan. This sheen was her reward for lying for hours in the sun as bare as the day she was born. Mitch found himself admiring the way her skin color contrasted with a tiny gold ring that glistened in her navel.

"Not true," Mitch said. "All I really want to do is make love to you, but I have to go to work because you refuse to support me in the manner I wish to become accustomed."

"Sorry about that. Tim's insurance money will just keep me and the kids fed and clothed for awhile until I rejoin the working class." Her ex-husband, Timothy Tilton, had been killed the previous September in a bloody gun battle when his gang of illegal military arms dealers was attacked by another. Jennifer's two small children were the beneficiaries of Timothy's modest life insurance policy and the family was living on that money.

His lanky body dried, Mitch went to the sink, drew an electric razor out of the vanity drawer and ran it over his neck, cheeks and chin, then gave a couple of quick nips to the ends of his neatly-trimmed, light brown moustache. Satisfied that his face was presentable to any prospective news source, he went back into the bedroom and dug into the overnight bag he brought along each time he spent the night with Jennifer. She wrapped herself in a pale pink, terry cloth robe and sat on the bed to watch.

Mitch pulled on a pair of khaki trousers and a light blue, short-sleeved shirt, quickly knotted a red-white-and-blue striped tie around his neck, zipped up the overnight bag and spread his arms. Jennifer went to him and turned up her round, snub-nosed face, which was framed by a tumble of light brown curls, and Mitch leaned down for a goodbye kiss. At six-foot-one, Mitch was eleven inches taller than the hundred-pound brunette. Sometimes when he bent to kiss her, or lifted her off her feet to bring her lips up to his level, he thought about what his mother had said to him when he started dating.

"You're tall, Warren," she had told him. "That means you should look for tall girls to go out with. A short girl can go out with anyone, but a tall girl needs a tall man in order to look good and you shouldn't waste your height on short girls." He had followed her dictum and dated tall girls all through high school and college.

His wife, Karen, whom he met at his first Navy duty station, had been tall—five-nine—and slender and vivacious. Vivacious, that is, until she and their newborn baby boy were killed in a horrific head-on crash on a California highway.

"I'll call you tonight," he said to Jennifer on his way out the bedroom door.

"Drive safe," she said, blowing him a final kiss.

"Don't worry, I want to come back to you in one piece." He walked out past the family room where Tracy Tilton, who had just turned seven, and Tony Tilton, soon to be six, were enjoying the first morning of their summer vacation from school by watching cartoons on television.

"Bye, kids," Mitch said as he went past.

"Bye, Uncle Mitch," said Tracy and Tony in unison.

It was Tracy and Tony who first brought Warren Mitchell into contact with Jennifer Tilton. The children had been kidnapped and the reporter-pho-tographer duo of Warren Mitchell and Alan Jeffrey, who covered the story for the Daily Dispatch, had actually rescued the children and carried them safely home to Jennifer. She showed her appreciation by inviting Mitch, who had been living alone and celibate for the three years following the California tragedy, into her bed.

Now, in Mitch's heart at least, what had begun as a physical attraction between two lonely people, was blossoming into something more substantial. He felt himself falling in love with Jennifer and with her two little children.

After Karen's death, Mitch promised himself he would never become emotionally involved with a woman again. Take them to bed and then move on would be his modus operandi. But he soon found that Jennifer's charms extended well beyond the bedroom. She was witty and clever and devoted to her children. He actually found himself thinking about a second marriage, but he hadn't summoned the courage to say that to Jennifer.

She, in turn, was still reeling from a rapid-fire series of painful events: a nasty divorce, the kidnapping of her children and the violent death of her criminal ex-husband. She had invited Mitch into her bed to enjoy a night of comfort, not to begin a long-term commitment. She immediately found herself enjoying his company, both in and out of the bedroom, and sometimes asked herself what she wanted from their relationship, but her primary concern was making a life for her fatherless children.

On his way to the car, Mitch paused a minute to take in the view. From her late father, Jennifer had inherited a sprawling L-shaped rambler, high on the bluffs above the St. Croix River. On this bright June morning, the fields and forests below the level of the house formed a shimmering green carpet and the ripples on the river beyond glistened like flashing strobe lights in the sunshine. A couple of small aluminum boats—one silver, one red—occupied by fishermen lucky enough to be either vacationing or retired, added another note of serenity to what could have been a Winslow Homer painting. Reluctantly, Mitch got into his aging, blue Honda Civic and started toward St. Paul.

The rush hour traffic had already passed through the Twin Cities suburbs, so the drive in from the River Hills section of Afton took only half an hour. Mitch parked the Civic five blocks from the Daily Dispatch in a Lowertown ramp where he had a monthly contract. Each time he left the ramp, he looked with amusement at the intriguing sign that read "No Trespassing Except Patrons" and a few minutes later he was at his desk in the newsroom perusing a packet of clippings he found there, along with a note instructing him to do a follow-up on that story for the city edition.

Don O'Rourke was busy at his desk dealing with two other reporters and didn't see Mitch come in. However, Alan Jeffrey appeared at Mitch's side within minutes. Shorter by four inches, but more muscular than Mitch, Al was dressed in the more casual clothes worn by newspaper photographers—in this case, blue jeans and a plaid, short-sleeve shirt. His round, usually-smiling face was encircled by a black beard, clipped to a moderate length and his upper lip was adorned with a matching moustache.

"Nice of you to drop by before lunch," Al said, with laughter in his brown eyes.

"What can I say? Jennifer won't let me go without a goodbye ... well, you know. And we're making up for lost time; she was gone almost a week for her high school class reunion in New Jersey."

"I never knew you were such a great lover."

"That's me—the great lover. Any time you want advice about your love life, just write to Dear Mitchy."

"Speaking of writing to Dear Mitchy, what did Mrs. Peterson have on her mind?"

"Her sister died suddenly last night and she wants me to handle any problems that come up in the building while she goes up to Askov to bury her."

"What did her sister die of?"

"She didn't say. Just said it was unexpected because she hadn't really been sick. What the hell, she was eighty-eight. Anything could have stopped working."

"That's the truth. Oh well, maybe Mrs. Peterson will feed you supper."

"Maybe. So what's going on here this morning?"

"Not much, unfortunately. However, I do have a chance for some freelance work. I'm meeting this afternoon with a guy who is looking for a photographer because he thinks one of his former employees who is drawing full disability pay is working at a strip club in Minneapolis. The guy supposedly has a bad back from lifting boxes at this guy's loading dock and is suing him for damages in addition to collecting disability."

"Well, that should bring in a few extra bucks."

"I'm going to need a few extra bucks. Carol is taking Kristin to the orthodontist today. She just turned eleven and it looks like it's time for braces."

"You might say you're facing the jaws of adversity," Mitch said.

"I'm preparing to bite the bullet."

"Ah, the joys of raising children," Mitch said. But there was envy in his heart as he watched his friend walk away. Still, he thought, if life continued on its present course with Jennifer, some day he might have a hand in bringing up Tony and Tracy Tilton.

CHAPTER 2

NO LAUGHING MATTER

Mitch arrived at his Grand Avenue apartment a little after five. He picked up the Sunday and Monday morning papers from in front of his door, turned the key and went in. Within seconds he was greeted warmly by his big, handsome roommate, Sherlock Holmes.

"How are you, old buddy?" Mitch asked.

"Meowr," said Sherlock, rubbing his furry head against Mitch's ankles.

"You must get kind of lonely when I spend the whole weekend in Afton," Mitch said as he leaned down to pet the well-fed, black-and-white tomcat. "Poor old Sherlock. You'd understand better why I stay out there with Jennifer if I hadn't had you fixed." Sherlock had been dumped off in the neighborhood by a previous owner and had adopted Mitch after hanging around the back door of the apartment building. Mitch had taken the half-starved animal to a veterinarian for shots and, at the vet's suggestion, a neutering job.

There were still a couple of bites of cat food and a bit of water in Sherlock's dishes, but Mitch dumped them both and refilled them with fresh provisions. He rubbed the cat's head and back a couple more times and said, "Sorry, pal, but I have to go see Mrs. Peterson before I can settle down. I'll see you in a few minutes."

Mitch knocked on Mrs. Peterson's door and heard her shuffling footsteps approach, then stop as she looked through the peephole to see who was knocking. After a moment, she opened the door and invited him in. She was white-haired and not much over five feet tall, but she was sturdy looking and she moved briskly for a person with eighty-year-old joints. She wore a Nordic-patterned sweater that was too warm for the season, loose-fitting gray slacks and a big pair of slippers that looked like koala bears.

"Sit down, please, Mr. Mitchell," she said. "Did you have your supper?"

"I've got a hot dish in the oven at my place," he lied, not wishing to intrude on her, even though the air smelled wonderfully spicy from something cooking on the kitchen stove.

"Oh, that's too bad; I got more Swedish meatballs here than one old lady can eat. I'll send some home with you and you can put them in the fridge till tomorrow."

Tomorrow, hell, he thought, they'll be gone in ten minutes after I get home. Aloud, he thanked Mrs. Peterson and asked about her sister.

"Grace's death was a real shock," she said. "She's been in this long-term care place since the first of May and she seemed to be doing just fine. She wasn't real active no more, but she'd just had a check-up the day before by a doctor who comes in there and the nurse said he never mentioned no serious problems. But when she didn't show up for breakfast on Sunday morning, someone went to her apartment to see if she was okay and they found her lay-ing dead in her bed."

"This wasn't her regular family doctor who saw her?"

"No, it was a doctor who just treats old people."

"A geriatric specialist?"

"Yah, that's what they called him. He comes in and takes care of the old folks at Cedar Gardens as part of what they pay for. I'm not sure what his exact name is; it sounded like Doctor Symphony or something like that. He come here from India originally. His main office is somewhere in Maplewood and he sees patients in the clinic at Cedar Gardens a couple times a week. Works it around his regular office hours. They called him right away when they found Grace, but she was past help."

"Did this Doctor Symphony tell you what caused your sister's death?"

"He had a fancy name for it, but he said what it meant was heart failure."

"Well, I'm sorry for your loss."

"I'm still in shock from the news," she said. "Grace was so cheerful and full of life when I saw her Saturday. But anyways, you're not here to listen to my troubles. I want to give you the master key to the apartments and a list of people to call if you have any trouble with the electric or the plumbing. I'll put up a notice for the tenants to call you if there's any problems before I get back. The funeral is Wednesday, so I'll probably be home some time on Thursday.

"No problem," Mitch said. "Take as long as you need. I don't have any plans other than my regular working hours until the weekend."

"Thank you. Let me get you the key and a pan of meatballs."

She went into the kitchen and returned a few minutes later with the mas-ter key, a sheet of paper with a list of names and phone numbers, a covered dish that emitted a tantalizing smell and half a loaf of homemade, whole wheat bread. "The bread won't keep till I come home," she said. Mitch almost said yes it would if she put it in her freezer, but he caught himself just in time. Why turn down something so good when she obviously was so capable of replenishing her own supply?

"Thanks," he said. "Have a safe trip and if there's anything else I can do, please let me know."

"Thank you, Mr. Mitchell. Them meatballs is especially good if you put them over a nice pile of hot egg noodles. You enjoy them and I should be seeing you on Thursday, then."

When Mitch walked through the door into his own apartment carrying the savory meatballs, he was greeted with astounding enthusiasm by Sherlock Holmes. The cat all but climbed his pants leg in an effort to reach the source of the ambrosial aroma that drifted downward from the pan.

"Okay, pal, I'll share the goodies with you," Mitch said. "But you only get one because we wouldn't want to load you up with cholesterol, would we?"

Sherlock's reply indicated that he wasn't at all concerned about cholesterol. Mitch thought briefly about Mrs. Peterson's suggestion of serving the meatballs over egg noodles, decided they would take too long to cook (if he even had any in the cupboard) and gobbled the meatballs right out of Mrs. Peterson's dish.

As he always did upon arriving home, Alan Jeffrey greeted his blonde, blue-eyed wife, Carol, with a hug and a kiss and a question: "Hi, Gorgeous, what's the joke of the day?" Al didn't care to devote much time to the world of computers and electronic networks, but his junior high school teacher wife was addicted to the machine in the corner of their dining room. The joke of the day was a regular feature that arrived via e-mail from a friend.

"I think it can wait awhile," Carol said. "There's a message on the answering machine for you to call your Uncle Charlie's wife."

"Diana?"

"Yes, believe it or not."

"That is strange. Did she say what she wanted?"

"Just that she needs to tell you about Uncle Charlie."

"Is there time to call her before supper?"

"You've got fifteen minutes, which is about fourteen and a half more than you've spoken to her in the last two years."

"Well, it must be damn important if she's willing to call me. Here goes." Al punched in the number.

"This is Al," he said when Diana answered. "What's up with Uncle Charlie?"

"He's in the hospital," she said. "He's had a stroke."

"Oh, God! How bad?"

"His left side is paralyzed and he can't talk. He's awake and he responds with his eyes and his right hand; he just can't say words. The doctors think it's possible his speech will come back, but they're not sure about the paralysis."

"Where is he? Can he have visitors?"

"He's in Regions Hospital, room 424, and he can have family. That's why I called you."

"I'll get over there right after supper. Carol too, if we can find somebody to take care of the kids on short notice."

"I'm sure he'd like to see you. His doctor said seeing family might help him recover. And contrary to what you're thinking, I do want him to get well."

"I wasn't thinking anything like that," Al said. "I'm grateful that you called."

"It wasn't easy, knowing how you feel about me."

"Shit!" said Al as he hung up. He explained what had happened to Carol and hunted for their list of baby sitters. Just as Carol was summoning everyone to supper, he found a sixteen-year-old neighbor who could come for a couple of hours to look after Kristin, whose eleventh birthday party balloons were still floating around the living room, and Kevin, who was a month short of nine.

Al told the children that Uncle Charlie was very sick, that Dad and Mom were going to the hospital to see he and concluded with, "Michelle is coming over to stay with you while we're gone."

The rest of the meal was eaten in virtual silence as the thoughts of both adults turned to Uncle Charlie, who had long been Alan Jeffrey's favorite relative. Al's father had been born with a heart defect and he died during Al's senior year in high school. Charlie, who was Al's father's older brother and had no children, had stepped forward immediately to fill the void. Uncle Charlie was there for all the big occasions in Al's life and was on hand whenever Al needed advice, a helping hand or just a conversation with an older, wiser man.

When Uncle Charlie's wife, Mildred, a long-time cigarette smoker, developed lung cancer and died, Charlie was left alone in a huge house in Roseville at the age of seventy. Al helped fill the void by frequently inviting Uncle Charlie to enjoy Carol's cooking, taking him on several fishing trips and just generally being available when companionship was needed.

However, the tight bond between nephew and uncle had been broken two years ago when Charlie, then seventy-three and still working part-time as a realtor, had married his secretary, Diana Davidson, after a whirlwind courtship that included a Caribbean cruise. Diana was a dark-haired, dark-eyed beauty, but she was forty years younger than Charlie and even a year younger than Al. Charlie had socked away a substantial nest egg during his long and successful career in real estate and Al suspected that Diana's interest in his well-to-do uncle was not altogether romantic.

Unfortunately, Al had let those feelings slip out at the wedding reception, which was a small affair for family and close friends held at the Minnesota Club in downtown St. Paul. After several glasses of wine, Al was dancing with the bride and feeling distrustful of her motives while trying to make small talk, when Diana commented on how lucky she was to have "captured the heart of such a sweet man as Charlie."

Al had noted that it was a lucky catch for her and made the mistake of adding, "But it's not surprising you caught him. After all, in mythology, Diana was the huntress, wasn't she?"

She had stopped in mid-waltz, stepped back and said, "What do you mean by that remark?"

"I mean that Charlie's quite a trophy for a woman who is hunting for security."

"Are you saying that I'm marrying Charlie for his money?"

"Well, he is living very comfortably and with the age difference he's likely to leave you quite a bundle when he passes on to that great real estate agency in the sky."

"I can't believe you're saying this to me on my wedding day!"

"Would you rather have me wait until after the honeymoon—providing Charlie survives it?"

"Fuck you!" she had said in a voice that carried through the reception hall as she turned and walked away. Those were the last words she had spoken to him, except for the times she had answered the phone when Al made a call to Uncle Charlie.

To his regret, Al saw very little of Uncle Charlie after the wedding. It seemed that the kindly old man who had always been available to Al for a day of fishing, a trip to the ballpark or a backyard barbecue and a beer, no longer was able to find time to spend with his nephew. Al was sure he knew why.

As he ate his dinner, he found himself hoping that Uncle Charlie's stroke would be a means of reconciling their differences and regaining the old, warm feelings. If his uncle's illness was not too severe, it could be a blessing in disguise.

CHAPTER 3

FROM GLOOMY TO GAY

"So what else is going on in the world?" Al asked as he and Carol drove toward Regions Hospital.

"Not much. My students were their usual, nasty selves today, but I didn't get to kill any of them. It's lucky for all of us that tomorrow's the last day of school."

Carol taught seventh and eighth-grade English at a school near their home on Hamline Avenue in the Midway district of St. Paul. It was a job that wore her down gradually during the year, so that by the final week of classes she was more than ready for the summer break. Al had noticed that her clear, Nordic complexion was looking paler than usual as the school year dragged on into the second week of June and when she took off her gold-rimmed glasses these days, he could see small, dark circles under her eyes. By nature, slender-hipped and small-breasted, she had lost some weight during the school year and her clothes hung a little loose on her five-foot, six-inch frame. Carol needed to get away from those junior high kids.

Regions Hospital is a large public, facility located three blocks north of the heart of the downtown St. Paul shopping area. Because its emergency room has an outstanding reputation, ambulance drivers automatically go there unless the patient's family requests otherwise. Diana had sent her stricken husband to Regions Hospital, knowing he would receive the best emergency care possible.

Diana was seated in a chair next to Uncle Charlie's bed when Al and Carol arrived. She stood and whispered, "Charlie is asleep." Quietly they exchanged stiff, self-conscious greetings and Al asked how Uncle Charlie was doing.

"He still can't talk," Diana said. "But his regular doctor was examining him when I got here and he said not to worry, that things will get better for Charlie."

"Was that good old Doctor Miller, the guy that Uncle Charlie likes to go golfing with?" Al said.

"Good old Doctor Miller has retired and moved to Florida where he can play fourteen rounds of golf a week. Charlie's been seeing a new doctor, a man who comes from India originally. He's a very gentle, calming person. He's not a golfer, but Charlie likes him a lot."

"Well, as long as he takes good care of the old boy."

"He's much quieter than Doctor Miller, but he seems to be very competent."

They stood without speaking for a few uncomfortable minutes. While Al seemed to be staring at the sleeping figure in the bed, he was studying Diana out of the corner of his eye. He was surprised at how pale and drawn she looked. He remembered her as lush and vibrant, with a complexion that glowed like the women in those skin moisturizer commercials.

Al finally broke the awkward silence. "Has Uncle Charlie been sick or did this come on all of a sudden?"

"He's been feeling kind of up and down energy-wise, but not really sick," Diana said. "He had a check-up with Doctor Sinfahdi a few weeks ago and got some iron pills for anemia, but otherwise he seemed to be okay."

"Doctor Sinfahdi is the new Doctor Miller?"

"That's right."

Just then Uncle Charlie's brown eyes flicked open. Al raised a hand in greeting and said, "Hi, Uncle Charlie" and walked to the bed. Uncle Charlie blinked his eyes and weakly opened his right hand to grasp Al's. The white-haired man's skin was so pallid it was almost transparent, the left side of his face sagged and his left eyelid drooped almost to the closing point, but the right side of his face moved into a hint of a smile. He opened his mouth, but no words came out.

"You don't need to talk, Uncle Charlie," Al said. "We love you and we're pulling for you to get well. I hear your doctor thinks you'll be getting better soon."

Uncle Charlie nodded his head ever so slightly to indicate agreement. Carol came to the bedside and put her hand on Uncle Charlie's and said she hoped he'd get well quickly. Al and Carol filled him in on how the kids were doing in school and how they were doing at work and then ran out of small talk. They discovered that chatting with a person who is involuntarily mute is not an easy exercise.

"Well, we'd better go and let you get some rest," Al said finally. Uncle Charlie's response was a blank stare, which Al took to mean, "Okay, coward, go away and leave me staring at the wall just because I can't talk back to you."

At five-foot-eight and 140 pounds, Charlie was a short, wiry man, but he looked smaller than life, lying helpless and speechless in the hospital bed. Al found himself wondering if the doctor was being overly optimistic in his prognosis, as Diana followed them to the door and bid them goodbye.

"Keep us posted," Al said. "If there's anything at all we can do, let us know. I think I'm the only blood relative he has left."

"Yes, I think you are," Diana said. "You'd be inheriting all his property when he goes if I hadn't married him." She turned quickly and walked back into the room.

"Obviously she hasn't forgotten your oh-so-clever remark at the wedding," Carol said as they walked toward the elevator.

"Obviously not," Al said. "Sticking my foot in my mouth that day made me a shoe-in for the title of biggest heel she's ever met."

"At least she hasn't had to listen to puns like that for the last two years."

"Maybe avoiding my tongue is her sole reason for staying pissed off. Could she just be stringing me along?"

On Tuesday morning, Alan Jeffrey was a half-hour late for work. After returning home from the hospital, he had called his mother who still lived in the house where he grew up in a rural area southeast of St. Paul, and told her about Uncle Charlie. They talked about old times for awhile and she said she would drive in to visit Uncle Charlie the next day. Then Al sat up awhile trying to read and found it impossible to concentrate on the book.

He went to bed after Carol was already asleep and couldn't settle his mind enough to doze off. Uncle Charlie had been the strong man in his life since Al was seventeen. Even these last two years, when they rarely saw each other, it was just good to know that Uncle Charlie was still going strong. The vision of him lying in that hospital bed, unable to talk and with half his body limp and useless, kept playing through Al's mind and sleep just would not come. He finally dropped off by something after three and when Carol tried to wake him at six-thirty, he groaned, rolled over and went back to sleep until a few minutes after seven. He finally dragged himself out of bed and went through the motions of his morning routine.

"You look like you lost your best friend," Mitch said as Al walked into the newsroom at 8:30.

"I almost did. Uncle Charlie had a stroke yesterday."

"Oh, no! How bad?"

"He can't talk and his left side is paralyzed, but his doctor told Diana that things probably would get better."

"Well, that's hopeful anyway. Did you go to see him?"

"Yeah. He looks awful. I couldn't get to sleep all night after seeing him that way."

"So how'd you find out about it? His wife doesn't speak to you, does she?"

"Diana actually called me. I have to give her credit for that. But she did let it be known that she hasn't forgotten what I said at the wedding."

"Ah, yes, your wonderful gift of tact."

"That thing about Diana the Huntress started out to be a joke, Mitch. But she got so damn defensive and I'd had just enough to drink that I blurted out what I was really thinking."

"Do you still think that?"

"I don't know what to think. Every time I talked to Uncle Charlie after that it sounded like she was making him very happy, so maybe she wasn't just hunting for the first rich guy who came along."

"Well, if we stay in this business, we'll never have to worry about some woman chasing us for our money," Mitch said. "And speaking of money, what happened with the guy you saw about the freelance job yesterday afternoon? Is it a live one?"

Al had met with a man named Richard Bombardier who operated a small delivery and shipping service called Bombs Away Trucking, located on North Snelling Avenue. One of Bombardier's employees had injured his back while loading a truck and was collecting full disability because his doctor had certified that he was unable to do any sort of physical work. This employee was also suing Bombardier's company for damages, claiming the injury was caused by unsafe working conditions. Bombardier said he had heard that the man was working as an entertainer in a nightclub called Hurley's Hangout near the University of Minnesota campus in Minneapolis.

Al explained this to Mitch, finishing with, "Bombardier needs somebody to go to the club and see if the guy is really doing something physical and, if he is, get some photos for him to use in court."

"Why doesn't Bombardier go?"

"He's afraid the guy would see him and duck out. It's not a real big place, so it's hard to get lost in the crowd, especially with a camera."

"Did you say you'd do it?"

"I said I'd go over and check it out. Want to go along? I would hate to indulge in such stimulating entertainment without giving you the opportunity to share in my good fortune."

"Just what kind of stimulating entertainment are we talking about?"

"The dancers are a little different, shall we say?"

"How different? Are they old, fat, flat-chested, what?"

"They're female impersonators."

"Oh, shit! And I suppose next you're going to tell me this is a gay bar we're going to."

"With deductive powers like that, my friend, you should become an investigative reporter for a large daily newspaper."

"I should have my head examined for ever agreeing to work at the same place you do. Thanks to sharing various assignments with you, I've been beat up, shot at and grilled by a very nasty FBI agent. Now I will probably be able to add being propositioned in a gay bar to my life's list of thrills."

"I'll try to fight them off of you," Al said. "But with that sandy moustache and those baby blue eyes, you're so pretty it might be more than I can manage."

"Maybe you can go as a cross-dresser; with your sexy black beard, you'd look great in a dress and high heels."

"You couldn't drag me there in women's clothes."

"Don't try to skirt the issue. When do you plan to attend this cultural event?"

"How about tonight? After I visit Uncle Charlie at Regions?"

"I guess that'll work. I have to hang around the building part of the evening in case any tenants have complaints, but I'd guess any time after nine would be okay."

"Hey, no problem. The action doesn't really get going until well after nine at a place like that."

"There is one problem," Mitch said. "How the hell will we know this guy if we see him?"

"There is a solution to your problem. Bombardier takes mug shots of all his employees for their personnel files. He gave me this shot of the guy, whose name, by the way, is Dennis O'Neal." Al pulled a glossy, black-and-white, three-by-five photo of a young man staring straight at the camera like the subjects on a ten-most-wanted poster. His hair was matted in grungy-looking dreadlocks and his face was long and bony, with a couple of zits showing on the forehead. The straight-on camera angle made it impossible to gauge the length of Dennis O'Neal's nose, but the bridge was high, the nostrils were wide and Mitch was willing to wager a week's pay that the forward protrusion was substantially above average.

"A real beauty queen," Mitch said.

"Actually, he might be a two-way swinger and not strictly a queen," Al said. "Bombardier said he'd gotten complaints about O'Neal making suggestive remarks to employees of both sexes."

They spent the lunch hour discussing what they might wear, so not to be conspicuous in the crowd at Hurley's Hangout. Mitch found himself wishing he knew the whereabouts of Jennifer Tilton's gay former bodyguard, Piotr Borlishevski, who had long since come out of the closet, but who might have left some useful articles of clothing in there. Piotr had been hired to keep Jennifer's ex-husband from stealing the children from her, but after the death of the ex-husband, who had been paying substantial child support, Jennifer couldn't afford to keep Piotr as a live-in baby sitter. Piotr's wardrobe, or his fashion advice, would be useful now, but he had gone to live with a boyfriend.

After lunch, on a whim, Mitch called Jennifer and asked if Piotr had left any clothing items behind.

"Why on earth do you want to know that?" she asked.

"I'm going to a costume party," Mitch said.

"Without me?"

"This one you don't want to go to. Al and I are doing a little free-lance work at a gay bar tonight."

"And you want something Piotr would wear?"

"You got it."

"I'm pretty sure he didn't leave a thing. He was very meticulous, you know."

"So what did he wear when he went off to see his boyfriend on the weekends? He used to go into the Cities on Sundays, didn't he?"

"I remember he had a purple shirt that he liked a lot. He wore bright colors, mostly. Are you looking to get picked up or what?"

"Oh, please! We're looking to be part of the crowd so we don't draw attention to ourselves as a couple of straight stiffs."

"I could loan you a dress and a handbag."

"I'd respond to that, but Al and I have been through that entire line of puns already. So, I'll just purse my lips and stay quiet. I won't let you drag so much as one more word out of me."

"Have a good time with the guys, sweetie," Jennifer said, getting ready to hang up. "But not too good."

CHAPTER 4

HANGING OUT AT HURLEY'S

Alan Jeffrey arrived home at 5:15 to find Carol alone in the house. "The kids are over at the playground shooting baskets," she said, pressing her body tightly against him as they hugged. She was wearing faded jeans and a pastel blue T-shirt and had her hair pulled back in a pony tail that made her look almost like a teenager.

"Both of them?" Al asked.

"It's a mixed group. Girls are allowed to shoot baskets with the boys as long as the girls don't do it better."

"Okay, so what's the joke of the day?"

Before Carol could respond, Kristin and Kevin came charging through the front door and the conversation took on a much more modest tone.

After supper, Alan Jeffrey went alone to visit Uncle Charlie at Regions Hospital. The plan was to go directly from the hospital to Grand Avenue to pick up Warren Mitchell and head out to Minneapolis. Al had dug around in his closet and found a pair of bright blue slacks, a gift from his mother that he had never worn. In a dresser drawer he found a red-and-blue striped, short-sleeved golfing shirt, a birthday gift from his children that he wore once or twice a year so they wouldn't think he didn't like it. He decided to change into these at Mitch's apartment rather than to appear in this costume at the hospital.

"Maybe you should put them on now," Carol had said. "Seeing you in that get-up might shake some words out of Uncle Charlie."

"It would more likely give him another stroke," Al had said.

Diana was at Uncle Charlie's bedside, holding his right hand in both of hers, when Al entered the room. The color had come back to her cheeks and she looked more like the luscious brunette beauty he remembered from the wedding. Charlie's color also was better and his grip was firmer when Al grasped his good hand in greeting.

"He still can't talk," Diana said. "But Doctor Sinfahdi says there's some sign of improvement."

"You look better," Al said to Uncle Charlie. "They'll be kicking you out of here before you know it."

"That's what I told him," Diana said. "We're going to set up his bed right in front of the big window in the family room so he can watch the bird feeders and see the flowers bloom."

"You must be practically living in the hospital right now."

"Just about. I slept in this chair last night and went home for a while this morning to take a shower and put on some fresh clothes. I got back here just as the doctor was coming in to look at Charlie."

Al pulled another chair to the bedside, sat down and told Uncle Charlie about the mission he and Mitch planned to set off on later in the evening. The right side of Uncle Charlie's mouth turned slightly upward in a half-smile and his eyes brightened a bit during the story. When Al finished speaking and sat back, Uncle Charlie opened his mouth, but again, no words came out. His eyes showed frustration and he struggled again to make a sound.

"Relax, Uncle Charlie," Al said. "Give yourself time to heal. Doctor Whatshisname will have you chatting with us before you know it."

Uncle Charlie blinked his eyes and then closed them. This is a man who loves to joke and tell stories, Al thought. The inability to speak must be driving him up the wall. Al briefly considered passing on the joke of the day to Uncle Charlie, but decided it might not go over well with Diana at this particular moment. So he said his goodbyes, again told Diana to let him know if there was anything he could do and took his leave.

Ten minutes later he was knocking on Warren Mitchell's door, which opened to reveal his partner decked out in green golfing slacks and a baggy purple pullover purchased that afternoon at the Salvation Army store.

"You're gorgeous," Al said, patting Mitch on the cheek. "Mind if I come in and slip into something comfortable?"

"Do hurry," Mitch said. "I just can't wait to see those lovely dancers."

"I'll step lively," Al said, heading into the bedroom followed by Sherlock Holmes. Sherlock had been keeping his distance from Mitch ever since he donned his unusually gaudy get-up and now the big tomcat seemed pleased to encounter a more familiar figure. Poor Sherlock, his pleasure didn't last long.

Hurley's Hangout was on the fringe of an area known as Dinkytown, where University of Minnesota students and faculty members could purchase anything they wanted, from books and breakfast to pot and prostitutes. Al parked his red Toyota in the small lot at the rear of the building, noting that there weren't many other cars there. "I hope we're not too early for the floor show," he said.

"Where's your camera?" Mitch asked.

"This is a dry run," Al said. "Tonight we check out the joint to see what kind of equipment we need. Never fear, tonight's time will be figured into my bill."

They were greeted just inside the front door by a very large man with a shaved head, wearing dark clothes and a huge gold ring in his left ear lobe, who informed them that there was a five-dollar cover charge. He looked them up and down while they dug out the money and offered the backs of their hands to be rubber-stamped. When they got further inside, they saw why the man had given them such a thorough examination. Almost everyone else in the dimly-lit barroom was dressed in everyday street attire. Khaki slacks were much in evidence, along with the same array of light and dark-colored shirts one would find in any straight bar in the city. Only an occasional bit of purple or something bright could be seen as they scanned the crowd.

"Shit!" said Mitch. "We stand out like a red-hot stove in a snowstorm."

"Thank God it's dark in here," Al said. "Let's grab that table over on the side and stay as far back from the stage as we can so we don't spook our boy."

The stage, located in a corner opposite the bar, was small, maybe eight feet by ten, and not very high. A curtained opening at stage right apparently led to whatever dressing room facilities were behind the wall. At the back of the stage, against the wall, was a table with a tape player that was hooked up to a pair of heavy-duty amplifiers.

It was, as Al had said, quite dark in the room. Thick swirls of smoke, not all of it from tobacco, reduced visibility even more.

"We'll both need to check into Hazelden just from breathing the air in here," Mitch said. Hazelden was a treatment center for chemical abusers where he had gone two years earlier to break his dependence on alcohol.

"I'll be too high to drive home," Al said. "We should have brought a portable oxygen tank."

A waiter appeared beside their table. Al ordered a beer and Mitch ordered a Coke. A minute later the drinks were on the round table, which was barely big enough to hold them.

"Bigger crowd in here than I expected from the number of cars in the parking lot," Al said.

"Must be a lot of foot traffic. Between the booze and the pot, it's a good thing they don't all drive."

Suddenly the stage was illuminated by a spotlight. A short, bald man, dressed in a paisley-print shirt that was stretched so tight across his bulging belly that he could barely button it and a pair of khaki pants that were slung below the paunch, stepped onto the platform. He picked up a microphone that had been lying next to the tape player and announced that the first show of the evening was about to begin.

"Let's have a hand for our opening performer who comes to us direct from a highly-acclaimed engagement in one of the finest clubs in San Francisco, California," he said. "Let's hear it for Big Betty Boobs from Biloxi!"

The applause was not deafening, but the music soon was. Big Betty Boobs, who pranced onto the stage in four-inch spike heels, stood well over six feet tall and looked to weigh about two-hundred and ten. "She" stuck a tape into the machine, punched the play button and cranked the volume to the threshold of pain.

Big Betty Boobs wore a curly blonde wig, a heavy layer of lipstick and a long, full-skirted, bright turquoise dress, trimmed with layers of ruffles below the waist and glittering sequins on the tight-fitting top. The bodice barely held in what appeared to be at least a forty-four-inch, double-E-cup bust. Gyrating slowly at first, Big Betty Boobs moved about the stage, leaned down to say something obscene to the line of young men seated at the edge of the platform, which sent them into gales of laughter, and then gradually picked up both speed and intensity.

"Those heels must be made of titanium to support all that weight," Al said.

"The stage must be made out of twelve inch butcher block or they'd punch right through," said Mitch. Big Betty Boobs' dance evolved into a series of bumps and grinds, punctuated by increasingly enthusiastic whoops from the spectators and ended abruptly when the tape ran out. Big Betty Boobs then quickly yanked down the front of the turquoise dress, taking with it the attached, overstuffed bra to reveal a flabby, hairy, male chest. Now boobless, Big Betty whipped off the blonde wig, exposing a thinning head of hair with more than a few flecks of gray and took a bow. Without the wig, Big Betty Boobs looked like a candidate for AARP membership.

"Well, that sure as hell ain't our guy," Al said.

"You think our boy will be a dancer?"

"What other type of entertainers do they have here?"

"Maybe a comedian?"

"Don't make me laugh."

"Well, whatever he does, I hope he comes on soon. I'd rather be home watching reruns of 'Who Wants to be a Millionaire' than sitting through this kind of shit."

"Different strokes for different folks," said Al as the potbellied master of ceremonies stepped up to introduce the next performer.

It was the third dancer on the program, introduced as Lou'siana Lou, who caught their attention. Lou had a younger-looking, angular face with a prominent nose, and a slender, athletic build. Lou's dance quickly turned into a twisting, turning, high-energy strip routine. First "she" bared a long, shapely, cleanly-shaved pair of legs, then eventually got down to a bulging G-string and a bra that looked like two ice cream cones sticking out at ninety degrees. When the wicked-looking bra came off, it exposed a hairy, muscular chest. A moment later, when the black wig was removed, Al pulled the mug shot of Dennis O'Neal from his pocket, studied the dancer while he was taking his bows and said, "That's our Dennis."

As if to confirm his judgment, the master of ceremonies was on stage with the microphone shouting, "Let's hear it for lovely Lou'siana Lou, better known as Hurley's own favorite dancing artiste, Dennis da Menace!"

"Does it look to you like he's suffering from a bad back?" Al said.

"If he is, somebody must have given him a spinal injection."

"I think our discovery will strike a happy chord with Mr. Bombardier. Tomorrow night we'll pay a return visit with my little spy camera and some high-speed film. If we dress a little more normal, we can sit right down front and snap a few pictures for the benefit of Mr. Bombardier."

Al was slipping the photo of Dennis O'Neal back into his shirt pocket, when he felt a hand grasp his left shoulder in a firm grip and his body jerked involuntarily as he heard a stern male voice say, "All right, what are you two characters doing in here?"

CHAPTER 5

BAILING OUT AND MOPPING UP

The heavy hand on his left shoulder and the demanding voice in his ear, startled Alan Jeffrey and he pivoted his head to look up. As his eyes passed Mitch, he saw a large hand in a similar position on Mitch's right shoulder. When he got his head turned all the way around, he found himself looking into the grinning face of Piotr Borlishevski, Jennifer Tilton's former bodyguard.

"Jesus! You could get shot sneaking up on a person like that," Al said.

"Don't blow our cover," said Mitch. "Sit down like we're old friends and don't get everybody looking this way."

Piotr pulled an empty chair away from a nearby table and squeezed in between Al and Mitch. He seemed both delighted and puzzled to see them. "Don't tell me you're doing a story on this dump," he said. "I can't imagine you two being fans of female impersonators."

"You're right; we're not in Hurley's for the entertainment and definitely not for our health," Mitch said. "The smoke in here is heavy enough to cure a ham."

"So what are you up to? And where did you get those clothes?"

"Does our sartorial splendor dazzle you?" Mitch said.

"Dazzle doesn't begin to describe their effect," said Piotr. "But, once again, what are you guys doing here?"

"Do you know any of these so-called entertainers?" Al asked.

"Not a one. I just drop in here sometimes to talk to friends. I don't pay any attention to these scuzzy dancers. On a scale of ten, they rate about a one-point-five. They're not in the same league with the real professional female impersonators."

"I believe that. Anyway, I was hired on a freelance deal to get action pictures of a guy who supposedly has such a bad back he can't do any kind of physical work," Al said.

"I don't see a camera."

"This was a scouting trip," Mitch said.

"We need to shove off now," Al said, pushing back his chair and rising.

"Good to see you again, Piotr."

"Good to see you," said Piotr. "If you ever want to watch some female impersonators with some real talent, call me and I'll show you where to find them. And say hello to Mrs. Tilton for me."

Mitch said thanks but no thanks to the invitation, but promised that he would greet Jennifer and they walked out the door, happy to breathe smoke-free air for the first time in more than an hour.

Shortly after nine o'clock Wednesday morning, Al called Richard Bombardier at Bombs Away Trucking. Bombardier was pleased to hear that they had seen Dennis O'Neal prancing around the stage with no sign of a back injury.

"We'll go back tonight with a mini spy camera I've got and try to get some pictures of Dennis da Menace in action," Al said.

"Sounds good to me," Bombardier said. "Just give me enough to pin that little asshole to the wall."

"You got it," Al said. "I'll bring you a package as soon as I get the pictures." And I'll also bring you a handsome bill, he thought as he hung up. Richard Bombardier was going to pay through the nose for subjecting his nostrils to the air and his eyes and ears to the entertainment at Hurley's Hangout.

Al went out to talk to Mitch and arrived at the reporter's desk just as he was hanging up the phone and saying, "Shit!"

"Why shit?" said Al.

"That was a woman named Martha Todd who lives in my building. The washing machine in the basement blew a filler hose and dumped water all over the floor and there isn't any drain. Since I'm in charge, I have to go see that the mess gets mopped up and the hose gets fixed."

"Lucky you."

"What a hell of a time for Mrs. Peterson's sister to die. Anyway, I've got a list of service people she gave me back in my apartment. I hope it includes somebody who replaces washing machine hoses." He bounced out of his chair and went to the city desk to explain the situation to Don O'Rourke.

Mitch was gone—on his way to Grand Avenue—when the photo editor summoned Al to the phone at the photo desk. It was Diana calling with a report on Uncle Charlie. "Charlie is a little bit stronger," she said. "He's making sounds with his mouth and his heart and blood pressure are holding steady under the medication."

"That's great," Al said.

"What I called to tell you is that they're sending him home this afternoon.

I'm setting up a bed for him in the sunroom."

"He's going home already?"

"Doctor Sinfahdi said he will come to the house to check on Charlie every day and there will be a nurse on call around the clock. They're going to teach me to monitor the feeding tube he's hooked up to."

"Your insurance will pay for all that?"

"Not completely, but there's enough money to take care of it. Doesn't look like we'll be going on any more Caribbean cruises, so we might as well spend it to have Charlie home where he's happy and comfortable."

Al almost said, "But won't that leave a lot less for you when he dies?" He caught himself and said, "If there's anything Carol and I can do to help, please let us know. Maybe we can give you a hand sitting with him or making meals or something."

"All of a sudden you want to hold my hand? Thanks, but I think I'll get along just fine by myself."

"Whatever. It's your call. Is it okay if we come visit him?"

"He's your uncle and for some reason he seems to cheer up when he sees you. I won't lock the door."

"Thanks. We'll come over tonight after supper if that's all right."

"He might be really tired from the move. Why don't you wait until tomorrow?"

"Good point. We'll see you tomorrow, then. And meanwhile, keep us posted if there's any change, like he starts talking or walking or something."

"He might be talking tomorrow. Walking looks a lot farther away."

"Imagine that," Al said to himself as he hung up, "a doctor who'll make house calls in this day and age. Doctor Sinfahdi must be a hell of a guy."

Warren Mitchell found a nasty mess in the basement of the apartment building on Grand Avenue. The cold water hose had popped between the main valve and the washer, allowing the water to flow onto the floor until Martha Todd, whose clothes were in the machine, went down to remove them. By that time the water was so deep she decided to go back to her apartment and put on a pair of rubber snow boots before wading over to the wall to turn off the main valve. There was no drain in the floor, but the water was very slowly seeping away through cracks in the concrete slab and between the floor and the block walls when Mitch arrived. The janitorial service that cleaned the building's common areas once a week hadn't swept the basement recently and the water looked disgustingly murky beneath a grungy film of floating crud.

In addition to the laundry facilities, the basement contained locked storage areas enclosed by heavy mesh fencing for the residents' use and whatever touched the floor in these cubicles was soaked. After Mitch had called a plumber to request a vacuum that would pick up water and a set of replacement hoses for the washer, he put on his rubber boots and sloshed over to check his own storage spot. He found that some cardboard boxes he hadn't looked into since leaving California would have to be repacked and a pile of old magazines he had been meaning to clip had been reduced to a soggy pulp.

Mitch was still peering into his storage area, when a female voice just behind him said, "Some mess." He turned and saw Martha Todd, the woman who had found the flood and called him. She had moved into the building only a month before and they had introduced themselves to each other in the hallway one morning as both were leaving for work. He had noticed that she was tall—her dark brown eyes were almost level with his—and slender and she had a pleasant smile.

"I don't know why it had to happen on my watch," Mitch said. "It could have waited until Mrs. Peterson got back."

"Want some help?" she asked. She was still wearing her snow boots and they were standing almost ankle deep in brownish-gray water. Their eyes met and Mitch thought again about his mother's admonition to go out only with tall women. It was a good thing mom couldn't see Jennifer, he thought.

"There's a plumber coming with a shop vac to suck up the water so we can dump it down the laundry tub drain," he said. "He's going to put the new hoses on, but I suppose after the water is vacuumed up, the floor will need to be mopped. I wouldn't mind having a hand with that if you've got time later on."

"Sure. It was my load that the hose broke on, so I feel kind of responsible. Give me a yell when you're ready, Mr. Mitchell; you know where I live."

"It could have happened to anybody. But I won't turn down your offer to help. And most people call me Mitch, Ms. Todd."

"It's Martha. See you later," she said. As she turned and walked toward the stairs, Mitch noted that she was wearing faded blue jeans that fit like a second skin and the thought "nice ass" involuntarily cruised through his mind.

He guessed that Martha was maybe a couple of years younger than his thirty-six years of age. Her round face was plain, but pleasant to look at, her skin was the color of coffee laced with a generous splash of cream, her smile was inviting and her body was that of a woman who watched her diet and did her roadwork. He knew she was a runner because he had seen her leaving the building in sweats and running shoes.

Mitch's only problem with Martha was her hair, which was cut shorter than his own—so short, in fact, that she was almost qualified to stand inspection with the Marines. If her hair had been blonde instead of black, it would have been invisible. Nevertheless, Mitch liked what he had seen and heard, and he would have invited Martha out to dinner if he had not been so thoroughly involved with Jennifer Tilton.

Soon the plumber arrived and Mitch set about vacuuming up the water and dumping it into the wash tub while the man disconnected the old hoses and attached the new ones. It was tedious, backbreaking labor and Mitch was beat when he finally hoisted the last canister of water over the edge of the waist-high tub.

Mitch signed the bill presented by the plumber and took the proffered copy to his apartment to save for Mrs. Peterson. She'll just be thrilled, he thought. And so would the building's owner when he made the payment and heard from pissed-off tenants who lost items of value when their storage areas were flooded.

"Not my problem," said Mitch to Sherlock Holmes as the cat presented himself for petting and scratching. While performing this service, Mitch looked at the clock for the first time since he had called the plumber and discovered that the afternoon was gone. It was almost five and he hadn't even thought about lunch. His back and shoulders ached and he was facing still more cleanup work in the basement. No way was he going to Hurley's Hangout with Al to photograph a phony bad-back case prancing around the stage in drag tonight. He called the Daily Dispatch and explained the situation to Al.

"Okay," Al said. "Take it easy when you finish tonight and we'll fly our photo-recon mission tomorrow night."

"You probably want to spend some time at the hospital tonight, anyway."

"Oh, you haven't heard the latest. Uncle Charlie was going home this afternoon. Doctor Sinfahdi is going to make house calls, would you believe, and a nurse is going to stand watch during the night."

"Doctor whatever you said his name was is actually going to come to the house?"

"This doctor comes from India, so maybe he doesn't have American doctors' aversion to making house calls. And his name is Doctor Sinfahdi, by the way."

"That's odd," Mitch said.

"That he's from India?"

"No, I mean it's odd because his name is a lot like the doctor who was seeing Mrs. Peterson's sister before she died. She wasn't sure exactly what the guy's name was, but she said it sounded like 'Doctor Symphony.' Come to think of it, she said he was from India, too."

"Might be the same guy," Al said. "This one has an office on Roselawn Avenue in Maplewood."

"I'll check it out when Mrs. Peterson gets back. It's a small world."

"That's what they say in Disneyland."

"Now you're talking, Goofy."

"Just a Minnie joke," Al said. "Anyway, do you think you can handle the mop up or do you want me to come over and help?"

"No, I don't need another swabbie on deck. The woman whose clothes were in the machine when the dam broke has volunteered to help. Stay home with the wife and kiddies and I'll see you in the morning if I'm not too stiff to get out of the sack."

Mitch hung up and went to the refrigerator hoping to find something he could eat. He located a couple of hotdogs that were still their normal color, heated them in the microwave, split them lengthwise the way the cook did at one of the restaurants Mitch frequented downtown and stuck them between two slices of bread coated with mustard. Some rippled potato chips from a half-empty bag and a glass of root beer that had lost its fizz while sitting for a week in an opened two-liter bottle, completed the meal.

"One of these days I've got to start thinking about eating healthy," he said to Sherlock. "Not getting any younger, you know."

"Meowr," said the cat, looking up hopefully as Mitch bit into the sandwich. He pinched off a small bite of hot dog and passed it down. The morsel disappeared quickly into Sherlock's pink mouth.

When he had finished eating, Mitch sat back, belched loudly, put his rubber boots back on, said "so long, old buddy" to Sherlock and walked down the hall to knock on Martha Todd's door.

Martha opened the door and said, "Oh, hi." She was wearing a half-size-too-tight T-shirt with the words "So many books, so little time" stretched across her breasts, which were smaller than average for a woman her height. The outline of the bra that supported them was clearly visible through the T-shirt, as were the faint, round-button impressions of her nipples. Martha's long legs and slender hips were still encased in the skin-tight blue jeans. Mitch felt his face grow slightly warmer as his eyes traveled quickly from bra to bottom and back again.

In Martha's hand was a wooden spoon and the smell of garlic was floating like incense in the air. "I was just cooking up some vegetarian pasta sauce," she said. "There's enough in the pot for two if you'd care to join me."

"Oh, no thanks, I just ate," he said. "I kind of lost track of what time it was. I'll go down and start mopping while you finish your dinner."

"Oh, why bust your butt all by yourself? It'll only take me a few minutes to eat and then we can go down together. Come on in. You can watch me eat if you're sure you're not hungry. What did you have?"

"Oh, just some leftovers." How could he tell a woman whose cooking smelled so wonderful—and who sounded like she might be a vegetarian, as well—that he had nuked two hot dogs for dinner?

"Sure you won't have just a little?" Martha said as she dished herself up a plate of spaghetti and covered it with a thick, red sauce from a pot on the stove.

"Well, maybe just a little." The smell and the sight of the sauce had activated his salivary glands and the hot dogs and chips hadn't really filled him to capacity. She waved him toward a chair at one end of a small dinette table and he sat down.

"Say when," she said, piling a plate with almost as much spaghetti as she had served herself.

"When! You're going to stuff me so full I won't be able to swing a mop."

She set the plate in front of him. "How about a little wine with that?" she asked, indicating a box of burgundy on the kitchen counter.

"No, thanks."

"A beer maybe?"

"No. Water would be fine."

"You're a teetotaler, are you?"

"I'm an alcoholic."

"Oh!" she said, and her face flushed a darker, reddish shade of tan. "I didn't mean to get personal."

"It's okay," Mitch said. "I'm used to saying it at my AA meetings."

"Do you mind if I drink this wine?" She had a nearly-full glass beside her plate on the opposite side of the table.

"Go ahead. Watching other people drink doesn't bother me. In fact, last night I was in a room literally filled with drinkers and pot smokers."

"Why?" Martha asked as she set a tall glass of water in front of him.

Mitch explained that he had been tagging along with Alan Jeffrey on a freelance photo mission.

"Warren Mitchell and Alan Jeffrey!" she said. "Aren't you the guys from the Daily Dispatch who got involved in the kidnapping and rescue of those two little kids last fall? I saw you on TV and read the stories in the paper." She sat down across from him at the table.

"That's us," Mitch said.

"You guys were terrific."

"Thanks," Mitch said. He went on to describe the previous evening at Hurley's Hangout, ending with, "I'd be there again tonight if the washing machine hose hadn't crapped out."

"Sorry about that," Martha said. "I was just trying to wash some clothes when I had a few minutes."

"What keeps you so busy you have to do laundry on a Wednesday afternoon?"

"School and work. I just finished spring semester at Hamline's Law School and now I'm working as a clerk at a law firm three days a week and waitressing at a restaurant on some nights and weekends."

"Doesn't leave much time for socializing."

"I haven't been much in the mood for socializing," she said. "I moved in here after getting a divorce from a guy I was married to for three years."

"Oh, sorry. That must have been tough."

"I should have got out sooner. He was a great guy when he was sober, but he could get pretty mean when he drank too much, which was more often than not. But what about you? Do reporters get time to have a life outside of rescuing children and watching female impersonators strut their stuff?"

"A little. Some of the guys I work with even have wives and children."

"But you don't have a family?"

"I had a wife and a son, but they died in an auto accident. That's what put me on the road to alcoholism."

"Oh, swell; I did it again. Asked too many personal questions." Martha stood abruptly and walked away into the kitchen, where she stood at the counter with her hands cupped over her nose and mouth. "I'm sorry," she said.

"Don't be," he said. "It was a perfectly logical question and those things happened long enough ago that I can give a straight answer."

"One of the things they teach you in law school is never to ask one question too many," she said, uncovering her face, but not turning around. "I wish they'd teach you how to apply that to your personal life."

"It's no big deal," Mitch said, carrying his silverware and empty plate to the kitchen counter. He stood beside her and put his right hand on her left shoulder. "What do you say we go mop the basement?"

Martha turned her head toward him and gave him a quick little smile. "I hope I can handle that without putting my foot in my mouth," she said. "Those rubber boots wouldn't taste very good."

CHAPTER 6

A HUNTRESS DISARMED

Thursday began like any other work day at the Daily Dispatch in downtown St. Paul. Photographer, Alan Jeffrey and reporter, Warren Mitchell arrived almost simultaneously from their respective homes and met at the photo desk coffee pot. While they drank their first cups, Mitch described the mess in the apartment building basement and the work needed to clean it up.

"This Martha that helped you—is she as old as Mrs. Peterson?"

"Not hardly. She's about our age, actually."

"Is she cute?"

"I wouldn't say cute. Attractive in a way. She's tall, slim. Nice ass."

"Well, she won't be the butt of any jokes then."

"I'm glad you won't get cheeky."

"So what did you and the lady with the nice ass do after you finished mopping the basement together?"

"What any tired, sweaty, grungy person would do. I went to my apartment, took a shower and went to bed and she went to her apartment and I assume did the same."

"How boring. I expected more from you, or are you being loyal to Jennifer?"

"I was filthy dirty and tired as hell and so was Martha. She was nice enough to feed me spaghetti in her apartment before we went down to mop. And, in answer to your question, yes, I would feel kind of strange making a move on somebody besides Jennifer right now."

Mitch was scanning the morning papers—both St. Paul and Minneapolis—when he and Al were sent to cover a press conference at the mayor's office. Minutes after they returned to the office, Al was summoned to the phone.

"Alan, this is Diana," she said in a voice that sounded like she was close to tears. "I don't know how to tell you this, but your Uncle Charlie passed away this morning."

Al felt like he had been punched in the solar plexus. It took him a good thirty seconds to respond. "Uncle Charlie died?"

"This morning." He could tell that Diana was crying now.

"But you said he was getting better."

"He was doing good last night when Doctor Sinfahdi was here and the nurse said he was resting peacefully when she left, but when I went in this morning to see if he was awake, his face was all gray and his hands were ice cold. I called 911 and Doctor Sinfahdi, but there was nothing anybody could do."

"I'm sorry, Diana. Can I do anything to help with the arrangements?"

"Charlie wanted to be cremated, so they took his body there," she said. "If you want to talk about planning a funeral service, I guess you can come over here."

"I'll be there in half an hour or so." He hung up, explained the situation to Bob Franklin, the photo editor, and walked over to Mitch's desk.

"You look like you have some really bad news," Mitch said.

"Uncle Charlie died this morning," Al said.

"I thought his wife said he was doing better."

"I guess she thought he was. Maybe he should have stayed in the hospital a little longer. I don't know. Diana didn't say what the doctor said today."

"Well, I'm sorry that he's gone. Are you bailing out for the day?"

"Yeah. I told Diana I'd help with the funeral arrangements."

"Well, let me know if there's anything I can do and keep me posted on when and where the services will be held."

"Thanks, I will. Could you maybe call that Bombardier guy for me and tell him there's a delay. If he's in a hurry because of a court date or something, you might have to go take the pictures at Hurley's all by yourself."

"God, I hope not. I need you to protect me from the regulars."

"I'm sure you'll have a gay old time."

"Well, at least you haven't lost your punishing sense of humor."

"It's all I have right now," Al said. And there were tears stinging his eyes as he went out the door and walked toward the elevator.

Diana met Alan Jeffrey at the door of the sprawling ranch-style home she shared with Uncle Charlie in the northern suburb of Roseville. Diana's eyes and nose were red from crying and the rest of her face was unusually pale in comparison. She invited Al in and steered him toward the kitchen, saying she had made a pot of coffee and wanted help drinking it.

"Did your Doctor Sinfahdi say what happened to Uncle Charlie?" Al asked as they sat on opposite sides of the kitchen table.

"He said Charlie's heart just stopped beating," said Diana. "The doctor was here just before the ten o'clock news last night and he said Charlie had been having some pain, so he gave him a shot to relieve it. Sometime between when the night nurse left at six o'clock and I went in at seven this morning, Charlie's heart stopped beating. Like I said on the phone, I found him gray and cold and not breathing."

"So what can I do to help?"

"The first thing you might do is check over the obituary that's going to be in the paper," she said. "I've listed you as the only blood relative surviving. I think we agreed that that's correct."

"I'm afraid it is. It was just him and my dad in that family, and I'm an only child, so there aren't any more nephews or nieces."

"Just you and me to settle everything," she said in a hard voice. She passed him a form that had been provided by the funeral director. "I filled in as much as I could. If you can think of any other organizations he belonged to or things he did, write them in."

Al studied the sheet for a minute and said he couldn't think of anything more. He noticed that the funeral was to be held in a nearby Methodist church, but that the date was still blank.

"Is this the church you were going to?" he asked.

"When we went. Charlie preferred to attend services on the golf course on Sunday mornings any time the weather allowed. Sometimes I went to church without him. What we need to do is pick a date. The minister said he's available both Saturday and Monday."

"Either one is all right with me. Which do you prefer?"

"The funeral director said the ashes will be available Saturday, so I'd just as soon do it then," Diana said.

"Makes no difference to me," Al said.

"Good," Diana said. "That's done. Now I suppose we should decide what to have for food after the service."

"Maybe you and Carol should talk about that. I'm not much of a refreshment planner."

"Okay. Why don't you have her call me?" Diana stood up.

"Is that it?" Al asked. He was only halfway through his cup of coffee.

"Unless you want to read your uncle's will. I don't get everything. He left you some stuff."

"I'm not concerned about that."

"You sure as hell were the day we got married."

"I didn't mean that I was worried about losing anything. Looking at you on your wedding day, it just struck me that you could have been marrying somebody a lot younger than Uncle Charlie."

"And poorer."

"I guess it came out that way," he said. "Anyway, you're the wife and you're welcome to everything Uncle Charlie left you."

"Your generosity is overwhelming."

"I'll see you Saturday," Al said curtly, rising and walking into the living room toward the front door, with Diana following. When he reached the door, the sound of a sob stopped him and he turned to find Diana collapsed on the couch, shaking and crying uncontrollably. He went back, sat near her head, pulled her up to a half-sitting position and wrapped his arms around her. She buried her head in his shoulder and continued to shake and sob.

Feeling as awkward as a drunk at a temperance convention, Al held Diana for what seemed like hours before she regained a semblance of composure. "This is really weird," she said, raising her head off his shoulder and leaning back against his arms. "I've hated your guts ever since you called me a fortune hunter at my wedding and here I am blubbering all over you."

"I think Uncle Charlie would want us to patch up our feud," Al said. "I'm just sorry I opened my big mouth that day."

"It really hurt," Diana said. "I got married to a guy my own age when I was in my early twenties and he turned out to be a total asshole. After I divorced him I didn't want anything to do with men, until I went to work for your Uncle Charlie. Charlie was sweet and kind, more loving than any man I ever met, and I really did love him. I'd have loved him and married him even if he didn't have a ton of money."

"For what it's worth, I believe you."

"It's worth a lot if you really mean it."

"I really do. I can see it in your face."

"My face? My face must be an awful mess. Look, you can go now, if you want. I'm okay again."

"You sure? I hate to leave you here alone."

"My parents are driving down from Hibbing," Diana said. "They should be here before long."

"Okay, then. I'll have Carol call you tonight about the food." Al bent forward and kissed Diana lightly on the forehead, then rose and went out the front door. As he started for home, he decided he'd like to talk to Doctor Sinfahdi himself, so he turned east instead of west and headed for Maplewood and Roselawn Avenue.

CHAPTER 7

THE DOCTOR IS IN

After downing a sandwich and a cup of coffee at one of the many restaurants in the St. Paul Skyway system, Warren Mitchell called Bombs Away Trucking Co. to tell Richard Bombardier there would be a delay—if he didn't mind—in the Hurley's Hangout photo shoot. The woman who answered the phone said Mr. Bombardier was not in, but would return Mitch's call later in the afternoon.

It was after four o'clock when Richard Bombardier finally called and said he had been visiting his grandfather in Maplewood. "He's ninety-one years old and he isn't doing so well," Bombardier said. "We may have to move him to a nursing home or a long-term care center. My mom and dad and I have been trying to keep him going, but I think he needs full-time care. Mom is just wearing herself out."

Mitch told Bombardier about Al's Uncle Charlie and asked if the photos of Dennis O'Neal were needed immediately.

"No, don't worry about getting the pictures this week," Bombardier said. "It'll be a couple of months before we actually have to be in court on the lawsuit, but I would like to blow the whistle on his disability claim as soon as possible."

"I'm sure Al will get on it right away next week," Mitch said. He hung up and sat back, relieved that he wouldn't have to venture into Hurley's hellish Hangout alone.

The phone was still in Mitch's hand when he realized he hadn't talked to Jennifer since the basement flood, so he punched her number. After four rings, he got her voice on the answering machine. He left a message saying he still had a mess to clean up in his building and that he'd call her in the evening to explain. Then he decided to swing out to Al's house on the way home to see how he was doing.

Mitch parked his Honda Civic on the street in front of the Jeffreys' house and went up and rang the bell. When Carol opened the door, she said, "Hi, Mitch, what brings you here?"

"I just came by to see how Al was doing. Is he home?"

"No. Wasn't he at the office?"

"No, he left about noon to go talk to Diana and never came back. I figured he must have come home."

"Why was he going to talk to Diana?"

Her question startled Mitch. Then he realized that if Al hadn't come home, nobody had told her about Uncle Charlie's death. He wished he could take back his question about Al's whereabouts.

"Me and my big mouth," he said. "I guess you haven't heard."

"Heard what?"

"About Uncle Charlie. Diana called Al at the paper and said he passed away this morning. That's why Al went to see her."

Carol felt her knees get weak and she put a hand on Mitch's shoulder. "Uncle Charlie died?"

"Diana found him this morning a little while after the night nurse left. Al went to help her make funeral arrangements. I thought he'd be home by now and would have told you. I'm sorry."

"I haven't heard from him at all. He must still be at Uncle Charlie's house, or maybe they went to the funeral home. The way he and Diana hate each other, I hope there's not another death." Carol's knees had stopped wobbling and she released her grip on Mitch's shoulder.

"Want me to go out there?" he asked.

"No, I hear you've got your own problem to deal with in the basement of your building. I'll call give Diana a call."

At about the time Warren Mitchell was discussing nightclub photography with Richard Bombardier, Alan Jeffrey was parking his Toyota at a small strip mall on Roselawn Avenue. The block-long, one-story building was one of those put up a few years before the larger, enclosed malls came into vogue. The outside had been neglected since the original retailers moved away to greener pastures and the paint was peeling so badly that the building appeared to be suffering from the heartbreak of psoriasis.

Al spotted Doctor Ravi Sinfahdi's office at one end of the building, which, instead of shops, now housed a dentist, a podiatrist and a chiropractor in addition to Uncle Charlie's doctor. The sign on Doctor Sinfahdi's door said he specialized in the care of the elderly.

When Al walked through the door, he found himself in a small waiting room, lined on three sides with chairs. On the fourth side, at right angles to the door, was a high counter and a hallway that led to the doctor's office and examining rooms. Two of the chairs were occupied, one by a white-haired woman who appeared to be pushing ninety, the other by a sixty-plus woman who Al took to be her daughter.

Al approached the counter and a matronly-looking woman in her mid-forties, wearing a white blouse and a light blue skirt that was several inches too short and at least one size too tight for a person of her age and weight, rose from behind a desk and walked over to meet him, saying, "May I help you?"

"I'm wondering if I could talk to Doctor Sinfahdi for a minute," Al said. "I'm the nephew of one of his patients."

"Which patient?"

"I guess former patient would be more accurate. It's Charlie Jeffrey. He died early this morning."

"And why did you want to see the doctor?"

"I just wanted to talk to him about the cause of Uncle Charlie's death."

"Didn't the doctor discuss that with Mr. Jeffrey's wife?"

"What I got from her was kind of vague. I was hoping to get something more, I don't know—definitive, maybe—from the doctor."

"You say Mr. Jeffrey was your uncle?"

"Yes. I'm the only relative he had left, other than his wife."

"Doctor Sinfahdi is with a patient right now, but I'll find out if he can see you when he's finished." She turned and walked back to her chair and Al noted that the outline of her underpants was visible through the tight blue skirt. He estimated their size as extra large.

"Thanks," he said. "I'll be glad to wait."

The choice of reading material in the waiting room was limited to the likes of *Modern Maturity, People,* and *Country Living.* Even if this doctor specializes in geriatric patients, you'd think he could provide something more lively for the younger people who bring the old folks in, Al thought. He had flipped most of the way through a six-month-old copy of *Country Living* without really seeing what was on the pages when the receptionist said the doctor would see him. Two more chairs had become occupied during the interim as another elderly woman, also escorted by a middle-aged daughter, had come in.

As Al walked past the sixty-something woman who had been waiting when he entered, she glared at him and muttered a couple of words under her breath. "I'll only be a minute," he said to her. He offered a smile which she did not return.

Al was met at the entrance to the hallway by a fortyish blonde woman in a white nurse's uniform with a name tag that said "Emily Darnell, RN" and the thought went through his mind that not many nurses dressed like that anymore. Her body looked firm and muscular and she was nearly as tall as Al. Her expressionless blue eyes looked squarely into his when she directed him to follow her. Al decided that if any of Doctor Sinfahdi's elderly patients needed physical support, Nurse Emily Darnell was capable of providing it.

"Right in here," she said crisply, pushing a half-open door the rest of the way. "Have a seat and the doctor will be right with you." She disappeared down the hall.

Al had been seated only a couple of minutes when a short, skinny man with snow white hair and wrinkled skin the color of strong tea walked in. "Good afternoon," he said. "I'm Doctor Sinfahdi. What can I do for you?" He offered his bony right hand in greeting and Al rose and grasped it with his. The doctor peered up at Al through rimless bifocals as they shook hands. Al was surprised at the strength of the little man's grip.

"I'm Charlie Jeffrey's nephew," Al said. "I just wondered if you could tell me what happened to him. He seemed to be regaining his strength from the stroke and then all of a sudden ... well, you know."

"Your uncle died of a myocardial infarction, more commonly known as heart failure," said the doctor. "This is not unusual with patients who have suffered a stroke." He spoke in a gentle voice—almost a whisper—with a touch of a British accent.

"What brought on the heart failure? Was he released from the hospital too soon?"

"I would have preferred that he stayed in the hospital for another day or two, but his wife was quite insistent that he would recuperate better at home. However, you must realize that these things are unpredictable, especially in patients of your uncle's age and physical condition."

"His age? He was only seventy-five," Al said. "It wasn't like the man was ninety years old."

"Unfortunately, his arteries were those of a person nearly ninety years of age, Mr. Jeffrey. Your uncle had severe arteriosclerosis, which is, no doubt, what brought about the stroke."

"He always seemed so healthy. I mean, he was always out on the golf course with his friends."

"Sometimes one's outward vigor masks problems within, Mr. Jeffrey. We've all heard of athletes much younger than your uncle who collapsed unexpectedly and passed away suddenly. I am sorry for your loss, but it seems that his heart could not cope with the stress of the stroke, coupled with the condition of his arteries."

"You saw him the night before he died?"

"Yes, I saw him that evening. His wife had called here and told my nurse that your uncle seemed to be in pain, so I gave him an injection to alleviate his discomfort. He was resting quietly when I left. If it's any comfort to you, I'm sure he died peacefully and painlessly, Mr. Jeffrey."

"That is a comfort," Al said.

"Your uncle's condition was such that he never would have completely recovered from the paralysis on his left side and I'm not sure how much, if any of his speaking capabilities he would have regained."

"I can't imagine Uncle Charlie paralyzed and speechless. Maybe it's best that he passed away."

"No doctor would ever agree with that," Doctor Sinfahdi said with a smile. "We always make every effort to preserve life."

"Thank you for your time," Al said. He shook the doctor's hand again and left the room. He found Nurse Darnell standing in the hallway near the door and she silently escorted him back to the waiting room where he was glad to see that the woman who had glared at him and the older woman she was escorting were no longer seated.

Back in the car and headed toward home, Al thought about what Doctor Sinfahdi had said. Diana had insisted on bringing Uncle Charlie home. Diana had called the doctor's office and said Uncle Charlie needed a painkiller. If she had been less demanding about leaving the hospital or more specific about the pain, would Uncle Charlie still be alive?

"No," he said to himself. "It's not fair to blame Diana. She's more broken up than I ever imagined she would be. Maybe she's feeling like she made some mistakes and is blaming herself for Uncle Charlie's death." He wondered if he should say something to Diana or just let it ride. Maybe Carol could give him some advice along that line.

"Oh, shit!" he said aloud. "I should have called to let Carol know." Oh well, he thought, it will be better to tell her face to face when I get home.

When Warren Mitchell got back to the basement of his Grand Avenue apartment building, he was hoping to find Martha Todd cleaning out her storage area—maybe bending over in those tight blue jeans. Instead, the only person there was an old fart who lived alone on the second floor and routinely grumbled about everything from the next day's weather forecast to the price of white bread.

Mitch had arrived in the basement later than he intended. He had stopped at a Chinese restaurant to pick up some take-out Kung-Pao chicken and fried rice on the way home, greeted Sherlock Holmes appropriately, fed both the cat and himself and watched the evening news before rousting himself out of the chair. At this hour, he figured that Martha must have finished her cleanup before he got started. Thus, he was pleasantly surprised when he heard a familiar female voice say, "Hello, down there," from the stairway while he was opening a box of waterlogged summer shirts and shorts.

"Welcome to Water Wonderland," Mitch said. "I thought you'd be finished mopping up your mess by this time."

"I've been working," she said. "Just got off the waitressing job after spending all day at the law office."

Mitch was pleased to see that she had changed into the jeans he had been hoping for. On top, she wore a T-shirt that wasn't stretched quite as snug across her breasts as the previous day's model had been. This one said, "Runs With Sharp Scissors" and Mitch decided that Martha must dress herself from the Wireless catalog.

Her storage area was close to Mitch's and they made small talk while dredging up soggy items and separating them into piles, either to be cleaned and dried or to be bagged and dumped. By keeping a judicious watch out of the corner of his eye, Mitch was able to enjoy the scenery almost every time Martha bent over or squatted in those wonderful jeans.

"Well, I'm done for now," Martha said finally.

"Need any help?" Mitch asked, hoping he could follow her up the stairs.

"No, but I wouldn't mind an escort to the trash barrel. Going into a dark alley at night isn't my favorite activity."

It occurred to Mitch that the back doorway, the path to the alley and the area in which the trash barrels were located, were very well lit, but if Martha wanted an escort, why not provide such a service. "I've done all I want to do tonight," he said. "Let me lock up and I'll be right with you."

Mitch enjoyed the view all the way up the stairs, which were at the front of the building, but when she reached the top, she stopped to wait so he was forced to walk beside her rather than behind her on the way to the back door. Back inside they said goodnight in front of Mitch's apartment and Martha asked if he had a busy day ahead.

"In my business you deal with whatever comes up," he said. "You never know where they'll send you. The only thing I know for sure about tomorrow is that the photographer I usually work with on stories won't be there. He had a death in the family—his favorite uncle—and he'll be off for the rest of the week helping the guy's widow."

"Oh, that's too bad," said Martha. "It's tough to lose someone like that. My grandfather died about six months ago and I miss him a lot."

"Yeah, this hit Al pretty hard. His dad died when he was just a little kid and this uncle was sort of an adoptive father to him when he was growing up."

"Had he been sick very long?"

"Only a couple of days. He had a stroke Sunday and seemed to be coming around, then early this morning his wife found him dead. The doctor told Al that his uncle had hardening of the arteries and his heart couldn't carry the load any more."

"Grampa's heart gave out, too. Mom had to put him in kind of a nursing home because he couldn't see good and was forgetting things and couldn't take care of himself any more. Then, all of a sudden, he was gone and the doctor said it was his heart."

"It happens to everyone, sooner or later. And on that happy note, I'll say goodnight again."

On Friday morning Mitch realized he hadn't talked to Jennifer since Uncle Charlie's death, so he rang her number. The phone was answered by a teen-age neighbor who said she was babysitting while Jennifer was out interviewing for a job. Mitch thanked her and left a message for Jennifer to call him.

Friday normally would have been Mitch's second day off this week, but he had swapped working hours with another reporter so he could attend Uncle Charlie's funeral on Saturday. As a reporter for the afternoon edition, Mitch always had Sundays off and his other free day rotated through the week. He usually went to Afton to visit Jennifer on both days and she would be expecting to see him this afternoon

Finally, near noontime, the phone on his desk rang. It was Mrs. Peterson.

"I just wanted to let you know I come back home this morning," she said. "I hear you had a big mess while I was gone."

"It was kind of nasty, but we handled it. Martha, the woman in the front apartment, helped me mop up after the plumber left."

"Yah, she's real nice girl, that Martha."

"Did everything go well in Askov?"

"Oh, yah. We had a nice service for Grace and I saw some family I hadn't seen in a long time. Weddings and funerals, don't you know?"

"Her sudden passing must have been a shock to the family."

"Oh, yah. Her daughters was really shook up. Kind of mad at the doctor who said she was okay, but what can you do? They can get fooled too, you know."

Mention of the doctor triggered a question in Mitch's mind. "Did you ever remember the doctor's name?" he asked. "The one in Roseville that you said sounded like Doctor Symphony?"

"Well, no. But come to think of it, he signed the death certificate and I kept a copy of that. If you want to hold on, I can go look."

"Oh, I don't want to be a bother ..."

"No bother. Won't take a minute."

It didn't. She was back in fifty-five seconds by the clock on the wall of the newsroom. "Here it is," she said. "It's spelled S-I-N-F-A-H-D-I."

"Sinfahdi," said Mitch. "It's a small world."

"How do you mean?"

"My photographer friend's uncle died yesterday morning and Doctor Sinfahdi was his doctor, too."

"Well, now, ain't that a coincidence?"

"Like I said, it's a small world," said Mitch. "Anyway, thanks for looking it up. I'll bring back your key tonight when I get home."

After that, time became a blur for both Alan Jeffrey and Warren Mitchell. Al and Carol, who finally was free from her teaching job for the summer, spent most of that day with Diana and her parents. They checked with the funeral director on the progress of the cremation, discussed the memorial service with the minister and made the final arrangements.

On Saturday Mitch drove out and picked up Jennifer who accompanied him to the funeral. The day's weather was appropriately gloomy with a dreary procession of dismal clouds providing alternating periods of drizzle and showers. They were spared the additional agony of standing out in the cemetery because Charlie had requested that his ashes be scattered on the farm, north of the Twin Cities where he had been born.

After the service and a lunch for friends and family at Charlie's (now Diana's) house, Mitch and Jennifer drove back to Afton. Mitch stayed and they warmed themselves after the soggy, gloomy day by making love far into the night. They were awakened at about nine o'clock Sunday morning by two curly-haired, brown-eyed children leaping onto the bed. Luckily the two lovers had pulled the covers up far enough to hide their nakedness before they had gone to sleep.

"I told you not to come bouncing in here when Uncle Mitch is visiting us," Jennifer said.

"We're hungry," said Tony.

"We want waffles," said Tracy.

"Scoot out and get the Sunday paper and pour yourself some juice,"

Jennifer said. "I'll be out to make waffles as soon as I take a shower." Obediently, they scooted, but they promised to return if their mother's shower took too long.

"Guess we'd better get up then," Mitch said when the children had left. "It would be fun to fool around a little, but not so good if they come back."

"Definitely not. I'm not quite ready to explain the facts of life to them yet." She kissed him quickly on the lips, rose and went into the bathroom with Mitch watching the tantalizing movement of her bare bottom all the way.

Jennifer had delivered one piece of good news on what had been an otherwise bleak Saturday morning. Her Friday job interview had been successful; she had been hired as a physical therapist by a firm that serviced nursing homes in the northern suburbs of St. Paul and she was scheduled to report for an orientation session on Monday afternoon. She had done physical therapy work in New Jersey before she married Timothy Tilton, but her job search, which she launched a month after his death the previous October, had been met with a series of negative responses all through the winter and spring.

"I'll have regular rounds at these nursing homes, working with patients who need rehab after surgery or strokes or heart attacks," she had told Mitch. "The pay isn't great, but with the insurance money it will keep me and the kids fed and clothed."

"No Caribbean cruises?" Mitch had said.

"Not on the salary they're going to pay me for this job, I'm afraid. But maybe some angel will come along and sweep me away for an exotic vacation." Jennifer had been looking him squarely in the eye.

Mitch chose to side-step her challenge. "If some angel does carry you off on a trip to the moon and the stars, say 'halo' for me and ask if I can come along."

"Only an angel could stand your devilish sense of humor."

"Okay, I won't harp on it."

"Thank heavens."

Now, as Jennifer's round, bare backside disappeared into the shower, Mitch was thinking how heavenly it might be to make this a permanent arrangement and spend every star-studded night of the rest of his life in the celestial pleasures of her empyrean bed. Maybe this would be a good day to muster up his courage and ask her to marry him. If she said yes, he'd be floating on Cloud Nine.

CHAPTER 8

SMALL WORLD

The world seemed more normal on Monday morning. Al was back at work and Mitch was fifteen minutes late. He and Jennifer did get up before any hungry children invaded their cozy love nest, but not in time for Mitch to arrive in St. Paul at eight o'clock.

"A whole weekend with Jennifer?" Al asked, not really needing an answer.

"A whole weekend in paradise," Mitch replied. "It was so good that I almost worked up the nerve to propose to her, but I couldn't quite get the words out."

"Well, I'm glad somebody enjoyed the weekend."

"Sorry. I hope yours wasn't too rough."

"Uncle Charlie really was a second father to me. It was tough to look at that urn full of ashes and think that's all that's left of him." Al also had been brooding over Doctor Sinfahdi's comments about Diana's insistence that Uncle Charlie be allowed to come home sooner than the doctor thought wise. Would Uncle Charlie still be alive if he had stayed longer in the hospital? Would Uncle Charlie want to be alive if he couldn't walk or talk? At least Al had managed to keep his mouth shut about this to Diana. He wondered if he should—or would—bring it up later.

"It is hard to believe," Mitch said. "Especially since he seemed to be getting stronger after the stroke."

"Well, Doctor Sinfahdi wasn't so optimistic when I talked to him after Uncle Charlie died. He thought the paralysis would be permanent and the speech thing was kind of iffy."

"That would be tough to live with. And your mentioning the doctor reminds me, Mrs. Peterson looked up the name of her sister's doctor and it was the same guy, Doctor Sinfahdi."

"No kidding? Tough week for the doctor, losing two patients like that."

"Well, I suppose you learn to deal with that when you specialize in geriatrics."

"Glad it's not my job. Which reminds me that it's time to get back to what actually is my job, both officially and unofficially. What's the status of the photo-recon mission to Hurley's Hangout?"

"It's on hold until you're ready to go," Mitch said. "Bombardier said there's no rush to meet a court date, but he would like to bag the little bastard for collecting disability pay as soon as possible."

"Want to go tonight?"

"Better ask me will I go, not do I want to go."

"Well, I'll get the candid camera loaded. We're going out to expose some hidden treasures tonight."

"I shutter to think of it."

The burly man at the door of Hurley's Hangout greeted them coolly as he collected their cover charge payments. They were dressed more appropriately, in sports shirts and khaki slacks, but the guardian of the gate did not seem at all happy to see them.

This time they found a table much closer to the stage. The miniature Minolta spy camera was in a pack of cigarettes in Alan Jeffrey's shirt pocket with the lens looking through a tiny hole in the bottom of the pack. If Al put the pack on the table and pretended to play with it nervously, he could surreptitiously aim the camera, click the shutter and advance the film. He would be shooting without the benefit of looking through the viewfinder, but there were twelve exposures on the roll and he planned to use them all. One thing they weren't worried about was anybody hearing the shutter click. The noise level had been beyond the pain threshold when Dennis da Menace danced.

Al and Mitch nursed a beer and a Coke, respectively, while they endured the gyrations of two less-than-graceful dancers and the revoltingly raunchy repertoire of a comedian whose sole topics were oral sex, anal sex, public urination and nocturnal defecation in unusual places. Even the regulars weren't laughing very much.

"Little Mitchy may fwo up," Mitch said midway through the comedian's routine.

"If you do, he'll tell some jokes about puking," Al said.

At last the onslaught of awful jokes ended and the comedian took his bows to sparse applause. Then the pot-bellied master of ceremonies stepped up to announce that there would be a brief intermission before the second half of this evening's show.

Their glasses were empty and the waiter was standing over them. They had little choice but to order another round of drinks. "We're running up an awfully big expense tab for Mr. Bombardier," Al said, as the four-dollar beer and the three-dollar coke arrived.

"It could be worse," Mitch said. "Some of the patrons are slipping tens and twenties to the dancers."

The pot-belly hauled himself onto the stage again to announce that the evening's entertainment was about to continue. Kicking off the second half would be Dirty Doris from Des Moines.

"Oh, God, a hog from Iowa!" Mitch said. But the performer, who wore a belly-dancer's costume made of a filmy, pale green material, with a see-through veil to match, looked familiar.

"Get out the cigarettes," Mitch said. "I think this is our buddy Dennis."

"I think you're right," Al said. "I'd know that schnoz anywhere, even poking out under a veil."

As Dirty Doris from Des Moines, Dennis O'Neal performed basically the same dance he did during their previous visit when he was billed as Lou'siana Lou. Apparently his repertoire was limited to bumps, grinds and a little mincing two-step on his toes. As he pranced and bumped and ground, Al fiddled with the pack of cigarettes on the table, hoping he was getting the man's face in some of the shots.

Al saved the last two frames on the film for the finale when Dirty Doris dropped her top, whipped off her veil and revealed her true identity. On the last shot, Al picked up the pack and aimed the bottom directly at the dancer's face—he had to make sure of at least one easily identifiable photo.

He had just put the pack of cigarettes back into his shirt pocket when, once again, Al felt a strong hand on his shoulder and heard a male voice asking, "What are you two doing here?"

He turned, ready to give a smart-ass answer. But this time the questioner was not Piotr Borlishevski.

The man with the hand on Alan Jeffrey's shoulder was big, at least six-two and broad-shouldered, and wore a dark business suit, white shirt and striped tie. Al twisted away from his grip and said, "We're watching the show; what's it to you?"

"I'm Derek DelMonico, the owner of this establishment," the man said. "I make it a point to get acquainted with all my new customers."

"That's very hospitable of you," Al said.

"I see you're a smoker," Derek said. "Can I bum one of your cigarettes?"

"Actually, I'm just about out," Al said. "I've got barely enough to get me home."

"Which is where we should be going right now," Mitch said, pushing back his chair and getting to his feet.

As Mitch stood up, two large, stern-looking men in dark T-shirts and black trousers appeared behind Derek. "My assistants will make sure you get to your car without any problems," Derek said. The two men moved into position, one on each side of Al and Mitch, and walked in lock step with them to Hurley's front door.

"We're parked out back," Mitch said when they were outside.

"We can get to our car with no problem," Al said.

One of the goons grunted and the other did nothing. They stayed beside the two newsmen all the way to Mitch's Honda, which was parked at the rear of the small lot, and stood by while Mitch unlocked the door on the driver's side, got in and reached across to raise the lock on the passenger side. One of the men followed Al around the car and as Al opened the door the man said, "I want a cigarette."

"Sorry, I'm fresh out," Al said, sliding into the seat.

"I see some in your pocket," the man said, reaching toward Al's chest through the open door.

"I said I'm fresh out," Al said, and he pulled the door shut hard on the man's arm, catching him right at the elbow. The man yelped in pain and tried to pull his arm out, but Al, using both hands, held the door hard against it. "I think I bumped his funny bone," he said to Mitch, who had locked his door, started the engine and was ready to roll.

"Is he laughing?" Mitch asked.

"No, but I'm getting a chuckle out of it."

"Shall we let him trot alongside the car for a little while or do you want to give him back his arm?" Mitch asked.

"He looks like he could use a little exercise."

Mitch put the car into first gear, let out the clutch and rolled slowly toward the street with the trapped man running alongside and screaming profanities. The other man followed, pounding on the rear fender and yelling his own wide-ranging selection of choice four-letter words.

"Time to say goodbye," Al said when the front wheels hit the street. He opened the door just far enough to let the man's arm slip out, then slammed it and locked it as they turned right and drove away.

"Parting is such sweet sorrow," Mitch said.

"Amazing what some Romeos will do for a cigarette," Al said.

"Maybe now he'll realize that smoking can be hazardous to his health."

"On the other hand, Virginia, he did get a slim bit of exercise out of it."

Tuesday morning Al souped his film in the Daily Dispatch darkroom and was pleased to see he had captured Dennis O'Neal's face in five of the twelve pictures, even though all but the last one were taken at weird angles.

"Looks like he's defying gravity," Al said, looking at a print that showed Dennis leaning at a ninety-degree tilt on one foot.

"The camera never lies," Mitch said.

"I'll give Mr. Bombardier a call and see when he can pick them up." Al picked up Mitch's desk phone and punched in the number. After a short wait, Richard Bombardier's voice said, "Hello."

Al explained that he held in his hand pictorial proof that would put Dennis O'Neal out of the dance club business.

"That's great, but I got other things to worry about just now," Bombardier said. "I just got off the phone with my mother. She said she needs my help to move her father out of his apartment and into a long-term care facility. He's been going downhill steady ever since my grandmother died last month."

"I'm sorry to hear that," Al said. "Sometimes that happens with older couples; the survivor feels lost without the one who died."

"Yes, Grandpa took Grandma's death very hard and it hasn't gotten any better."

"Was your grandmother sick a long time?"

"No, her dying was kind of a shock, actually. She was 90 years old and almost blind, but she hadn't really been sick—just kind of, you know, getting older. Matter of fact, the geriatric specialist at the home saw her the night she died and didn't report any unusual problems to Grandpa."

"Did he usually give your grandfather a report?"

"Yes, if there was anything to be concerned about. He seemed like a very kind and caring guy. He comes from India, originally."

"From India?" Al said. "What's his name?"

"It's, uh, Sin something ..."

"Not Sinfahdi?"

"Yeah, that's it, Doctor Sinfahdi. How'd you know?"

A bell was clanging so loud inside Alan Jeffrey's head that he almost didn't hear the question or anything else Richard Bombardier said before he hung up.

CHAPTER 9

LET'S GET ONE THING STRAIGHT

Al put the phone down and fixed his eyes on some distant place, far beyond Warren Mitchell's face.

"What was that all about?" Mitch asked.

"You're not going to believe this," said Al as he came back to earth.

"Try me."

"Richard Bombardier's grandmother died last month in a nursing home, shortly after a visit from her doctor."

"So? That happens with old people. Your Uncle Charlie, for example."

"That's what I'm getting at. Grandma's doctor was a guy from India named Doctor Sinfahdi."

"No shit?"

"No shit. Our small world keeps getting smaller and so does Doctor Sinfahdi's list of living patients."

"You're not thinking that the good doctor is having something more than a run of bad luck with his patients, are you?"

"Three dead in a month? I suppose it could be bad luck. I don't know what the average geriatric specialist's patient death rate is, but this does seem like a lot. And these just involve people we know."

"Oh, come on, Al! Think about it. Why would a doctor, who from what we've heard is very popular with his patients, do something to shorten their lives?"

"I don't know. But three so close together ..."

"It makes no sense," Mitch said. "It would be stupid monetarily, if nothing else. Unless the patients are leaving the doctor a bundle in their wills."

"I know that Uncle Charlie didn't. But it does make you wonder—about his competence, if nothing else."

"Now that possibility I can buy. My father always said to be careful when you choose a doctor because somebody has to finish at the bottom of every class in medical school. It's beginning to sound like Doctor Sinfahdi was the anchor man in his."

"Well, anyway, I guess I can stick those pictures of dancing Dennis in the file for awhile until Mr. Bombardier gets his personal affairs settled."

"At least the gang at Hurley's will be happy for a few more nights."

"Ah, but some day my prints will come and one less queen will be enthroned on that stage."

After lunch, Alan Jeffrey drove out to an attorney's office on Victoria Street in Roseville to join Diana for the opening of Uncle Charlie's will. Al had suggested that Diana just pick up the will, which the attorney was holding, and bring it to the house where they could read it together, but Diana insisted on a formal session with the attorney present. "That way there won't be any doubt in your mind that everything is on the up and up," she said.

Al had told Diana that he had no fear she would rewrite the will, but she said the appointment had been made and she expected Al to be there. During the drive out to Roseville, Al decided it probably was a good thing, given his misgivings about Diana's actions after his conversation with Doctor Sinfahdi. On the other hand, he now had concerns about the doctor, as well. The guy might just be having a run of bad luck with his elderly patients. On the other hand, maybe he was not giving them proper treatment. Al wondered if Uncle Charlie's stroke might have been prevented or its devastating effects reduced if the doctor had done something different. It could be more than mere coincidence that Uncle Charlie, Mrs. Peterson's sister and Richard Bombardier's grandmother all died a few hours after a visit by Doctor Sinfahdi. It was possible, Al thought, that the doctor had given them the wrong medication, either through ignorance or by accident.

Another, less pleasant thought still lurked in the back of Alan Jeffrey's mind. He didn't want to consciously acknowledge this thought, but it finally pushed its way forward. What if Doctor Sinfahdi had knowingly given one or more of these patients the wrong medication?

As Mitch had said, this idea didn't make sense. First of all, it was unthinkable that a doctor would intentionally let a patient die. And secondly, even if a doctor was tempted to dabble in euthanasia, the loss of a patient meant the loss of a check from Medicare. Still, the similarities of the three old people's deaths were undeniable. Three in a month. Al wondered how many patients Doctor Sinfahdi lost during, say, a year, and what the normal loss rate was for geriatric specialists.

All this was still rattling around in Al's brain as he listened to Uncle Charlie's attorney read the will. Almost everything went to Diana, as expected. Al got his uncle's fishing gear, the aluminum fishing boat and trailer, which hadn't been used for several years, and a few odds and ends. The only surprise came when the lawyer announced that Uncle Charlie had left his entire coin collection to his nephew, Alan Jeffrey. There was some real value here, as Uncle Charlie had put substantial research, care and money into compiling an extensive collection of high-grade, ancient Greek and Roman coins that he had shown to Al with great pride.

"Whoa!" Al said to Diana as they left the office. "I never dreamed Uncle Charlie would leave his entire coin collection to me."

"He knew you were interested in it," she said. "To me they were just old pieces of metal with pictures of dead emperors. A lot of them aren't even perfectly round."

"The amazing thing is that they've survived all these centuries in such an excellent state of preservation."

"Whatever. They're all in a big safe in the bedroom closet and he had a little book listing everything he ever bought, so you can check them out and make sure I haven't taken any and sold them."

"I'm sure you haven't. But I'd love to come over some time soon and take a quick look at them. Would you mind?"

"Come over now if you want to. My parents have gone back home and I'm not doing anything special."

Al looked at his watch. It was nearing two-thirty. "Okay," he said. "I'll call the desk and tell them I'm not coming back to the office this afternoon. See you soon."

The long, low rambler that Uncle Charlie had built nearly forty years earlier for himself and Aunt Mildred, seemed cold and empty when Al followed Diana into the front entryway. He remembered having a similar sensation fifteen years before when he escorted Uncle Charlie home after Aunt Mildred's funeral, but the feeling of emptiness was even more intense now.

Diana led Al to the master bedroom at the rear of the house and opened a large walk-in closet with a sliding door. On the floor, beneath a row of Uncle Charlie's shirts, was a small, but solid safe.

"Here's the combination and here's his book," she said, handing Al a slip of paper with three numbers written on it and a little red loose-leaf notebook. "You start to the left, stopping at the first number on the fourth turn, go back and stop at the second on the third turn, the third on the second turn and then go right until it stops at ten. When you can't turn it any more, it's unlocked."

She watched while Al twirled the dial and eventually hit the final number and turned the handle that opened the safe. He found it packed with long, narrow cardboard and plastic boxes that contained coins packaged in two-inch-by-two-inch holders.

"Can I get you some coffee or a beer or anything?" Diana asked.

"No thanks," Al said. "I'm just going to take a quick look and then get out of your hair."

"You're not in my hair. Anyway, I'll be in the kitchen if you decide you want anything." She turned and went out of the bedroom, leaving Al to pull a few boxes out of the safe and quickly flip through the contents. He was thrilled at the number and the quality of what he found. He decided to take a couple of boxes home with him to peruse at his leisure after supper.

He was about to pick up the coin boxes when Diana appeared in the bedroom doorway. For the first time that day, Al took a really good look at his uncle's widow. She was dressed appropriately in black, but the clingy silk blouse and the hip-hugging slacks emphasized every curve of her luxuriously feminine body. Her face had regained its natural glow, her long, dark hair glistened in a shaft of sunlight coming through the bedroom window and her lips, which never needed lipstick, were red and full. Al remembered seeing pictures of Aunt Mildred that showed she had been quite a looker in her younger days too, and the thought struck him that Uncle Charlie had been blessed with a hell of a good eye for women.

"I really want to thank you for being such a help these past few days," she said in a silky voice.

"Well, I hope Carol and I have given you some comfort."

She raised her head and smiled. "Oh, you have," she said.

"Well, good," Al said. He was beginning to feel like Tweetie Bird being watched by a puddy tat and decided it was time to pick up the coin boxes. Before he could move, Diana walked purposefully across the bedroom, placed her hands on his shoulders, looked directly into his eyes and said, "Just having you acknowledge that I'm more than a greedy old gold-digger has been the most comfort of all."

Al felt the temperature in his face go up a degree as he gazed into the dark brown eyes only inches from his and said, "I just wish I hadn't made a fool of myself at your wedding so I could have known you better these last two years."

"You could get to know me better now," she said, barely above a whisper.

Wondering how much better she meant, Al said, "Yeah, I'd like us to get closer."

"Is this close enough?" she asked. She took her hands off his shoulders, wrapped her arms tightly around his body and pressed her soft breasts against his chest.

"Well, you can't get much closer," Al said as glistening beads of sweat popped out all across his forehead.

"Sure I can," Diana said. She tilted her face up to his and pulled his lips onto hers. Al's temperature rocketed up another couple of degrees as her tongue played along the perimeter and then pushed its way into his mouth.

The kiss went on so long that when it ended, Al was aware that more than his temperature had risen. Diana pressed her body tightly against the hardness in his groin, moving her hips in a slow circle as she reached up and placed the tip of her tongue in his ear. He gripped her upper body tightly as he felt her hands slide down his back and move around the front toward his zipper. He wanted desperately to undo the buttons on the back of her blouse, but instead he took a hard, deep breath and forced himself to lean his head back far enough to say, "Diana, we can't do this. You're a gorgeous woman and I'd love to keep going, but I'm a happily married man and I want to stay that way."

She released her grip quickly, pulled away and said, "You're right. We can't do this to Carol. I'm sorry. It's just that it's been an awful long time without—you know."

"Charlie wasn't a great lover?" Al said.

"Not after the first few months. He had prostate surgery and it left him … well, he couldn't do it, even with one of those pills. God, I'm sorry I came onto you like that. I really started out just to say thanks, but once I felt your body I forgot about everything."

"Don't be sorry. It's the biggest ego boost I've had in years. If I wasn't married, we'd be on that bed right now."

"You'd better leave before we change our minds."

"You're right," he said, picking up the two boxes of coins from the nightstand. "I'll bring these back in a couple of days."

"I'll see if I can find a mover to take the safe to your house," Diana said. "It's probably not a good idea for you to keep coming to my bedroom. One of these times you'll get into more than the safe."

"I suppose you're right. But I sure don't know where I'm going to put that thing. The safe, I mean."

"It's better you should keep it at home. And I'm talking about more than the safe. Now go!"

Without another word, he went.

On the drive home, the bedroom scene replayed itself in Al's mind. He was amazed at how easily Diana had turned him on. After two years of considering her to be nothing more than a cold-hearted gold digger, he had been ready to undress her in a matter of seconds when she presented herself as hot-blooded and available. Oh, how weak and vulnerable we poor men are in the arms of a beautiful woman, he thought. No wonder so many lonely sailors were lured to their deaths by the Sirens' call.

When Al got home, he found Carol in the kitchen with her hands smeared with blood and grease from cutting up a chicken. He set the boxes of coins on the hall table, went to Carol, turned her body toward his, hugged her tight and gave her a long, lingering kiss. Then he whispered the words she always wanted to hear, "Hi, gorgeous; what's the joke of the day?"

"I'm not sure I can remember it after a greeting like that."

"I always greet you with a hug and a kiss."

"Not with that kind of a hug and a kiss. Not since you used to go away for five or six months at a time in the Navy."

"Maybe I'm flashing back," Al said. "Uncle Charlie's death has my mind all mixed up. Especially after what I heard this morning."

"And what was that?"

Al went on to tell her about the death of Richard Bombardier's ninety-year-old grandmother last month and the identity of her doctor. He reminded her that the sister of the woman who manages Mitch's apartment building also had been seen by Doctor Sinfahdi shortly before her death. "I just wonder what the odds are on three of any given doctor's patients dying within a month of each other like that."

"Well, they were all older people," Carol said. "Uncle Charlie was the youngest and he was seventy-five with hardened arteries and he had suffered a severe stroke."

"I suppose it happens that way, but it does make you wonder about the doctor."

"You're not wearing your investigative team hat and thinking that there's anything funny going on, are you?"

"Maybe a little. I guess I'm thinking more about whether Doctor Sinfahdi knows what the hell he's doing. He admitted to me that he let Diana talk him into sending Uncle Charlie home from the hospital sooner than he wanted to let him go."

"Well, I imagine Diana can be pretty persuasive."

Al thought, "You have no clue how persuasive."

CHAPTER 10

ALL SHOOK UP

The rest of the week was uneventful. On Wednesday, Alan Jeffrey took the boxes of coins back to Uncle Charlie's safe and took out two more boxes. Diana Jeffrey, dressed in shorts and a sun top, greeted him without so much as touching his hand and stayed in the kitchen for the whole time he was in the bedroom. As he was leaving, she offered a handshake and said a mover was coming Friday to transport the safe to Al's house. Their hands stayed clasped and their eyes met for a long time before he thanked her and said he'd have to get right home and find a place to put the safe. Al's pulse was racing as he walked away toward his car and he avoided looking back to see if Diana was still in the doorway.

This was the week that Mitch had Saturday off and he was able to spend the entire weekend in Afton with Jennifer Tilton, whose fitness program included thirty laps of her swimming pool during the day and an exhilarating regimen of sexual exercises at night. Mitch couldn't keep up with her in the pool and he did all he could do to match her energy in bed, but he found it to be well worth the effort. He wondered where Jennifer had learned some of the more stimulating moves she used during their lovemaking, but he thought it wise not to ask.

Since his second day off rotated back to Monday, Mitch could have stayed in Afton for a third day, but Jennifer was working Monday through Friday on her new job, so he decided to be up and out of her house before the babysitter arrived that morning. He was surprised to receive a phone call from Jennifer at his apartment only a couple of hours after he had left her bed.

"I need someone friendly to talk to," she said, and the words came tumbling out. "I've just found out that one of my patients died suddenly. This is the first time it's happened to somebody I've been working with and it's got me kind of shook up. I did range of motion exercises with this woman twice last week. Her name was Irene. She was a sweet little old lady in her nineties who was trying to get strong enough to use a walker after having a series of little strokes."

"Where are you, anyway? Do you want me to come out?"

"I'm in Golden Pond Manor in Maplewood. You don't need to come out. Just talk to me for a minute."

"I know it's hard to lose a patient, but you're going to see more of this if you keep working in nursing homes."

"I know. I've got to get used to it. But even Doctor Sinfahdi, who must see a lot of deaths, seemed kind of sad about Irene."

"Whoa!" Mitch said. "Who did you say her doctor was?"

"His name is Doctor Ravi Sinfahdi. He's a sweet old gentleman from India who specializes in geriatrics. All the patients seem to adore him."

"I'll bet they do. And I'll bet his office is right close by in Maplewood."

"You're right. How do you know that?"

"Jen, this is really weird. Doctor Sinfahdi was the doctor for Mrs. Peterson's sister, for Al's Uncle Charlie and for the grandmother of that freelance customer of Al's I told you about Saturday."

"Oh, God! No wonder he felt bad. Imagine losing four patients in that short a time. The poor man!"

"I'm not so sure he's the one we should be feeling sorry for," Mitch said.

"What do you mean?"

"I mean that with four deaths that we know about occurring in a little over a month, maybe Doctor Sinfahdi's patients aren't getting the best of care."

"Oh, come on, Mitch. He treats old, sick people. You just got done telling me to expect to see more deaths if I keep working with patients in nursing homes."

"Okay," Mitch said. "I'll give Doctor Sinfahdi the benefit of the doubt. But do me a favor."

"What?"

"See if you can find out how many other patients in that nursing home were being treated by Doctor Sinfahdi when they died within the last six months or so."

"I don't think I can do that. Medical records are confidential."

"Yeah, but the nursing home must keep some sort of a daily log or something that's not part of the patients' confidential files."

"I don't know about anything like that. I suppose I can ask around."

"Try to be cool about it. You don't want to get anybody upset or suspicious if you can help it."

Mitch hung up and decided to relay what he had just learned from

Jennifer on to Alan Jeffrey, who also had this day off. He punched in Al's home number and said, "Guess what?" when the photographer answered the phone.

"Jennifer's pregnant?"

"No, it's nothing childish, but it is kind of strange and she is shook up. It seems that Doctor Sinfahdi has lost another patient."

"No shit? Who now?"

"A woman at one of the nursing homes where Jen does therapy," Mitch said. He told Al what Jennifer had said about the death of Irene at Golden Pond Manor. They agreed that the pattern being woven before them smelled strongly of malpractice—if not of something even more repugnant.

"There's still no way I can believe a doctor would intentionally be doing away with his patients," Mitch said. "Even supposing they asked him to help them commit suicide, it violates his oath, not to mention the law. This is a big issue with doctors and politicians and the courts."

"Okay, let's operate on the assumption that he's innocent of anything criminal, but may be some kind of a malpracticing quack," said Al. "Whatever he is, this is a personal thing with me because of Uncle Charlie. The first thing we need to do is find out what the normal death rate is for patients of a geriatric specialist. Next we need to figure out what that rate is for Doctor Sinfahdi. Now, how in the hell do we do either one?"

"I've got Jen looking for a legal way to find out how many patients the good doctor has lost at Golden Pond Manor. Maybe the AMA could give us some numbers on average geriatric death rates."

"I'd also like to know more about how the other three patients died. We know that Doctor Sinfahdi visited Uncle Charlie and gave him a shot of a pain killer a few hours before he died. What do we know about the others?"

"Not much. We need to ask Mrs. Peterson and Mr. Bombardier some questions and ask Jen to find out what details she can about Irene."

"Let's get on it. In addition to satisfying my personal curiosity, we may have a story here."

They decided that their first move would be to call the American Medical Association office in Minneapolis. Al made the call and got a dumbfounded response from the woman in the AMA's public information office.

"Why would you want to know that?" she asked.

"I'm part of a team working on a story on geriatrics," Al said

"I doubt that we have statistics on anything like that," she said. "May I take your number and call you back?"

"I'd better call you back later today. I'm going out on an assignment soon and you might miss me. My name is Alan Jeffrey." He didn't want her to call the newspaper office when he wasn't there because it might arouse the curiosity of whoever picked up the phone on the photo desk.

Meanwhile, it was Warren Mitchell's task to question Mrs. Peterson. This was a call he didn't relish making. Quizzing the old lady about the details of her sister's death so soon after the fact was not going to be easy. He punched in the number and told her who he was when she answered.

"Is anything wrong, Mr. Mitchell?" she asked. She rarely got calls from renters unless there was a problem.

"No, nothing's wrong," Mitch said. "But I want to ask you some questions that are kind of personal about your sister. The one you lost last week."

"What is it that you want to know?"

"I'm wondering when was the last time Doctor Sinfahdi saw your sister and what, if anything, he did in the way of treatment or medication."

"Well, I remember the nurse at Cedar Gardens saying she called the doctor in to see Grace late Saturday afternoon because she was having quite a lot of pain in her joints. She had arthritis pretty bad, you know."

"Did the nurse say whether the doctor gave Grace any kind of medication when he saw her that day?"

"No, I don't think she did."

"Could you call her and ask her? As Grace's next of kin, you have a right to know these things."

"What's this all about, Mr. Mitchell?"

"I don't want to alarm you, Mrs. Peterson, but a photographer I work with and I know of several other patients of Doctor Sinfahdi who have died recently. In fact, one of them was my photographer friend's uncle. Probably it's just a coincidence, but we're trying to figure out if there are any similarities."

"You don't think the doctor did something wrong?"

"We don't know, Mrs. Peterson. That's what we're trying to figure out."

"I feel kind of funny doing it, but I'll call that nurse and see if she knows if the doctor did anything for Grace."

Al's next call went to Richard Bombardier. He was told by the woman who answered the phone that Richard was at the Cedar Gardens long-term care center making arrangements for his grandfather to move in. Al then phoned Cedar Gardens and, after a considerable wait, heard Bombardier's voice say, "Hello."

"This is Alan Jeffrey from the Daily Dispatch," Al said. "I'm sorry to bother you at a busy time like this, but I need to ask you a couple of questions about your grandmother's passing."

"What the hell for?" was the brusque reply.

"I don't want to upset you, but we're looking at how some of Doctor Sinfahdi's patients died. We're trying to make sure that everything is the way it should be."

"You think the doctor might have screwed up?"

"We're hoping to make sure he hasn't."

"So what do you want to know about Grandma?"

"Just a couple of things. You said that she was in some sort of senior home, didn't you?"

"Yeah, Cedar Gardens, right where I am now. Nice place."

"And you said Doctor Sinfahdi came to examine your grandmother the night before she died?"

"Yeah. She seemed okay, but she was having headaches."

"Did he give her anything for the headaches?"

"Jesus, I don't know. We were leaving from a visit when he came in and, like I said, the doctor didn't report anything to Grandpa." Al could sense the Richard Bombardier's patience was wearing thin.

"I don't want to ask you to go to a lot of trouble, Mr. Bombardier, but could you, when you have a minute, ask the people there at Cedar Gardens if the doctor did anything like, say, gave her pills or a shot?"

"What the hell are you aiming at?" Bombardier asked. "Are you people cooking up some kind of a sensational story?"

"Probably not," Al said. "But the information would be helpful and if we do find that everything isn't the way it should be, we'll certainly let you know."

"All right, I'll try to talk to the nurses here, but I'm pretty busy right now."

"I know, Mr. Bombardier. There's a lot of work involved in moving somebody. Please give me a call when you find out something"

Al hung up, called Warren Mitchell and asked, "Where'd you say your building manager's sister died?"

"Cedar Gardens in Roseville."

"Guess what? Cedar Gardens is where Richard Bombardier's granny was when Doctor Sinfahdi paid her a final visit."

"Why am I not surprised? And did Doctor Sinfahdi give the Bomber's granny a shot for something?"

"We don't know that yet. He's going to find out and I hope he does it soon because Cedar Gardens is where he's planting his grandfather."

"Let's hope Doctor Sinfahdi doesn't call on him or the old man might end up planted six feet deeper somewhere else."

The next time Mitch's phone rang it was Jennifer Tilton. "I don't think I can help you guys much," she said. "They do keep a daily log of patients entering and leaving—and whether they went home or to a hospital or to a funeral home—but it is strictly confidential."

"There's no way you can sneak a peek?"

"Not without risking losing my job."

"We don't want you to do that, but there is one other thing," Mitch said. "Do you know if Doctor Sinfahdi gave any kind of medication to your late patient the last time he saw her?"

"One of the nurses said Irene was having migraines and he gave her a shot that seemed to help a lot."

"Yeah, well, the pain certainly went away, didn't it?"

"Forever, I guess." Noting that she still sounded shaken by Irene's death, Mitch suggested that he pick up some take-out Chinese and bring it out to Afton for dinner.

"Will you stay over?" she asked.

"If you promise to let me get to work on time."

"Hey, you could have got to work on time today. Becky will be here at 7:30 again tomorrow and we don't want to be demonstrating the facts of life for her." Becky was the 14-year-old neighbor Jennifer had hired to stay with Tony and Tracy every day during the summer school vacation.

When the phone rang a few minutes later, it was Nellie Peterson.

"I just wanted to let you know, I spoke to the nurse and she remembered the doctor giving Grace a shot of pain medicine when he saw her because her arthritis was acting up," Mrs. Peterson said.

"He gave her a shot for arthritis pain?"

"Yah, that's what the nurse said. She seen him do it. She said Grace felt better and was able to relax and go right to sleep a little while later."

"Thank you, Mrs. Peterson. I'm sorry to put you to this trouble."

"Oh, that's okay, Mr. Mitchell. If I can be any more help, you just let me know."

Mitch relayed this information to Al as soon as soon as his conversation with Mrs. Peterson ended.

"A shot?" asked Al.

"A shot."

"You're not needling me?"

"No, but I'll bet I'm getting under your skin."

"All the way to the bone. It is now my turn not to be surprised."

"If you don't mind, I'll pass on my next turn for that. I don't like the non-surprises we keep turning up."

"Me neither. What we do need to turn up is information on more of Doctor Sinfahdi's patients. But how the hell do we get it?"

Mitch pondered Al's question all the while he was picking out a change of socks, shirt and underwear to take with him to Afton. He was carrying them out the back door to his car when he met Martha Todd on her way in from her parking place behind the apartment building.

"Going away?" she said, eyeing the bundle in one hand and the shirt he carried on a hanger in the other.

"Just for a little while," Mitch said, feeling his face growing warm with a blush. "My ... uh, the woman I'm seeing has had a traumatic day and I'm going out to have supper with her."

"How nice of you. What happened to her?"

"She works as a physical therapist with patients in nursing homes and when she arrived for her first appointment this morning, she was told the woman had died."

"Oh, that's too bad. Does your friend work here in the city?"

"In the northern suburbs. This happened in Maplewood at a home called Golden Pond Manor, would you believe."

"No kidding? I would believe. Remember I told you my grampa died just before Christmas? That's where he was, Golden Pond Manor."

Mitch could hardly wait for the answer to his next question. "Tell me, who was your grandfather's doctor?"

"Oh, I have no idea," Martha said.

"Can you find out?" He realized he had asked the question with the intensity of a leopard pouncing on its prey.

"Why?" she said, backing away a step. "Is it important?"

"It could be." He lowered his tone, trying to sound serious but casual. However, Martha had already sensed that something was wrong.

"I guess I could ask my parents; they'd probably know. Look, has this got something to do with your work at the paper?"

"It might, or it might be nothing at all, but I'd appreciate it very much if you'd find out for me."

"Sure," she said. "Well, have a nice time at dinner."

"Thanks," he said, starting toward his car. He heard Martha say, "Glad to see you're dressing for it," and turned back to see a playful smile on her face. He felt his blush grow a deeper red and he hurried to the car.

CHAPTER 11

FRIENDLY PERSUASION

The need to be out of the shower and dressed before Becky, the baby sitter, rang the bell at Jennifer Tilton's front door allowed Warren Mitchell to arrive at the Daily Dispatch office on time Tuesday morning.

Alan Jeffrey, who was already at the photo desk, sipping his first cup of coffee and reading the morning paper, looked up, looked at Mitch and suddenly slumped in his chair, feigning a dead faint.

"Very funny, but if you think I'm going to wake you with a kiss, you'll be zonked out there one hell of a long time," Mitch said.

Al raised his head. "It's just too much for me to see you here at this early hour after you've spent an evening comforting the fair Jennifer," he said.

"The fair Jennifer also has a job, and her hours aren't quite as flexible as those of us who pursue the small daily events that shape our world for a living."

"For your sake, I hope all of her clients make it through this day alive. I would hate to see you wearing yourself out providing solace in her bed every night of the work-a-day week. I'm not sure you could keep it up."

"Your concern for my well-being is most touching, but I can assure you that with Jennifer's help I can keep it up any time I want it up."

"Ah, it's wonderful to be young and upright," said Al. "Pour yourself a stiff cup of coffee and catch up on the world while I try hard to think of a way we can find out more about our Doctor Sinfahdi and the death rates of geriatric patients." He tossed the newspaper to Mitch, reached for the phone and punched in the number of the AMA. He asked for Ellen, and when she came on the line he said he was Alan Jeffrey, the newspaper photographer who had inquired about geriatric death rates the day before.

"I meant to get back to you yesterday afternoon but some other assignments got in the way," Al said.

"It really doesn't matter," said Ellen. "I'm afraid I can't help you. There are no statistics like that available. I'm sorry."

"I'm sorry, too. This makes it tough to develop our story."

"You might try talking to some geriatric specialists. They won't discuss their individual patients but they might give you some blind numbers."

"That's a great idea," said Al. "Thank you very much for your help."

"What's a great idea?" asked Mitch after Al hung up.

"Talking to some geriatric specialists about their experience with dying patients."

"You think they're going to discuss that kind of information with some schmuck who calls up and says he's working on a story for the paper?"

"Yeah, you're right. That's very touchy stuff."

"Doctors are even more protective of their secrets than nursing homes, and you may remember that Jen ran into a dead end there—no pun intended for a change."

"Ah, yes, Jennifer," Al said, taking a sip of coffee and putting on his thoughtful look. "I'll bet she sees a lot of doctors in her travels out there from nursing home to nursing home."

"What is on your devious mind?"

"Jennifer is aggrieved over a patient's dying just a few days after she started her job. Could she maybe, in all the sweet innocence of her moment of sorrow, ask a few of the doctors she encounters just how frequently, in their experience, patient deaths occur?"

"You are one sneaky son of a bitch," Mitch said. "I'm proud to be associated with you. Jen might be willing to serve as our spy if I asked her very nicely at just the right time."

"You guys want me to do what?" Jennifer Tilton said as she and Warren Mitchell lay side by side in her bed. She had been half dozing after a leisurely round of love-making when Mitch began talking about doctors, elderly patients and death rates.

"The timing is perfect," Mitch said. "You can play on your genuine grief over your friend Irene's death to ask some doctors how often they experience the loss of an elderly patient."

"What's that going to prove?"

"It won't prove anything, but it might give us some perspective on Doctor Sinfahdi's rate of loss, which, at the moment, seems kind of high. In fact, Doctor Sinfahdi is one of the doctors you could ask."

"And the reason I give the doctors for asking is …?"

"You're new on the job and very emotional and you're wondering how often you'll have to deal with death, or something to that effect, however you want to say it." He kissed her gently on the earlobe nearest him.

Jennifer pulled away slightly and turned her face toward Mitch. "I could get my ass fired if one of these doctors finds out I'm passing information about his practice on to you guys."

"How would they ever find out?" He stretched toward her, intending to kiss her lips, but she slid her face away across her pillow.

"I'll think about it," she said. "Now don't try to muddle my mind with your lovey-dovey stuff while I'm making my decision." She rolled away across the queen-size mattress and turned her back to him.

"Wouldn't dream of muddling your mind," Mitch said as he slid across and pressed the length of his body against her. One hand crept up her belly and came to rest on her right breast. His fingers toyed with the nipple, which immediately sprung to attention, and she felt the heat of him rising against her flesh just above the crease between her buttocks.

"Oh, Christ, go ahead and muddle," she said, rolling over to face him, pulling him tight against her breasts and belly. Even while she was enjoying the solid feel of his muscular arms and chest, she silently scolded herself for being unable to resist this man, even when he clearly was trying to manipulate her.

Timothy Tilton had been a master manipulator all during their courtship and marriage and now Warren Mitchell was leading her down the same path. It's my own damn fault, Jennifer said to herself as Mitch's lips caressed her left nipple, I've got to learn to say no sometimes. She sucked in her breath as his teeth tightened on the same nipple, and she told herself that saying no would be a hell of a lot easier if she didn't like Warren Mitchell so much.

"Jen's not terribly comfortable with the idea of talking to doctors about their patients dying, but she'll do it," Mitch reported to Al at the Daily Dispatch office on Wednesday morning.

"You must have been very persuasive."

"She deals with different doctors and clinics throughout the week, so it will take at least a week to talk to all of them. Maybe more, depending on their schedules. The really interesting quiz session could be on Friday when she expects to see Doctor Sinfahdi at Cedar Gardens."

"Friday always was my favorite day of the week," Al said.

"While Jen's busy with her survey, as you call it, I was thinking on the way in this morning that there's something else we can do to check on Doctor Sinfahdi's recent mortality rate."

"What's that?"

"We could look at the death notices that have been in the paper."

"Where will that get us?"

"Most of them tell where the person died and they all list survivors. I'm talking about the obituaries in the news columns, not the ones in fine print that just give the bare essentials. We could list the people who died in the good doctor's geographic territory during the last six months or year or whatever. Then, if what Jen finds out makes it look like Doctor Sinfahdi's loss rate is above average, we could contact some of the survivors to see who their dear departeds' doctors were."

"How do we dig back through a year's worth of obituaries?" Al asked.

"It's all in our library computer files. I could look through them"

"Sounds like a lot of work, but it might be interesting."

"I'll come in and give it a try sometime after regular working hours," Mitch said. "I don't want O'Rourke the worry wart to know I'm doing this until I'm sure we have a story that's going to be worth printing here." The city editor was noted for taking a super-cautious approach to controversial stories that had any possibility of bringing forth a libel suit.

"Good thinking. No use getting Don all worked up over nothing. But beyond that, what makes you think any of the survivors will tell us who their lost loved ones' doctors were?"

"I'll think of a scam. Remember, I'm the great persuader."

When Mitch arrived home that evening, Sherlock Holmes greeted him at the door, as usual, jumping down off his sleeping spot on the sofa and presenting himself for petting. After the prescribed homecoming ritual of ear scratching and belly rubbing, the cat went back to his comfy cushion on the sofa. Mitch had decided to use the computer in the Daily Dispatch library, which couldn't be seen from the newsroom, for his obituary search, so he had asked the librarian to call him when the room was empty and nobody else needed that machine. While waiting for the call, he began to think about supper. Not surprisingly, he found his choices limited to a can of spaghetti and meatballs on the kitchen cupboard shelves and an unidentified variety of sandwich meat in the refrigerator.

Cooking was an art that had never really been of interest to Mitch, even though he loved to eat a well-prepared meal. His mother, who could make almost anything taste good, had taught his sister to cook but Mitch had resisted all efforts to drag him into the kitchen during his teenage years. Then he went off to college and subsisted on whatever could be scrounged up. After that, the Navy fed him until he married Karen.

Among her many attributes, Karen had been an excellent cook, so Mitch never found it necessary to try his hand in the kitchen during the few years of their marriage. For a short while after Karen and little Billy died, Mitch ate out a lot. Then, during his subsequent bout with depression and alcoholism, he subsisted mostly on booze and an occasional fast-food cheeseburger with fries.

Now that he was productively employed and no longer drinking, he again ate out a lot. His home cooking repertoire consisted mostly of boxed macaroni and cheese, canned soups and frozen dinners. Not even these old reliables were available on this particular night and he was wishing he didn't have to wait for a call from the Daily Dispatch librarian when he heard a knock on the door. He opened it to find Martha Todd standing before him.

She was dressed in a smartly-tailored dark blue business suit, with a pale blue blouse that opened in a V down the front and contrasted dramatically with her coffee-with-cream complexion and jet-black hair. Obviously she had just returned from an afternoon of clerking at the law office.

"Hi," Mitch said. "Come on in."

"I just dropped by to tell you I have the answer to your question about Grampa Mendes's doctor," Martha said.

"Well, come, sit and tell me," he said, motioning toward the end of the couch not occupied by Sherlock Holmes. "You're not allergic to cats or anything, are you?"

"I love cats," she said, seating herself beside Sherlock. Before she could even cross her legs, the cat responded by crawling onto her lap and nuzzling her ribs with his head. "Well, hello. What's your name?"

"Al Jeffrey's wife suggested the name because she thought it was appropriate for a reporter who goes around snooping into other people's lives. It's Sherlock Holmes."

Martha laughed. "Al Jeffrey's wife is pretty good at naming things."

"She's a very clever woman. Al is very lucky to have her."

"It's nice that some people are lucky in love." She was stroking the fur all along the back of Sherlock Holmes, who had hunkered down on her lap and was purring his loudest purr.

"Well, I have Sherlock Holmes," Mitch said. "Unless he decides to go home with you. He's usually a little more reserved with strangers."

"He just knows a friend when he sees one. Don't worry, I won't steal him, although I'd love to have him around." She smiled down at the contented bundle of black-and-white fur on her lap.

"Anyway, you were going to tell me about your grandfather's doctor."

"Yes," she said. "I talked to my mother last night and she said Grampa's doctor was named Ravi Sinfahdi. He's from India. She said he's a very sweet, soft-spoken, sympathetic man."

Mitch tried not to react to this revelation but Martha saw a quick change of expression flash across his face. "Is something wrong?" she asked.

"Maybe ... and maybe not," Mitch said. "It's kind of a long story."

"Why don't you come down to my apartment and tell it to me? I'm about to cook up some spaghetti and I can easily throw in enough for two. It's the same sauce I fed you the other night."

"I'd love to join you, but I have to stick here and wait for a phone call. It's kind of important or I'd be happy to take you up on the invitation. Cooking is not my bag."

"Well, maybe some other time," she said. The look of disappointment on her face matched the frustration Mitch was feeling. "With work and school and all, I don't get to cook nearly as much as I'd like to."

"Could you cook it here—in my kitchen?" he asked.

The smile returned to Martha's face and eyes. "No reason I couldn't," she said. "I'll go get everything if you'll take the cat. I don't have the heart to move him."

Sherlock was sound asleep on Martha's lap. Mitch leaned down, slipped his hands between the slumbering cat and Martha's thighs and slid Sherlock smoothly over to the open end of the sofa. He noticed that the thighs felt firm against the backs of his hands and his nose detected a subtle, pleasant odor of either perfume or bath soap when he was close to her. He felt his pulse quicken and he straightened and stepped back.

Martha rose and walked to the door. "See you in a few minutes," she said as she stepped into the hallway. "I want to change clothes before I start slopping around in spaghetti sauce."

"Hurry back," Mitch said. "I'd go along and help you carry stuff but that's when my call would be sure to come."

When Martha Todd returned ten minutes later she was wearing the faded, skin-tight jeans he loved to watch and a navy blue T-shirt with a Minnesota Twins logo on the front. She was carrying a plastic grocery bag loaded with a box of spaghetti and the raw materials needed to create a sauce, along with salad greens and a couple bottles of dressing. Mitch watched with approval as she strode past him and set her burden down on the small kitchen counter.

"You a baseball fan?" he asked.

"My favorite spectator sport," Martha said. "But I haven't seen a game yet this season. No time."

"You should make time. We could go together. I love baseball, too."

Mitch seated himself at the kitchen table where he could watch Martha from the rear while she prepared their dinner. He wondered if she could feel his eyes riveted on the undulations of her beguiling bottom while she moved from counter to stove and back again. She had just dumped a handful of spaghetti into a pot of boiling water and given the mixture on the other burner a stir when she turned and caught him with his eyes fixed on her body, just below belt level.

"Are you thinking I need a new pair of jeans?" she asked. The playful grin Martha had displayed when she'd seen Mitch carrying a change of clothes on his way to have dinner with Jennifer was back.

Mitch felt the blood rush to his face. "Oh, no," he said. "There's nothing better than a comfortable, well-broken-in pair of jeans."

"They are very comfortable," she said as she settled onto a chair across the small table from Mitch. "I just wonder if they're getting worn a little thin across the seat."

"They look pretty sturdy," Mitch said and he felt the blush grow deeper. Silently he asked himself why he always behaved like a babbling idiot when he was close to a desirable woman.

"Good. I was afraid you could see right through them."

Don't I wish, Mitch said to himself. He felt a need to change the subject. "Could I get you something to drink?" he asked. "I can't offer you wine or anything like that but there is some cold root beer in the fridge."

"I'd love some. I almost brought a bottle of Merlot with me and then I remembered what you told me when I stuck my foot in my mouth that night."

"You never did," he said, rising to get the root beer from the refrigerator. He poured them each a glassful and sat across from Martha again. Her nose is a little too flat, but she looks pretty good from the front, too, he thought. If only she'd quit clipping her hair almost down to her scalp. "Cheers," he said, raising his glass.

"Cheers," she said, reaching across the table to clink his glass with hers. At close range, their eyes locked for a lingering moment and Mitch felt a strong urge to lean a little further and kiss her on the lips. Then the phone rang.

"Must be my call," Mitch said. He stood up quickly and crossed the room to answer it. But it wasn't the librarian on the other end of the line.

CHAPTER 12

PLAYING THE NUMBERS

"What are you doing?" asked Jennifer Tilton in her cheeriest voice.

"I'm, uh, getting ready to eat supper," Mitch said.

"Macaroni and cheese from a box or Spaghettos from a can?" She loved to tease him about his inadequacies as a cook.

"Oh, well, neither one, actually, but I guess it's closer to Spaghettos."

"Don't tell me you're actually cooking something!" Her voice vibrated with mock shock.

"Hey, I can boil water with the best of them," Mitch said. Martha pointed to herself and pointed toward the door. He shook his head "no" and said into the phone, "To what do I owe this most welcome call?"

"I just wanted to tell you that I talked to a doctor from one of the clinics I work at today. He told me not to worry about losing my patients; that it doesn't happen all that often."

"Did he give you any numbers?"

"I asked him how often is 'not all that often' and said he could remember only three of his patients dying over the last couple of years."

"Three in a span of two years?"

"That's what he said. Which is about what your Doctor Sinfahdi has lost in the last month."

"Maybe Doctor Sinfahdi is just having a streak of bad luck," Mitch said. "And then, again, maybe not. Keep asking around and we'll see if we can work out an average after you've quizzed a few more doctors."

"I feel like a character in a spy novel."

"Well, don't get captured and thrown into a dungeon. I gotta go now; water's boiling." Martha was signaling that the spaghetti and the sauce were ready to serve. She opened a cupboard door, hauled out some plates and salad bowls and put them on the table with a moderate clatter.

"Is someone there?" Jennifer asked. "I thought I heard dishes rattling."

"Must have been Sherlock Holmes banging his bowl into the wall," Mitch said. "I'll call you later and we can chat."

"Okay, but if you get a busy signal it means I'm on the internet and I might be on quite awhile. Bye."

Martha was slicing some mushrooms over the top of a three-lettuce salad she had concocted. "Sorry if my presence put a damper on your conversation," she said.

"Don't worry about it. Jen's helping Al and me with the project I'm going to tell you about and she was just passing along some information. It's not like we're engaged or anything." Now why in the hell did I think I needed to say that, he asked himself. They damn well could be engaged if he had just had the balls to open his mouth and ask her a few days ago.

"Everything's ready," Martha said. "I'll pour us some more root beer and you can tell me all about this project while we eat." They were joined at that moment by Sherlock Holmes, who obviously had smelled the spaghetti sauce and seemed interested in sampling it.

"Would Sherlock eat a vegetarian sauce made of peppers, onions, garlic and tomatoes?" Martha asked. "There's no meat in it and it's pretty spicy stuff."

"Better cool it," Mitch said. "All I need is a cat with diarrhea." Then he launched into his lengthy story, beginning with Mrs. Peterson's phone call about her sister's death. Martha listened intently to the entire monologue.

"So, what exactly are you and your photographer friend driving at?" Martha asked when Mitch had finished. "Do you suspect Doctor Sinfahdi of malpractice?"

"It looks like a real possibility," Mitch said. "If we figure out that the death rate of his patients is way out of line with other doctors in the area, it might be a good idea for some of the survivors to bring it to the attention of the AMA. In all the cases Al and I are familiar with, the patients didn't seem to be pounding at death's door, so to speak."

"I guess you could say that about Grampa Mendes, too. He was frail but nobody was concerned about him dying. Then, boom, he was gone. Mom and Gramma Mendes still haven't gotten over how sudden it was."

"That's pretty much been the pattern."

"So, what happens next?"

"We run whatever numbers we can find and see where it leads. Which reminds me, the Daily Dispatch librarian still hasn't called to say her computer's available."

"Must be a busy night in old St. Paul. Anyway, I should gather up my dirty cooking pots and take them home to wash."

"I've got a dishwasher; you could do them here," Mitch said. "That way you could stay awhile longer and keep Sherlock Holmes happy." The cat again was curled up in Martha's lap, having jumped up the minute she pushed her chair back after finishing her meal.

"I'd love to stay but I really do have some homework that has to be done before tomorrow morning. Sorry, Sherlock." She eased the bulky tomcat off her lap and onto the floor, from where he looked up at her indignantly before walking away to the sofa with an air of "I was ready to get down and go into the other room, anyway."

Together they loaded Mitch's plates, silverware and salad bowls into the dishwasher and packed Martha's stuff back into the plastic bag. At the door, she stopped, turned back and said, "You don't think Doctor Sinfahdi is doing something ... how shall I say it ... worse than malpractice, do you?"

"The thought has crossed our minds," Mitch said. "The problem there is we can't figure out why he would intentionally do anything to hasten the death of a bill-paying patient."

"Can you keep me posted on what you find out? I kind of have a personal interest in this." Her eyes were moist, as though she was on the verge of tears.

Mitch went to her and touched her hand as he said, "Absolutely. You and a lot of others may have yourselves a lawsuit."

"I'm not much interested in a lawsuit, but if Doctor Sinfahdi is a quack I am interested in seeing that no more families get a shock like mine did."

"I think that's Al's major interest, too. If the guy can't take care of his patients, he ought to be put out of business before he causes any more pain."

Again their eyes met and held for a moment and again Mitch thought about how pleasant it would be to lean forward a few inches and kiss Martha's full, magenta lips. Then the phone rang again and she whispered "good night" and slipped out the door. This time it was the librarian on the line.

Carol Jeffrey was clearing away the dinner dishes when she suddenly remembered something. "I almost forgot to tell you," she said to Al. "Your Aunt Diana called just before you got home and asked me to have you call her back."

"My Aunt Diana?" he said, with a heavy emphasis on "aunt."

"She was married to your Uncle Charlie; that makes her your aunt."

"Diana's the same age I am. Aunts are supposed to be your mother's age, not your own."

"Apparently your Uncle Charlie didn't subscribe to that theory."

"Well, she sure as hell never acted very aunt-like." He was thinking of the two years of non-communication that followed Charlie and Diana's wedding. Then his mind moved onward to the more recent moment when he had suddenly found her melting in his arms. "She didn't say what she wanted?"

"She said she found some more of Charlie's stuff that you should have. She wants to know when you can come and get it."

Alan Jeffrey was not so sure that it would be wise to make a return visit to Diana's house. He had never been so close to straying from his marriage vows as he was that afternoon when Diana pressed her body against his and made it clear that she was ready and willing to forget about the two-year chill that followed his insulting remark at her wedding reception. Technically Diana might be his aunt, but realistically she was a voluptuous woman in the prime of life who was, at least at that particular moment, in desperate need of some sexual release.

Well, what the hell, he couldn't avoid Diana forever. Al made the call, learned that Diana had found some more coins in the house and wanted to give them to him, along with whatever items of Charlie's fishing and outdoor gear that Al might find useful. He agreed to stop by after work the following day to look things over and take what he wanted. Later, when Al and Carol went to bed, he took a long time making love to her, draining the well of his sexual energy to the bottom in the process.

At 9:45 P.M., Warren Mitchell parked his Toyota on Kellogg Boulevard near Cedar Street and walked to the Daily Dispatch. He checked in with the security man in the lobby and went up to the newspaper's library, which was in a corner with one open doorway that faced the newsroom and another that was on a back hallway leading to the men's and women's restrooms. Mitch went in through the back hallway and sat down at a computer in the far, rear corner.

Mitch decided to start with the most recent deaths and work backward, looking for persons who died in St. Paul's northern suburban area—Roseville, Falcon Heights, Little Canada, St. Anthony and Maplewood. Each time he found one in that area, he wrote down the name, place of death and names of all the survivors (except those who lived in some distant state).

It was tiresome, eye-straining work, with the boredom relieved only when he found the occasional familiar name. They were all there: Charles A. Jeffrey, Grace (Peterson) Nordstrom, Renee (Fortier) Bombardier, Valdis J. Mendes.

Mitch had worked his way back to the previous July and was ready to shut down the computer and leave the building when a voice at his shoulder said, "What the hell are you doing here?" He jerked his head around quickly and found himself looking up into the face of Jerry Granger, a columnist whose work appeared in the morning paper every Sunday, Tuesday and Thursday.

"Oh, hi, Jerry. I'm ... uh ... I'm looking up an old obit for a friend," Mitch said. "A mutual friend of ours died last summer and we both missed it at the time."

"Sorry, I didn't mean to startle you," said Jerry Granger. "I just didn't expect to find a day-side reporter working in here at midnight."

"No problem," Mitch said. "I didn't expect anyone from the newsroom to walk in here at midnight."

"Sometimes we work funny hours," Granger said. "Hey, you do some investigative stuff, don't you? Didn't you and that photographer, Al Somebody, get involved in a kidnapping last fall?"

"Yeah, that was Al Jeffrey and me," Mitch said.

"I really would like to talk to you sometime," the columnist said. "I've come across something that might be worth digging into."

"Call me any time and tell me what you've got," Mitch said. He was closing files and shutting down the computer as he spoke, eager to leave before Granger asked any more questions about his late-night obituary search.

"Well, it won't be for awhile," Granger said. "I'm going to Kansas for a week's vacation. Going to visit some 'rellies' at the old family homestead near Wichita."

"Okay, we can talk when you get back. Now I'd better haul ass out of here or there won't be any point in going home before starting work. See ya around, Jerry."

"Yeah," said Jerry. "See ya, Mitch."

"You'll never in a thousand years guess who Martha Todd's grandfather's doctor was when he died," Mitch said to Al over a cup of coffee Thursday morning.

"It couldn't possibly have been Ravi Sinfahdi, could it?" Al said.

"Damn! A thousand years just flashed by before my very eyes."

"You do look a little older than you did a minute ago."

"I hope the aging has improved me, like a good wine. Anyway, Martha is now very interested in our little investigative reporting project. It seems that Grampa Mendes, as she calls him, didn't appear to be anywhere near death's door when the grim reaper, or his emissary, Doctor Sinfahdi, snuck up and pushed him through. Her mother and grandmother are still in shock."

"How much did you tell her?"

"Everything. It seemed like she should know, being as how her family is intimately involved with the doctor."

"I guess that makes sense, but I don't think we should be blabbing about Doctor Sinfahdi to too many people before we have something more concrete to go on."

"Something concrete to go on. You mean like a cement toilet?"

"Oh, can it!"

"Well, I trust it won't piss you off that I collected a few more prospects from the obit files late last night."

Before Al could respond, the voice of city editor Don O'Rourke was heard summoning Mitch to the city desk for an assignment. It was the last the pair of would-be medical investigators saw of each other that day.

Friday was one of those days when a person hates to stay inside—sunny bright blue skies accentuated by passing windrows of fluffy white clouds, a slight breeze from the west, low humidity and temperatures rising gradually all day to a high of eighty degrees by mid-afternoon. It was the sort of day that inspired the poet to write: "What is so rare as a day in June?"

And, in sharp contrast to the previous day, nothing of great importance was happening in the city of St. Paul. Except for a handful of minor rewrite jobs and a couple of quick phone checks, Warren Mitchell spent the morning searching through telephone directories for numbers of survivors listed in the obituaries that he had perused on Wednesday night. Trial phone calls to a couple of those numbers yielded one "it's none of your damn business who my mother's doctor was" and one "I think his name was Johnson ... or maybe Jenson ... what difference does it make?" All this after carefully explaining to each person called that the purpose of the question was to help fill in the gaps on a press release from the American Medical Association, which was trying to compile some much-needed statistics on doctors specializing in geriatrics.

Jennifer called Mitch soon after lunch to report that another of the doctors she worked with told her he had lost two elderly patients in the past year and a half, and one of them was 102-years-old.

"This gets more and more interesting," Mitch said to her. "When do you talk to Doctor Sinfahdi himself?"

"Last thing this afternoon," she said. "I'm kind of scared to ask him about patients dying. What if he suspects that I'm checking up on him?"

"Be an actress. Don't let him suspect."

"I'm trained to be a Florence Nightingale, not a Katherine Hepburn."

"You're not old enough to be either one. Just act natural and the doctor won't be suspicious."

In mid-afternoon, after Mitch had done some additional number hunting and made four phone calls that found nobody at home, Alan Jeffrey came by to announce that he was going out to look for some color shots of people enjoying the beautiful day.

"I can't stand to sit around here twiddling my thumbs, waiting for the desk to give me something to do, when I know how gorgeous it is outside," Al said. "And also I have to stop at Uncle Charlie's house to pick up some more goodies on the way home."

"I hope those goodies don't include his lovely widow," Mitch said.

"As my darling wife so thoughtfully pointed out last night, Diana is technically my aunt. One does not screw around with one's aunt, especially when one is happily married to an equally lovely lady."

"Just a thought," Mitch said. "Diana may be your aunt by marriage but she is also quite a hunk of woman. Maybe you should send me to pick up your goodies."

"Maybe I should, and then see what the fair Jennifer says when she finds out you paid a social call to my sexy Aunt Diana. Anyway, don't bust your balls too much longer over these phone calls. It looks like most of them will have to be made at night because nobody's home in the daytime. If the desk doesn't give you anything to do, get your butt out of the office and enjoy the sunshine while you've got a chance."

Fifteen minutes later, Al rang the doorbell at Uncle Charlie's house and when the door opened, after some delay, he was treated to the sight of a well-tanned Diana in a yellow thong bikini. Or, more accurately, in the bottom half of a yellow thong bikini. The top half was dangling from her right hand and Al observed that there was no area of lighter skin interrupting the even suntan all over her upper body.

"I was sunbathing by the pool," Diana said. "Shall I put this back on?" She swung the slender ribbon of cloth she was holding in a small circle. "Or shall I take this off?" While Alan Jeffrey stared in surprise and fascination, she hooked her left thumb into the waist band of the skimpy bikini bottom and stretched it down just far enough to reveal the first curls of black hair at the top of the pubic triangle.

CHAPTER 13

GETTING WARM

On his seventh phone call of the afternoon, to a woman listed as the sister of the deceased man, Warren Mitchell got the kind of answer he was looking for.

"The man's name was Doctor Something Sinfahdi," said Doris Lindblom. "He's a sweet old gentleman from India."

"Can you tell me a little bit about the circumstances of your brother's passing?" Mitch asked, noting that said passing of the 81-year-old man had occurred only four months ago.

"Well, John was slowing down a lot and his wife couldn't take care of him anymore—her eyes and her back ain't so good—so she persuaded him to go into a home," said Doris. "Doctor Sinfahdi went to see him there after he had a small stroke, but he died later that night."

"Did the doctor tell you the cause of death?"

"He gave us some medical term that basically means heart failure. John's heart couldn't handle the stress, he said. What sort of a study is the AMA doing that you want to know this kind of information?"

"They're trying to determine the comparative success of doctors treating certain ailments in the elderly and we're trying to localize their work for a story about doctors in the St. Paul area. Everything you've told me will be used without mentioning your brother's name and the doctors involved are not being identified by name, either, so no one has to worry. Thank you very much for your time. I'm sorry for your loss." Mitch hung up quickly before Doris could ask any more questions about the story he had told her he was trying to put together.

"Damn right the doctors won't be identified by name," he said after hanging up. "It looks like only one of them will actually get his name in the paper."

Mitch attempted two more calls, got no answer at either number, packed up the obituary information and the phone numbers, told the city desk he had some research to do for a feature he was working on and went out to enjoy the June sunshine, just as Al had suggested.

Meanwhile, Al was enjoying more than the sunshine.

"Your mouth is open but I don't hear anything coming out," Diana said. Her thumb was still hooked tantalizingly in the lowered bikini-bottom strap.

Al realized that his mouth was, in fact, wide open. It had dropped open in amazement at what came into view when Diana tugged downward on the bright yellow strap. He closed his mouth quickly, took a deep breath and said, "You'd better put them both back on."

"Too much for you?" Diana asked. She let the bottom strap go with a snap and slowly snuggled the tips of her breasts into the other minuscule bit of yellow material. It covered almost nothing beyond her nipples, which pressed boldly against their confinement in firm twin points.

"We agreed awhile ago that I am happily married," Al said, feeling his face grow hot with a rush of blood. "Besides, you're my aunt."

Diana laughed. "God forbid you should get it on with your old Auntie Diana," she said. "Not to worry; I wasn't going to rape you. I just wanted to give you a peek at what your Uncle Charlie got when he married Diana the Huntress."

"You'll never let me forget that dumb-ass remark, will you?"

"Why should I? I'll never forget it."

"I thought I was forgiven."

"Forgiven doesn't always mean forgotten. But let's cut the bullshit and get you what you came for. You did come for coins and fishing stuff, right?"

"Right. And that's all I came for," he said, wishing he could stop blushing and that the agitation going on in his groin would subside before an embarrassing tell-tale bulge became visible in his pants.

"Follow me," she said, turning and walking away. The sight of her bare buns swinging on either side of the thin yellow band that ran through her crotch did nothing to calm the activity in his jockey shorts.

In what had been Uncle Charlie's den, Diana turned around and indicated an array of coin boxes, fishing tackle and outdoor gear that she had stacked on and around Uncle Charlie's favorite recliner. "Take whatever you want," she said. Then, eyeing the area below Al's belt, she said, "Are we going camping now?"

"I don't think so," Al said.

"Then why are you pitching a tent?"

Al followed her gaze. Sure enough, a triangular bulge stood out in the front of his light-weight summer trousers. "I'm only human," he said, looking up again at the nearly naked woman in front of him.

"So am I," she said. "That's why it's so much fun to tease you. But teasing is all you'll ever get from me because I respect your wife."

"Only my wife?"

"You're doing better lately. Now show me what you want and I'll help you carry it out to your car."

Moving with self-conscious stiffness, Al gathered up all the coins, selected a couple of fishing rods and indicated some other odds and ends that Diana picked up.

"Find out anything more about Doctor Sinfahdi?" she asked as she put the items into the back seat. As she bent over to lean into the car, Al had to remind himself that she was only teasing him.

"We've turned up at least one more person who didn't survive under his care," Al said. "We're trying to determine if this many fatalities is anywhere near normal for a geriatric specialist."

"Let me know what you find out, will you please?"

"I'll keep you posted." Looking down again at his trouser front, he decided that this was a Freudian choice of words.

After a supper of take-out pizza, Warren Mitchell spent two hours phoning survivors of people whose obituaries might possibly fit the Doctor Sinfahdi pattern. It was not pleasant work—some of those who answered the phone were offended, some questioned his manhood and a couple of them began to cry. But with Sherlock Holmes purring by his side, Mitch plunged onward and was rewarded with the names of two additional patients who had died within hours of being treated by Doctor Ravi Sinfahdi during the past ten months. The list on Mitch's yellow legal pad was now longer than the combined two-year total reported to Jennifer Tilton by two other doctors.

Twice during his phone-a-thon Mitch took a break and punched in Jennifer Tilton's number. Twice the line was busy. "She's getting to be a real web freak ever since she got back from New Jersey," he said to Sherlock. "She never used to spend the whole evening on line." He tried her cell phone and got no answer. "Probably sitting on a shelf in the bedroom," he said. Sherlock Holmes yawned in response.

Mitch really wanted to talk to Jennifer about her interview with Doctor Sinfahdi that afternoon, so he tried her line again just before the ten o'clock news and found it still busy. He fell asleep during the report of the Minnesota Twins' latest diamond debacle and stumbled off to bed after waking up to find Jay Leno interviewing a woman who held a huge, hairy black tarantula in her hand. As he hit the remote's off button, Mitch wondered if Jennifer was still on the web.

"Yes, my dear, what would you like to talk about," Doctor Ravi Sinfahdi had said as he ushered Jennifer Tilton into the small office he kept in Cedar Gardens Nursing Home. He pointed her toward a chair near his desk and seated himself less than an arm's length away after she had crossed her legs and adjusted her skirt, which didn't quite stretch to her knees.

"Well, doctor, as you know, I'm very new at working with elderly patients," Jennifer said. "And, within a few days of starting, one of my favorite patients died, and this shook me up more than I expected. Now I'm wondering if this sort of thing—patients dying suddenly—happens so often that maybe I don't want to do this job."

"I don't understand how I can help you," he said.

"Well, I'm hoping you can tell me what you've experienced. Have you had very many patients die suddenly in the last year or two?"

Doctor Sinfahdi frowned before he answered. "There have been some deaths among those I treated, yes."

"Do you know how many you've lost? How frequently you lose them?" Jennifer hoped she was looking sufficiently naïve to ask these questions without setting off the doctor's mental alarm system.

"I don't count them, if that's what you mean. If you're asking about actual numbers, you'll have to speak with the head nurse in my office, Nurse Darnell. She is the keeper of the records for my practice."

"Oh, I'm not looking for strict statistics," Jennifer said, slightly flustered. "I just want, you know, an idea of how often I can expect to be forced to deal with losing a patient I've grown fond of."

"I really can't say," the doctor said, leaning forward and placing the tips of the fingers of his skeletal right hand on Jennifer's pantyhose-encased knee. "I try to deal with the patients I'm seeing at the present and not dwell on those I've lost in the past. It's the only way one can remain hopeful when treating the elderly. If you really want an estimate, as I said, you'll have to ask Nurse Darnell."

"I guess that's not really necessary."

"I can arrange to have her speak with you. If this information will guide you in your career, I'm sure she can provide it." He started to slide his fingers along her knee toward the edge of her skirt but stopped when she covered his hand with her own. At that, Jennifer took a deep breath and decided to plunge onward.

"Well, okay," she said. "Please set up a time that I can meet with Nurse Darnell. It really would help me decide if I'm in the right line of work or not."

Doctor Sinfahdi removed his hand from Jennifer's leg, picked up the phone and, after some discussion of what times were mutually available, Nurse Darnell agreed to see Jennifer at 3:15 P.M. the following Wednesday.

Mitch had barely reached his desk Saturday morning when the phone rang. It was Jennifer, ready to report on her meeting with the doctor.

"What did you find out?" Mitch asked.

"I found out he's an old letch," Jennifer said, and described the doctor's hand-on-knee maneuver. Mitch snorted his disapproval and Jennifer went on to tell him about her upcoming date with Nurse Emily Darnell.

"Good work," Mitch said. "But I can't believe the old fart doesn't know how many patients he's lost."

"Well, except for grabbing a feel of my leg, the man seems to be just kind of floating along in his own little world," Jennifer said. "Maybe he really is oblivious of the numbers."

"The body count is rising on this end," he said and went on to tell her about the additional names he had obtained by phoning survivors.

"This is getting kind of creepy," Jennifer said. "I wonder if Nurse Darnell thinks her boss is losing more patients than he should."

"Be careful what you say. She may be aware that he has a problem and be loyal enough to cover it up."

"You're asking me to be an actress again."

"Yes, we're at that stage."

"Oh, stop with the puns, will you. I've gotta go now."

"Okay, I'll drop the curtain. And I'll be out there about three today if you can stay off the internet long enough to see me."

"You were trying to call last night? I'm sorry. I was online and I just couldn't seem to get off."

"Yeah, I tried three times. You're turning into a real web fanatic. Anyway, I'll see you in a little while." Mitch hung up and walked over to the photo department just in time to flag down Alan Jeffrey.

"It's weird," Mitch said. "Doctor Sinfahdi said he can't even give her an estimate of his death toll. Set her up for a meeting on Monday with his head nurse to talk about the numbers."

"Oh, yeah, I've met her. She's all business, not much bedside manner. If there are numbers available, that nurse should have them, but will she just rattle them off to Jennifer for the asking?"

"Who knows? Apparently the doctor told her it was okay. Anyway, I'll see you here on Monday and I might have time to phone some more survivors on my own. And I'll try to look at some more obits on the library computer Monday night."

"No, you won't see me here on Monday. They've got me scheduled to work Sunday because of the mixed up holiday schedule, so I won't be around on Monday. But I do get to work the Fourth of July holiday, Tuesday."

On Monday night, the library computer became available at around 9:30 and Mitch sat himself down to another evening of flipping through obituaries. He had compiled an additional list of names and was resting his eyes from the strain of staring at the computer screen when a voice behind him said, "Well, if it isn't the late-night obit hunter again!"

Mitch turned to find the columnist, Jerry Granger, standing over him once more. "Hi," Mitch said. "I thought you were heading to Kansas."

"Leaving tomorrow morning," Granger said. "But when I get back I really want to get together with you. I have a damn good story idea for you."

"That's the best kind. What does it involve?"

"It involves something medical. I deal with a lot of medical stuff in my column—have contacts with a lot of doctors. There's one that I think bears investigating and I don't have the time to really dig into it."

"This is a local St. Paul doctor?"

"Very close. He practices in the near-northern suburbs—you know, Roseville, Maplewood, that area."

"Want to tell me his name now? Maybe I can get started digging while you're away in Kansas."

"His name is Sinfahdi. Doctor Ravi Sinfahdi. He's a geriatric specialist and he's from India originally. I've got a file on him I can let you look at while I'm gone. Just don't tell anybody where you got it, okay?"

"It couldn't be more okay," said Warren Mitchell. "I'd be more than happy to look at your file." He hoped his face was not revealing the rush of excitement that was flowing through his innards.

A minute later Granger's file was in Warren Mitchell's hands. He tried to keep his fingers from trembling as he took the manila folder from the columnist. He tried to sound casual as he asked, "How'd you happen to start this?"

"I'm pretty good friends with another doctor who practices in that area. One day we were talking about treating the elderly and he mentioned this guy from India who, my friend thought, was experiencing an unusually high death rate among his patients. My friend said he didn't want to bring this to anyone's official attention unless he could document it, so he asked me to do some research, and I agreed because it would make a great story if we find out this Sinfahdi guy is over here practicing medicine without the proper kind of training or something."

"So where do I come in?"

"You come in because I just plain don't have time to do this and I think it's worth pursuing as a news story, rather than a column. You think you want to take it on?"

"I think I do," Mitch said, trying not to sound too intensely interested. Five minutes later, as he went out the front door with Granger's folder in his hand, Mitch wondered if he should pinch himself to make sure he wasn't dreaming.

"You're shittin' me! Some other doctor thinks the paper should investigate Doctor Sinfahdi?" Al said when he heard Mitch's report Tuesday morning. Mitch was calling from Jennifer's, where he had gone to spend the Fourth of July holiday watching Afton's annual parade and picnicking with Jen and the children.

"I am not shittin' you," Mitch said. "I have Jerry Granger's Doctor Sinfahdi file to prove it "

"So what's in there?"

"Not much, really. Notes from his conversation with the other doctor, who seems willing to challenge Doctor Sinfahdi's competence if he has the numbers to back it up, and a couple of clipped obits that I assume were Doctor Sinfahdi's patients. I'll call some of the survivors to check that out right away tomorrow. I doubt they'd appreciate that kind of a call on the Fourth of July."

"Is the other doctor's name in the file? Can we talk to him?"

"Not yet. Granger is protecting his source for the time being. We won't know who the instigator of this little investigation is until the shit officially hits the fan."

"I'm thinking it had better be a pretty big fan because the shit seems to be getting deeper by the day. Well, start making those calls first thing tomorrow morning if Don doesn't send you out on something. This is fucking wonderful!"

"I thought it might perk up your Fourth."

"Makes me feel better than drinking a fifth."

"My sixth sense told me it would."

CHAPTER 14

NUMBERS GAME

On Wednesday morning, having failed once again to find the proper moment for a marriage proposal, Warren Mitchell found himself talking on the phone to Emma Hansen, who sounded very old and extremely cautious. She made him repeat—slowly and carefully—his pitch about working on a local angle for a story about the American Medical Association's study of geriatric specialists and how they related to their patients.

"My husband just died in May while being cared for by a very sweet old doctor from India," Emma said when she finally became convinced that Mitch wasn't trying to sell her something or swindle her out of her life savings.

Mitch had Ernest Hansen's obituary on the desk in front of him. "Yes, I know," Mitch said. "That's why you were chosen to participate in the local survey. We're trying to learn how family members feel about the medical care their loved ones received in their final illness."

"Ernie wasn't really all that sick," Emma Hansen said. "Just kind of run down and getting forgetful. Nobody thought he was going to die that quick."

"How old was your husband?" Mitch asked.

"He was eighty-one. Would have been eighty-two on the first of June."

"And who was the doctor who saw him last?"

"It was a Doctor Sinfahdi. From India. I think his first name was Robby or something like that."

"Could it have been Ravi?"

"Oh, yes, I think it was. Do you know him?"

"We know of him, Mrs. Hansen. Tell me, do you feel he took good care of your husband?"

"Oh, yes. He was so kind and gentle every time he saw Ernie. Always had a smile and an encouraging word."

"Can you tell me a little about how your husband died?"

"Well, like I said, he was kind of run down and getting forgetful so I couldn't take care of him no more. I'm eighty-two and I got back problems and a heart condition. So we put him in a long-term care center called Golden

Pond Manor, right here in Maplewood, where the nurses could take care of him and I could visit him whenever my son could give me a ride. I don't drive no more because of my eyes. Then one morning, they called and said Ernie had died during the night."

"'They' being the people at Golden Pond Manor?"

"That's right."

"Had Doctor Sinfahdi seen your husband recently?" Mitch asked.

"The night before. Ernie was coughing a lot and having trouble breathing, so the doctor gave him a shot."

"Do you know what kind of a shot?"

"Oh, no, I ain't got no idea what it was. I didn't ask; figured I wouldn't understand it anyhow."

"Did the doctor or anyone tell you what caused your husband's death?"

"The doctor said it was heart failure. There's a fancy medical name for it, but what he said happened was that Ernie's heart just gave out. That happens when people get old, you know."

"Well, I appreciate your talking to me, Mrs. Hansen," Mitch said. "I'm very sorry for your loss and I hope your husband is resting in peace."

"Well, we scattered his ashes over his favorite fishing lake up north, so he should be feeling real peaceful."

"Mr. Hansen's body was cremated?"

"That's what he said he wanted, so that's what we did."

"He told you that's what he wanted?"

"That's what he put on the form when he moved into Golden Pond Manor. They have a sheet you fill out about using heroic methods to bring you back and how you want to be buried in case anything happens while you're there."

"Thank you again, Mrs. Hansen," Mitch said. "You've been very helpful."

"So how helpful was she?" asked Alan Jeffrey, who had been leaning against a corner of the desk and listening to Mitch's end of the conversation.

"Damn helpful. Her husband, who is now Number Seven on our list, died during the night after getting a shot from Doctor Sinfahdi, supposedly to cure a cough and a breathing problem. And the body was cremated, as it seems many of his late patients have been."

"How convenient for him in case anyone wants to do an autopsy."

"That's what I was thinking. In this particular case, there will be no working in dead Ernest."

"That's the importance of being Ernest," Al said. "Now get back on the phone and make an earnest call to somebody mentioned as a survivor in the other obit in the Granger file."

"What am I getting myself into?" Jennifer Tilton asked herself as she turned off Roselawn Avenue into the parking lot of the small strip mall that housed Doctor Ravi Sinfahdi's office. She had been jittery all day about her appointment with Nurse Emily Darnell, so jittery, in fact, that one of her elderly patients had asked her what was wrong.

"Your hands are shaking, dear," the woman had said, and, indeed, they were. They were still shaking as Jennifer turned off the engine and stepped out of her Ford Escort in front of the geriatric office. Why did I let Mitch talk me into this, she wondered. I could lose my job if Doctor Sinfahdi ever gets the idea that I'm trying to wreck his practice, she said to herself. Spying, she decided, was not her cup of tea

She took a couple of deep breaths in an effort to quell the shaking and ran the opening lines of her self-introduction to Nurse Darnell through her head one more time before stepping out of the late-afternoon heat (according to the radio, it was ninety-five in the shade, but there was no shade in the black-topped parking lot) and into the air-conditioned office.

The temperature drop was startling—and not helpful to someone trying to control the shakes. Jennifer, who was wearing a short-sleeved blouse that was open at the neck and a lightweight pair of summer slacks, wrapped her arms across her body just below her breasts as she approached the receptionist's desk.

"I have a 3:30 appointment with Nurse Darnell," Jennifer said when the chunky woman looked up with no great interest showing on her face. Then, realizing she was hugging herself for warmth, Jennifer added, "It's kind of chilly in here."

"Actually, it's on the warm side," said the receptionist, who was wearing a thin, short-sleeved blouse and a very short skirt—too short for someone her age and weight, Jennifer thought. "Our patients are elderly people so we keep it at about 78. I'll tell Nurse Darnell that you're here. Your name?"

"Tilton. Jennifer Tilton. Doctor Sinfahdi arranged for me to have a talk with the nurse today."

"Please have a seat."

Jennifer unwrapped her arms, chose a chair next to a gray-haired woman wearing an orange cardigan sweater and picked a *People* magazine off the small table on the other side of the chair. The woman in the sweater looked critically at Jennifer's summery attire and said, "You should have brought a sweater, dear. They keep it so cold in here."

"I didn't know," Jennifer said. "I've never been here before."

"Well, next time remember to bring a sweater. It's always this cold in here."

"God forbid there's a next time," Jennifer said to herself. Aloud, she thanked the woman for the advice and said she certainly would remember. She had barely opened the magazine when a commanding female voice said, "Ms. Tilton?"

Jennifer looked up and saw a woman in a crisp white nursing uniform standing in the doorway that led to the doctor's office and examining rooms. The woman's tone of voice and military posture brought Jennifer to her feet and the nurse said, "Follow me, please." She led the way into a small office with a desk faced by a couple of chairs for visitors, indicated that Jennifer should sit in one of those chairs, closed the door and took a seat behind the desk. The name tag above her left breast said Emily Darnell, R.N.

"Now, what can I do for you, Ms. Tilton?" said Emily Darnell, R.N. The tone was pleasant enough, but her face was expressionless and Jennifer sensed no real warmth either in the greeting or in Emily Darnell's pale blue eyes. Doctor Sinfahdi's head nurse clearly was all business and didn't plan to spend a lot of time on this interview.

Crossing her legs and placing her hands in her lap to conceal their slight tremor, Jennifer began her well-rehearsed speech: "I've just begun a new career as a physical therapist, working with elderly patients, and I found I wasn't prepared emotionally when one of the patients I really enjoyed working with died suddenly about a week ago. Because Doctor Sinfahdi was that woman's doctor, I asked him how often I could expect to lose patients this way. You see, if I'm going to be shook up too often by the loss of a patient, I'm not sure if I should continue in this line of work. Doctor Sinfahdi was kind enough to send me here and said you could tell me how often his patients die."

The expression on Nurse Emily Darnell's face went from blank to quizzical. "You think that somehow knowing how frequently patients die is going to prepare you emotionally for the inevitable?" she asked.

"I think knowing the frequency with which I would be facing the death of a patient will help me decide whether I should continue in this line of work or look for another kind of job," Jennifer said.

"Have you talked to any other doctors about this?"

The question caught Jennifer by surprise but she quickly said "no" and hoped that Nurse Darnell didn't have a built-in lie detector. "Since the woman who died was Doctor Sinfahdi's patient, it seemed logical to discuss it with him," Jennifer continued. "And, as I said, he was kind enough to let me come here to get some information from you. He said you keep all the records." Somehow the room didn't feel so cold to Jennifer anymore and she noticed that her armpits felt moist after this bit of ad-libbing.

"I'm afraid I don't keep a tally of the patients who pass away," said the nurse. "I know there have been a couple within a week or so of each other recently—these things sometimes run in cycles."

"By a couple, do you mean two?" Jennifer thought she sounded like a fool the instant she asked the question.

"That's the usual definition of the word," Nurse Darnell said. "One was the woman you were working with and the other was a gentleman who suffered a stroke, which was followed by heart failure."

"Al's Uncle Charlie," Jennifer said to herself. To the nurse she said, "So, you're sure that's all there have been in the last six months or so?"

"I'm not 100 percent positive—as I said, I don't keep a tally and the doctor sees dozens of patients every month. If you've got a minute, I suppose I could flip through the files quickly and see if I've forgotten someone."

"I've got time, if you don't mind doing that."

The expression on Emily Darnell's face said that she clearly did mind, but she rose and walked to a file cabinet on the wall beside the desk. Opening the top drawer, she began looking at the names on folders, working from front to back. Watching her, Jennifer noted that she was sturdily built but not overweight and that her arms and shoulders looked muscular, as if she worked out with weights on a regular basis.

About midway through the row of files in the drawer, Nurse Darnell said, "Oh, yes, here's an elderly gentleman who passed away last December. So I guess you could say Doctor Sinfahdi's recent experience has been three deaths in a little over six months. But, as I said, these things tend to run in cycles— we might not see another patient pass on until some time next year."

Jennifer felt a jolt of foreboding strike her gut. She knew this was not the truth. Mitch had told her that he and Al knew of six persons who had died while under the care of Doctor Sinfahdi within the last six months. Was nurse Darnell lying to protect Doctor Sinfahdi? Or had the doctor tampered with the records to conceal the actual death count from her, as well? Either way, Jennifer again felt cold, but this time the chill was produced by what the nurse was telling her and she wanted to get up and leave.

"You look unhappy," said Nurse Darnell. "Are you thinking this is more than you can handle emotionally?"

"Uh, yes. Yes, I'm afraid it might be."

The nurse walked over and laid a cool but gentle hand on Jennifer's shoulder. "Then, I'd recommend that you do look for another line of work," she said in a softer, more sympathetic tone. "I know that Doctor Sinfahdi takes every loss very hard but he keeps on going because he loves his work and is deeply devoted to every one of his patients. You have to remember, these are old people, in their eighties and nineties, and old people in their eighties and nineties are going to die. If you can't face that fact, then you probably should be practicing your therapy with younger patients."

"You're probably right," Jennifer said, shrugging the hand off her shoulder and rising from the chair. "I'll really have to do some heavy soul searching. Thank you so much for your time and for the information."

"I'm happy to have been of help," said Nurse Darnell with the slightest hint of a smile. "Come, I'll show you out."

A minute later, Jennifer was back in the ninety-five-degree heat of the parking lot, but she felt a shiver go through her body nevertheless. Warren Mitchell was going to be extremely interested in the numbers that Nurse Emily Darnell had given her. Jennifer started her car, turned on the air conditioning and, with a hand that still trembled slightly, picked up her cell phone and punched the button that was programmed for the reporter's direct-line number.

CHAPTER 15

THE PERFECT HEALTH PLAN

Unable to contact any of the survivors listed in the second obituary given to him by columnist Jerry Granger, Warren Mitchell had decided to try the phone numbers again from his apartment in the evening. He had just finished the final unanswered call when Don O'Rourke summoned him to the city desk and sent him to the University of Minnesota campus in Minneapolis to interview a visiting physicist. Alan Jeffrey was dispatched to take photos at a crime scene where police were investigating a convenience store holdup. Thus, neither Mitch nor Al was available to answer the phone when Jennifer Tilton called the Daily Dispatch in the late afternoon.

Annoyed, Jennifer punched in the number for Mitch's apartment, got his answering machine, left a message and drove home to Afton. She was eager to pass on the information and a little frightened by the fact that Nurse Emily Darnell had given her a death count that was only half the total that Mitch and Al said they had compiled.

When Mitch finished his interview, he decided to treat himself to dinner at the Index Café, one of the hole-in-the-wall neighborhood restaurants dotting Grand Avenue. The Index was a homey place, containing maybe a dozen tables covered with light blue cloths. It adjoined a locally-owned bookstore in a mutually beneficial arrangement within a brick building that housed several other small shops as well. Mitch was perusing the menu when a familiar female voice said, "May I help you, sir?" and he looked up to find Martha Todd standing next to his table, with a smile on her face and an order pad and pencil at the ready.

"Oh, hi," Mitch said. "So this is where you do your waitressing."

"You mean I haven't told you?" she said. "I thought you came in here specifically to experience my expert service."

"Had I known, I'd have come here sooner. But, no, you never did say where it was you were working."

They exchanged small talk throughout the meal whenever she came to his table and he lingered over an extra cup of coffee in order to watch her walk past in her form-fitting black slacks and to enjoy her smile when she refilled the cup. When it came time to pay, he left a tip that approached twenty-five percent and as he was going out the door she caught him from behind and said, "Mitch, this is way too much."

"No, it isn't," Mitch said. "You gave me great service and I always like to help a struggling student."

"You're embarrassing me," Martha said.

"I don't mean to. Next time I'll stiff you; how's that?"

"I'd almost feel better it you did. It's awkward to take money from a friend. Maybe that's why I didn't tell you where I work."

"Well, now that I know, you're liable to see me more often. You know I can't cook worth a damn, so I like to treat myself to a decent meal out every once in a while."

It was after seven when Mitch arrived home and was greeted with a "meow" and a blatant plea for a tummy rub by Sherlock Holmes. The big cat rolled onto his back with his paws in the air, inviting the massage and, when he'd had enough, rewarded Mitch with a quick nip of his teeth and a kangaroo kick of his hind feet, with the claws extended only a fraction.

Mitch rubbed his hand where Sherlock's teeth had left an impression, checked his answering machine, heard Jennifer's excited voice and punched her number. He got a busy signal and hoped she hadn't settled down for another evening on the internet. Next he took out the list of phone numbers he had compiled for survivors named in the obituary of an 84-year-old woman named Margaret McConnell and punched in the number for her son.

When a woman answered, Mitch asked for James McConnell.

"Who's calling?" she asked sharply.

"My name is Warren Mitchell. I'm a reporter for the Daily Dispatch and I'm writing a localized a story about a survey of geriatric specialists done by the American Medical Association," he said.

"My husband is in perfect health."

"We're interested in your husband's opinion of the care his mother received from her geriatric specialist, if she had one. May I speak to him, please?"

"Jim's mother died and he's still very upset over her death. The doctor was very kind but Mother's death was a terrible shock and Jim's not talking about it to anyone."

"Was his mother seeing Doctor Ravi Sinfahdi?"

"Yes. How did you know?"

"As I said, I'm using information provided by the American Medical

Association."

"Well, I'm not sure that this Doctor Sinfahdi knows what he is doing. It didn't seem like Mother was all that sick and then boom, she's gone."

"She hadn't been ill?"

"She'd had a stroke but she seemed to be getting over it. At least the doctor led us to believe she was. Then her heart gave out. But, please, don't bother Jim about this."

"No need to," Mitch said. "You've been very helpful. Thank you very much, Mrs. McConnell."

Again he tried Jennifer's number and again he got a busy signal. "Get off the goddamn net," he said. He had better luck calling Alan Jeffrey.

"The body count is up to ten," Mitch said when Al answered. "And the woman I just talked to said her husband was very upset because his mother's death was a real shock. She seemed to be recovering from a stroke and then her heart gave out. Sound at all familiar?"

"All too," said Al. "What did Jennifer learn from Doctor Sinfahdi's nurse this afternoon?"

"I don't know. I missed her call and now I can't get through. I think she's on the goddamn internet again."

"She's really gotten into that lately."

"Yeah, ever since her trip to New Jersey. I don't know if she's in one of those chat room things with classmates she saw at the reunion or what, but she spends hours on the damn net almost every night."

It was almost time for the ten o'clock news when Jennifer finally called Mitch. "If you've been trying to get me, I've been online," she said.

"I've only been trying every half hour since a little after seven," Mitch said. "What do you do on that computer all night?"

"I communicate with friends. Is that okay?"

"Well, yeah, but it would be nice if you'd communicate with this friend once in awhile; especially when you've had a session with Doctor Sinfahdi's nurse."

"I tried to call you but you weren't at the office or at home. Anyway, Doctor Sinfahdi's Nurse Darnell didn't tell me the whole truth."

"What do you mean?"

"I mean she looked in the doctor's files and counted three patients who have died in the last six months. And you told me there have been six."

"Actually, we're now up to ten, although one of them might have been seven or eight months ago—I have to check the date. But his nurse told you there were only three in the last six months?"

"That's what she told me. She also passed on the startling news that people in their eighties and nineties have a tendency to die and suggested that I find another line of work if I can't stand to lose a patient every now and then. 'Death runs in cycles,' she said."

"Yeah? Well, it's a pretty fast-moving cycle in Doctor Sinfahdi's case, kind of like a revved-up Harley-Davidson. Do you think she was lying about the number of cyclists or—sorry, I can't resist this—do you think the files had been doctored?"

"Oh, please! I have no way of knowing if anyone doctored ... I mean messed with the files. The nurse could be lying to protect the doctor but he might be pulling things out of the files without her knowing it. It's hard to read her; she keeps herself very much under control."

After saying good night to Jennifer, Mitch called Alan Jeffrey.

"You're interrupting the news," Al said.

"Wait till you hear my news, hot off the medical press," said Mitch.

Al's reaction to Jennifer's report was exactly what Mitch expected. "I'm getting more and more convinced that we're dealing with something worse than mere incompetence here," Al said. "Why would Doctor Sinfahdi's nurse be putting out false numbers unless, for whatever reason, this guy is putting his patients away and either hiding it from his nurse or getting her to help him cover his tracks. What was Jennifer's impression of the nurse?"

"She said the nurse is very hard to read, that she keeps herself under perfect control."

"Which is an admirable trait for a nurse, but not a lot of help to us."

"So, where do we go from here?"

"God only knows. I'd like to see what's really in that filing cabinet that Jennifer said the nurse looked into."

"Fat chance of that. I can just picture Nurse Darnell opening the drawers and inviting us to thumb through the folders."

"Yeah, me, too. Hey, now that you mention drawers, I don't remember seeing any rings on Nurse Darnell's hand. If she's not married, maybe you, the noted resident stud, could take her out to dinner, invite her back to your place, persuade her to drop her drawers and eventually let down her guard as well."

"Maybe you can take that idea and stuff it up the dark place covered by the seat of your own drawers."

"She's not a bad looking woman, Mitch. Medium brown hair, blue eyes, a nice enough face and a good strong body that could support your weight."

"You're saying she's chubby?"

"No way. She's solid; looks like she lifts weights. Give you a hell of a ride."

"Forget it. I'd rather break into Doctor Sinfahdi's office than try to work my way into Nurse Darnell's panties."

There was a moment of silence before Al said, "That's an interesting thought."

"What is? Breaking into Doctor Sinfahdi's office?"

"It could be done."

"By an expert locksmith, maybe, which I am not," Mitch said. "Anyway, the place is sure to be alarmed. You open the door and bam! The cops are there with a SWAT team in thirty seconds."

"Yeah, you're right. But maybe a window—"

"You bust a window and you'll sure as hell set off an alarm. You might as well try hiding in the men's room."

"Hmm!" said Al. "I wonder where the men's room is."

"Oh, come on. I wasn't serious."

"Well I am. We need to find out how that building is laid out—what rooms are where and which ones have windows. Then maybe we can figure out a way to get in."

"What will you do if you get in there? All the life-and-death stuff is probably on a computer."

"Not all of it. I saw manila folders when I was there and you just said that Nurse Darnell looked at file folders for Jennifer. Those are the patient charts I want to see. I just don't know how to get in there and case the joint— both the doctor and his nurse know me and they know I don't have any further business there."

Once more there was a brief silence before Al said, "You, on the other hand …"

"Me again!" Mitch said. "First you've got me trying to fuck the doctor's nurse and now you've got me risking a jail term if I fuck up whatever goofy plan you have in mind for breaking into his office."

"That's the problem, I don't have a plan in mind. I can't think of a plausible reason for you to go there."

"Me neither. And I'm not trying to think of one. Good night, old buddy, I'll see you in the morning."

Mitch hung up the phone with more force than necessary. But like it or not, while he prepared for bed his mind went to work, trying to find a convincing excuse to get into Doctor Sinfahdi's office and look at how things were laid out. He was in bed, half asleep, when the answer came to him. It was so good he sat up quickly, spilling Sherlock Holmes off his comfy spot next to Mitch's backside, and was reaching for the phone to call Alan Jeffrey when he realized it was way past midnight.

"No sense waking up Carol," Mitch said to himself, settling back down and soothing the indignant tomcat at his side. "It can wait until morning. And it will work, if only Martha Todd will cooperate." Satisfied with himself, Warren Mitchell drifted off to a dream about crawling toward a huge stack of manila folders and never getting closer.

Mitch was up at six Thursday morning so he could get in his jogging exercise before the early-July temperature soared into the nineties again. He was also hoping to spot Martha Todd in her running clothes, for more reasons than his usual desire to get a look at her long legs and beautiful buns encased in shimmering blue Spandex. But Martha was nowhere in sight and Mitch was reluctant to rap on her door at that hour of the morning, even though he suspected she was up. "Never know who she might have for company," he thought. Although he was fairly certain Martha wasn't entertaining any men overnight, he could be mistaken and he didn't want to risk embarrassing her before he sought the assistance that his plan required.

Mitch showered, breakfasted on toast and peanut butter washed down with two cups of coffee and went to the office. When he explained his plan to Al, the photographer agreed that it had a very good chance for success.

"But will your friend Martha go along with this idea?" Al asked.

"Doctor Sinfahdi gave her grandfather his final shot on this earth," Mitch said. "If I tell Martha that her grampa might still be alive if he hadn't had that shot, I think she'll help us find the answer."

Mitch knocked on Martha Todd's door as soon as he got home that evening, but she did not answer. Impatient to present his plan, he decided to walk up to the Index Café to see if she was on duty there. The hostess informed him that Martha wasn't scheduled to work until the following day.

After supper, Mitch knocked again, with the same negative results. He went back, wrote a note asking Martha to knock on his door when she came home—no matter what the hour—and taped it to her door. He was only three chapters into a new mystery novel when he heard the requested knock.

"Hi," said Martha. "You wanted to see me?"

"I sure did, I mean I sure do," he said. "Come on in. I need to talk to you about an interesting little project I have in mind. How would you feel about letting me borrow your grandmother for a few hours?"

CHAPTER 16

A HIGH-INTEREST LOAN

The expression on Martha's face would have made a great movie close-up—mouth open, eyes wide, nostrils flared. "Did I hear you say you want to borrow my grandmother?" she said.

"You did," Mitch said. "Come in and sit down and I'll tell you why and what for." He gestured toward the sofa and watched her as she walked to it and sat down beside Sherlock Holmes. Mitch plopped down in the only armchair, facing her, and watched Sherlock Holmes glide smoothly onto her lap.

"So tell me what this is all about," Martha said, rubbing the cat behind his ears. "And I'll tell you if Gramma is available to be loaned."

"I think you'll be willing to make her available when you hear what Al and I have learned about Doctor Ravi Sinfahdi," Mitch said.

He proceeded to brief Martha on their search for additional patients who had not survived Doctor Sinfahdi's tender care and watched as the look of skepticism on her face turned to one of horror.

"I'm getting the feeling that you think Doctor Sinfahdi might be worse than a quack," she said.

"That would be correct," Mitch said. "We are getting the feeling that all these deaths are not the result of mere incompetence. But we need more information, and that's where your grandmother comes in."

"I doubt that she knows anything about Doctor Sinfahdi, other than that he gave Grampa a shot shortly before he died."

"It's not what she knows now that we need. It's what I can learn by accompanying her on a visit to the doctor's clinic as a potential patient."

"You want my Gramma to go see a doctor who you think might be killing his patients? No way!"

"Hear me out. I'll be with her and will make damn sure the visit is only a preliminary check up and that absolutely no medication is administered."

"What can you gain from this?"

"I need to look over the layout of the office—determine where things are—in case Al and I decide to pay an unscheduled visit after office hours.

Obviously I'm not old enough to pose as a geriatric patient, but if I bring your grandmother in ..."

"You guys are going to break into the doctor's office?"

"It's a thought. Like I said, we need more information about his patients—how many have died and anything we can find about how they died."

"This is crazy!"

"It's not so crazy if you look at what's going on. Martha, if this guy is killing his patients we need to put him out of business. We can't do that without evidence."

"Why don't you go to the police and let them get a search warrant?"

"Martha, the police would laugh in our faces. They'd say 'what's the big deal?' A geriatric specialist can be expected to lose some patients in their eighties and nineties. We need a better grip on the facts before we bring the cops into this or we'll just spook Doctor Sinfahdi and send him running all the way back to India."

"Well, that would put him out of business here."

"But would it punish him for sending people like your grandfather to an earlier-than-normal grave? Ask your grandmother how she feels about that."

"Gramma feels bad enough without me telling her that poor Grampa might have been murdered."

"So how do you feel about it? Do you want to just sit back and let him get away with what he's done?"

"On a personal level, I'd like to see him punished," Martha said as tears appeared in the corners of her eyes. "Grampa Mendes was such a sweetheart. But I don't want to drag my Gramma into this. Why don't take your own grandmother to see this weirdo?"

"They're both dead or I would," he said.

"Oh, God, I'm sorry. There I go sticking my stupid foot in my mouth again."

"Don't worry about it," Mitch said. "Look, I'll do my scouting while we're in the waiting room. I'll stay with your grandmother every second that she's with the doctor. Please, Martha, we have to nail this guy and your grandmother is the perfect decoy."

"You make her sound like some kind of a wooden object. She's a flesh-and-blood little old lady who doesn't hear very well and is all bent over with osteoporosis. It's a chore for her to walk from her chair to the dinner table, much less go to a doctor's office. My mother is just about ready to put her into a home where she can have twenty-four-hour care."

"And where Doctor Ravi Sinfahdi may be the staff geriatric specialist?"

"Oh, Jesus! I never thought of that."

"He's got the area pretty well covered," Mitch said. Martha's eyes told him that he had scored a point with this observation.

Martha bowed her head and covered her face with her hands. "Let me think about it," she said when she finally looked up. "I can't decide something like this on a few minutes notice. I need to think and then maybe talk to Gramma Mendes."

"While you're thinking, remember that it would be far better if she saw Doctor Sinfahdi in his office with me at her side than in the nursing home some night with nobody else around," Mitch said. "You may be helping her as well as us by loaning her to me."

Martha gently slid Sherlock Holmes off her lap and back onto the sofa cushion, rose and walked to the door. "I'll let you know as soon as I can," she said. He watched her walk away down the hall, marveling one more time at the perfect proportions of her gently-undulating derriere.

"So what kind of luck did you have borrowing a grandmother from she with the lovely ass?" Al asked the next morning as he perched on the edge of Mitch's desk, coffee cup in hand.

"I think my luck will be good," Mitch said. "Martha wouldn't commit to it last night, but she's definitely leaning toward saying yes."

"You are a persuasive devil with the women," Al said. "I'd never loan you my grandmother for a visit to a possible psychopath."

"I pointed out that if Martha's mother puts Gramma Mendes into a nursing home or long-term care facility—as mother is planning to do—Doctor Sinfahdi might be the geriatric specialist of choice. That scared her a bit."

"Ah, there's nothing like fear to motivate a person who otherwise might make a cold, rational—and wrong—decision."

The phone on Mitch's desk rang at a little after ten and he answered.

"Hi, it's Martha," said the caller. "I've decided that I'll loan you my Gramma on one condition."

"And what's that?" Mitch asked.

"That I go along to the doctor's office," said Martha Todd.

"You want to go along?"

"Yes. After all, she's my Gramma."

"Well, yes, but ..."

"But what?" she said, cutting off his protest.

"But how do we explain both of us being there," Mitch said. "I mean, one of us alone could take her in."

"What will they care? We can say that we're a married couple, or that we're brother and sister …"

"Yeah, we really look alike."

"Say whatever you want to, Mitch, but I'm not sending Gramma to see a new doctor with a total stranger, nice as you are. Besides, look at it this way: if I stay with her when she goes in to see the doctor, you'll have more time to snoop."

"Now you're making sense," he said. "Okay, suppose you call and set up the appointment, then."

"What should I say?" Martha said. "Why does Gramma want to see the doctor?"

"Oh, Christ, I don't know. Make it some simple ailment, but one that needs quick attention. Say she's having severe headaches and can't sleep nights. He's not likely to try to give her a shot for that."

"True. He'll probably say take two aspirin and call him next year."

"Which would be just fine. Anyway, call and get the earliest appointment you can without making it sound like an emergency."

"Okay. I hope he's not so busy we have to wait till next month."

"Make it sound like your grandmother can't wait that long," he said. "What does she think about all this, by the way?"

"She actually seemed to get a kick out of the idea. She thinks she's going to be a spy, just like in the movies."

"Does she know why she's going to see Doctor Sinfahdi?"

"I told her you guys are working on a story about the AMA checking up to see if geriatric doctors in this area are providing proper treatment for their patients. I didn't say anything about the possibility that Grampa's death might not have been natural."

"That's good. We don't want to worry her or make her feel bad. Call me back as soon as you get an appointment."

"Will do. Bye, bye."

"She really is loaning you her grandmother?" Al said when Mitch approached the photo desk to report on the call.

"Not only that, she's coming along to take care of the old lady so I'll have more time to check out the building. She's calling to make an appointment, even as we speak."

"Good deal!" Al said. "Let me know what she gets set up. Right now, I've got to go shoot a stupid press conference in City Hall."

Minutes after Al disappeared, Martha Todd called back.

"It took some talking, but I got Gramma set up for next Tuesday at five o'clock," she said. "For somebody who's losing patients right and left, Doctor Sinfahdi is pretty well booked up."

"Well, the book may end sooner than he thinks. Where do we go to pick up your grandmother?"

"I'll drive," Martha said. "She's used to riding in my car. I'll pick her up and then stop by your office for you."

"Sounds good," he said. "See you then if we don't run into each before that."

"Have a nice weekend with your friend in Afton," said Martha as she hung up. "The weather is supposed to be good, if you get outside at all."

"What a cheap shot that was," Mitch said to himself as he put down the phone. "She must think we spend all our time in the sack."

When Mitch arrived in Afton late Saturday afternoon, after finishing his shift at the Daily Dispatch, Jennifer seemed to have something distant on her mind. After a half hour of monosyllabic conversation, Mitch asked, "Want to take the kids out to Afton State Park?"

"Why don't you take them?" she replied.

"Aren't you feeling good?" he asked. She never turned down an outing with Tony and Tracy.

"I'm fine." Her tone was sharp, but she softened it by adding, "I just would like a little peace and quiet."

"Tough week at work?"

"Yeah."

Saying she wanted to flake out by the pool, Jennifer stayed home while Mitch drove Tony and Tracy to the park and hiked the river bluffs with them until dinner time.

Jennifer was emerging from the room where her computer was set up when they returned to the house in River Hills. Her face was slightly flushed and Mitch asked if she was running a fever.

"I'm fine," she said again.

Mitch grilled hamburgers and hotdogs for supper and most of the conversation during the meal was between him and the children.

Later, in bed, Jennifer said she was really tired and "kind of head-achy," so they went to sleep without the usual love making.

On Sunday morning, Jennifer was up, showered and dressed before Mitch's eyes fluttered open. She said almost nothing at the breakfast table and retired to the pool with the Sunday paper as soon as she finished eating, leaving Mitch to clean up the kitchen and put the dishes into the dishwasher.

Eventually, he joined her at the pool, read the sports section and glanced at the funnies. Finally, he asked, "Is something bothering you? Something I did or said?"

"Jesus Christ!" she exploded. "Do I have to entertain you every goddamn minute you're here?"

"Whoa! I didn't say anything about entertaining me. I'm just worried about you because you've been so quiet and distant—it isn't like you."

"What do you really know about what I'm like? Maybe you're seeing the real me and you can't take it."

"I know you're normally not this grouchy," he said. "Even when it's time for the dreaded PMS."

He meant the PMS remark as a joke, but it backfired. Jennifer rose from the poolside recliner and said, "You goddamn sexist pig! Sit out here and play with yourself. I'm going to check my e-mail." She marched into the house, swinging her hips with extra verve as she retreated.

Later she apologized for blowing her top, but the atmosphere remained cool and Mitch decided to go home before supper.

"I'll call you tomorrow," he said.

"Sure," she said. Their normally passionate parting embrace was reduced to a quick hug and a peck on the lips. Mitch was still feeling depressed when he walked into the Daily Dispatch office Monday morning.

Alan Jeffrey, on the other hand, arrived at the office bubbling with tales of family fun. He was in the middle of describing the hiking and picnicking the four of them had done at William O'Brien State Park on Sunday when he noticed that Mitch was staring gloomily into his coffee cup and barely nodding in response.

Al stopped his story and asked, "Why so cheery this morning? Something go wrong in the Afton love nest?"

"Oh, nothing, really," Mitch said. "Jen and I had a less than idyllic weekend in said love nest, but I didn't mean to put a damper on yours. Keep talking."

"No billing and cooing?"

"Damn little. That birdie's got quite a tongue when you piss her off."

Their conversation was interrupted by the photo editor summoning Al to the telephone. It was Richard Bombardier of Bombs Away Trucking Company. "Sorry it took so long to get back to you guys," Bombardier said. "It took a while to get grandpa moved and settled and to get my mother's guilt feelings taken care of."

"Everything is fine, now?" Al said.

"Yeah. We lucked into a vacant room at Golden Pond Manor. It's a long-term care center in Maplewood."

"I've heard of it," Al said dryly.

"So, if you don't mind, I'll stop in today and pick up that stuff on my asshole former employee, so I can shut off his disability pay as soon as possible."

"Fine. I'll be here most all day. And if I'm out on assignment, I'll leave it with a reporter named Warren Mitchell." Al hung up, went back to Mitch and said, "It's time to dig out the pix of dancing Dennis. Richard Bombardier has got his grandfather settled in at Golden Pond Manor, would you believe, and is ready to lower the boom on the supposedly incapacitated Mr. O'Neal."

"Did I hear you say Golden Pond Manor?"

"Yes, you did. He says he 'lucked into' an open room there. Probably one left vacant by one of Doctor Sinfahdi's patients who ran shit out of luck."

Mitch was writing a story about the surplus of soaring temperatures and the shortage of rain showers in the Twin Cities area thus far in July when his phone rang.

"Hi," said the voice on the phone. "It's Jerry Granger. I just got back from Kansas and I was wondering what, if anything, you found out about the little doctor from India that I gave you the file on."

"It's nothing I can write about yet, but I think you'll be interested," Mitch said. "Why don't you come by my desk this afternoon and we can talk."

"Sounds good. I'm coming back to work this afternoon, so I'll see you then."

When the columnist arrived shortly after Mitch returned from lunch, he was very much interested in the number of deaths and the similarities of the circumstances in which they occurred. Mitch didn't tell him about their suspicion of foul play, nor did he reveal what his next step was going to be, but he suggested that Granger pass on the information gathered so far to his doctor friend and see how he reacted. "I'd be interested in his comments on the stuff we've turned up," Mitch said.

"I'm sure he'll have some," Granger said. "He got me started checking on this in the first place because he had the feeling that Doctor Sinfahdi was losing more patients than normal. These numbers—and the way the deaths occurred—should give him something to chew on."

"Just don't let him go running to a gumshoe at the AMA while we're still working on this," Mitch said. "I'm trying to get a few more details about his operation so I can put together a page-one story that will close him down."

"Good idea. This guy sounds like the biggest quack since Donald Duck."

"Yes, and unfortunately, a lot of his patients are now pushing up daisies."

Richard Bombardier walked into the office shortly after Alan Jeffrey had finished lunch. Al showed him the photos of Dennis O'Neal, let him read through the brief report he had written to accompany them and presented him with the bill. Bombardier expressed disgust at the pictures and satisfaction with the report, grunted at the amount due shown on the bottom line of the bill and wrote a check.

"Thanks for helping me nail this asshole," Bombardier said as walked to the door. "I can't believe he actually prances around on a stage in that outfit."

"He's a real beauty," Al said. "And let me tell you, Hurley's Hangout is not the classiest place in town to view female impersonators. Let me know what happens when you show the pictures to a judge. The folks at Hurley's were so friendly I'd like to see this guy actually have to live off what he can make doing his thing there."

"Yeah, I'll be in touch," said Bombardier. "Oh, I was gonna ask you; did you ever dig up any dirt on that doctor whatever his name is that treated my grandma? You sounded like you thought he might not be so good."

"Nothing concrete," Al said. "But I wouldn't put him at the top of my list if I was looking for a geriatric specialist."

"The guy seemed nice enough, but we've got somebody else lined up to take care of Grandpa," Bombardier said. "So long."

At four-thirty on Tuesday afternoon, Warren Mitchell was standing in front of the office building in ninety-five-degree heat when a white, eight-year-old Honda Accord pulled up. He climbed into the back seat behind a tiny, white-haired woman in a purple flower print dress, greeted the driver, who was Martha Todd, and noted that the car's air conditioning was working.

"This is my Gramma Mendes," said Martha. "Gramma, this is that nice Mr. Mitchell I've been telling you about."

"Pleased to meet you," said the older woman without turning around. "I hear you've been very friendly to my granddaughter."

Mitch felt his face get warm and was glad he was behind the two women so they couldn't see him turning red. "Your granddaughter is very easy to be friendly with," he said. "And she's been very friendly with me, too."

"I hope we can help you with your story about Doctor Sinfahdi," said Gramma Mendes. "He seems like a very nice man. I'm sure you'll find that he's doing a fine job as a doctor."

"Well, I'll be interested in hearing about what he prescribes for your symptoms, and while you're talking with him I'll be looking into the office procedures used by his staff," Mitch said. "I hope you're right about him being a fine doctor."

Martha turned her head far enough to catch his eye with a look that said let's change the subject before it gets too deep in here. "How was your weekend?" she asked.

"Oh, just fine," he said. No need for her to know that Jennifer was acting strange. "We took Jennifer's kids to the beach Saturday and played in the park on Sunday."

"It's nice that you get along so well with her kids," Martha said in a tone that didn't sound entirely sincere.

"Yeah, they're a lot of fun," he said. "What did you do?"

"Oh, the usual. Worked at the restaurant mostly and got some reading done." He was wishing he hadn't asked and wondering how to respond when she said, "Where exactly are we going, by the way?"

They were on Highway 35E, heading north. "Just keep going to the Roselawn Avenue exit," he said. "Then go west half a block and we're there." They rode the rest of the way in silence.

They found two other patients—both of them elderly women—in the doctor's air-conditioned waiting room. Martha went to the desk, told the receptionist that Ana Mendes was here for her appointment and was asked to take a seat. They sat, and Mitch studied the room carefully while pretending to read a three-month-old copy of *Modern Maturity*. He could see that there were some patients' files on open shelves behind the receptionist, that the two windows in the waiting room were of the variety that did not open and that the corridor leading to the examining rooms was the only way into the waiting room other than the front door.

"Mrs. Mendes?" said a female voice about ten minutes after they had been seated. Both Martha and her grandmother responded and a woman in a white blouse and black slacks led them down the corridor to an examining room where she left them and closed the door.

After a few minutes, Mitch approached the reception desk and asked, "Is there a men's room available?"

"Straight back as far as you can go, turn left and it's the last door on the right," said the woman behind the desk.

"Thank you," Mitch said. "Perfect," he thought. "This gets me all the way back into the guts of the building." He walked slowly down the corridor, noting that the second door on the right was halfway open and he could see filing cabinets inside. At the end of the corridor he turned left and counted three doors on the right side. The second was marked LADIES and the third was labeled MEN.

He went into the men's room and discovered a small translucent window at belly-button level. He tried to raise the lower half, but it wouldn't budge. Reaching up, he discovered a locking lever, which he flipped with some difficulty. Apparently this lock had not been moved since the day that air conditioning was installed in the building. This, Mitch decided, was a good omen. It wasn't likely anybody would be checking this lock if he left it in the unlocked position.

He had to bang on the window frame with the heels of his hands a bit before he could get it to move. When he finally raised it, he found himself looking out onto the service alley at the rear of the building. There was no screen on the window, another indication that it was never opened any more. It would be a tight fit, but the opening looked big enough for a man his size to wriggle through if the sash was lifted all the way.

Relieved that no alarm had gone off, Mitch lowered the sash, leaving a crack big enough to insert his fingers into at the bottom. He flushed the toilet, left the men's room and intentionally made a false start down the hallway on the other side of the center corridor. He spotted a door marked "Emergency Exit" at the far end on the left side, but his exploration of the area was interrupted by a female voice saying, "May I help you, sir?" He turned to find himself facing a sandy-haired woman wearing a crisp white blouse with a name tag that said "Emily Darnell, R.N."

"Just trying to find the waiting room," he said with an embarrassed smile. "Always get lost in these places."

"You went by the exit right back there," said Emily Darnell, R.N., waving toward the corridor he had purposely bypassed.

"Thanks," Mitch said. "Without some help, I'd be likely to wander around here until I'm old enough to be one of Doctor Sinfahdi's patients."

Nurse Darnell gave him an accommodating smile and said, "You're welcome," and she stepped into a room beside Mitch. He got a glimpse of office type furniture inside during the brief moment the door was open before the nurse shut it behind her.

He returned to the waiting room after studying the location of doors along the hallway and had been engrossed in a magazine specializing in the treatment of osteoporosis for about ten minutes when Martha and Gramma Mendes reappeared.

"Shall we go?" said Martha.

Mitch rose and spoke in a low voice. "You should go first. Go to the bathroom, I mean."

"I don't think it's necessary."

"I think you have to go real bad," Mitch said. "And while you're there, you have to flip the lock at the top of the window, if there is one, and raise the window up just enough to get your fingers—or, better yet, my fingers—underneath it."

"Are you serious?"

"What are we here for?"

"You're serious." Martha explained to Gramma Mendes that she had to go to the bathroom and went off down the corridor. Mitch and Gramma sat down to await Martha's return.

"How'd you like Doctor Sinfahdi?" Mitch asked.

"He's a very nice man," she said. "Seems to be a very caring person; doesn't act like he's in a big hurry to get you out of the room so he can see the next patient, the way so many of them do."

"Did he give you something for the headaches you told him you've been having?"

"Tylenol," she said. "Same thing I'd have taken without seeing him—if I really had a headache." She said this loud enough to cause a waiting patient three chairs away to turn her head toward them.

"Well, that's good," Mitch said, wishing he had waited until they were outside to start this conversation. "That's good. He didn't put you on something that would cost a lot of money?"

"He wants to see me again," Gramma Mendes said in the same loud voice. "Shouldn't Martha be making an appointment for me?"

"She can do that later. She can phone in after she checks her schedule to make sure she can drive you here," Mitch said. To himself, he added, "That will be one cold day in hell."

"Oh, sure, I should have thought of that. Martha is so busy, with classes and jobs and all. I'm just lucky to ever get to see her at all."

"Yeah, me too," Mitch said. Come to think of it, he wouldn't mind seeing Martha more often.

Martha returned from the ladies' room, looking a bit flushed. "Let's go," she said. Once outside, she turned to Mitch and complained about the difficulty of opening the window in the ladies' room. "I broke a nail, I'll have you know," she said as she helped Gramma Mendes into the right front seat. "I should bill the Daily Dispatch for a manicure job."

"I'll put a manicure on my next expense sheet and see which upraised finger I get when I hand it in," Mitch said. "By the way, what did you think of Doctor Ravi Sinfahdi?"

"You can't help but like the man. He's very soft spoken and gentle and seems to have a genuine interest in the patient's symptoms, unlike some of the hurry-up types you run into nowadays. Gramma liked him, didn't you, Gramma?"

"He's very nice," the older woman said. "Very kind and patient for a doctor."

"No expensive prescriptions?" Mitch said. "No suggestions of shots?"

"Nothing like that," Martha said. "He gave her some Tylenol sample packs and said to come and see him again if the pain persists."

"That's all?"

"Pretty much. He did suggest coming in for an overall check-up as soon as possible, but I kind of slid around that so he didn't have his 'girl' make us an appointment."

"Good slide," Mitch said.

"Keep me posted about what happens," Martha said as Mitch got out of the car at the Daily Dispatch building.

"Knock on my door when you're around," Mitch said. "It seems like I can never find you at home."

"I didn't know you'd been looking all that much," she said. "Maybe I should tack up my schedule on the door."

"Good idea. If nothing else, the burglars will appreciate it." She laughed and drove away, and Mitch went up to the Daily Dispatch office to sketch out Doctor Sinfahdi's floor plan while it was fresh in his mind. Then he called Alan Jeffrey at his home and said, "How about a little office call very late tonight?"

"Can we get in with our health insurance plan?" Al asked.

"The only health insurance we need is two bathroom windows that Martha and I left unlocked. I figured two would be healthier than one, in case somebody got pushy around one of them."

"In that case, I don't have a medi-care in the world. Make a house call here and pick me up at midnight. By that time Carol will be in a coma and I won't have to make any embarrassing explanations about where I'm going. Meanwhile I'll dig out the set of lock picks I acquired while I was doing some dirty work for a private investigator a few years ago."

CHAPTER 17

PICKY, PICKY, PICKY

Mitch parked his Honda on a dark side street a block and a half from Doctor Sinfahdi's office and he and Al walked to the parking lot where they checked the front of the building for lights to make sure nobody was working late. Once satisfied that the building was dark, they moved swiftly around the end to the back side. Both were dressed in dark clothing—black trousers and long-sleeved black pullovers—and were wearing latex gloves from the Daily Dispatch darkroom so not to leave any fingerprints. This apparel was not ideal for a muggy July night and both Al and Mitch were sweating freely by the time they located what Mitch believed to be the window of the men's room.

The window had been at belly-button level when Mitch stood inside the men's room, but now, with the added elevation of the building's foundation, it was at shoulder height for Mitch and chin height for Al—and it was not an easy climb up the clapboard side of the building. Mitch slid his fingers under the sash and found it still open.

Al grabbed onto the window sill and, with Mitch pushing against his butt, got his head and shoulders through the opening.

"Suck in your gut and I'll make like a catapult down here," Mitch said. A couple of grunts later, Al was through the window and landing on his hands on the floor of what turned out to be the ladies' room. "I'll have to be sure to wash my hands after using this rest room, employee or not," he thought as he pulled himself upright and turned to help Mitch scramble up. It was a tight fit, but with Al pulling and Mitch squirming like an eel on a fisherman's line (and swearing softly under his breath), they got him inside.

"Easy does it until we're sure nobody is working back where we couldn't see a light from the front," Al said as he opened the bathroom door a crack. Seeing nothing but darkness down the hall, they slipped out of the ladies' room and moved toward the corridor that led to the room with the filing cabinets. Mitch went first, shining a tiny flashlight on the floor to keep from bumping into any of the small tables and carts that stood along the walls.

"I hope the individual rooms of this rat trap aren't alarmed," Al whispered.

"It looked to me this afternoon like the front door was the only thing that had an alarm. That and probably the emergency exit—I didn't have time to inspect that before your friend, Nurse Darnell, sent me back to the waiting room."

The door to the room Mitch sought was closed. It was marked "Staff Only" so he felt certain it was the right room.

"Time for your lock picks," he said softly. Al stepped forward with the assortment of picks and skeleton keys he had collected during his association with the private eye and began trying them on the keyhole in the doorknob. The fourth key did the trick and they slipped quickly into the room. Mitch locked the door behind them with a twist of the lever on the inside knob, whispering, "Can't be too careful."

The beam of the flashlight revealed a row of filing cabinets against the far wall, each of which was secured by a steel bar ran through the handles from top to bottom and fastened to a steel loop with a padlock.

"This is what's known as easy picking," said Al, opening a padlock with the first pick he chose.

"You've really got a nose for picking," Mitch said.

"Careful, or I'll pick your seat," Al said, making a jabbing motion toward Mitch's backside.

"Better pick some other time for playing grab ass. I'd like to haul ass out of here as fast as possible."

"Picky, picky picky! Okay, let's see what's in here." Al slid the steel rod up and out of the way and opened the top drawer. Mitch pointed the flashlight into the drawer and they saw a row of hanging files with names on the tabs. The tabs also were marked with stickers of several different colors, indicating a code of some kind.

"Can you find a name we know?" Mitch said.

"These are A's and here are some B's," Al said. "Hey, here we go. Bombardier." He pulled out a folder with a red tab and the name "Bombardier, Linda M." on top. It was the file for Richard Bombardier's grandmother.

They leafed through the contents of the folder, finally coming to the bottom page that concluded with the notation that Mrs. Bombardier was deceased. The date of her death was noted and the cause of death was listed as myocardial infarction.

"Heart failure; just what Richard Bombardier said the doctor told the family," Al said. He laid the file down, took a small notebook and a ballpoint pen out of his pants pocket and wrote down the name and date of death. "Let's see if we can find some more," he said, returning the Bombardier file to the drawer.

He pulled out a file with a green tab and discovered that this patient was still being treated. Then he tried a yellow tab and learned that this patient was no longer being seen by Doctor Sinfahdi, but there was nothing about that person dying.

"Do you think all the red tabs mark the charts of dead folks?" Al said.

"Let's try them," Mitch said.

It turned out that they did. Out of twenty folders in the drawer, three had red tabs. They recorded the names and dates and causes of death in Al's notebook. Two, including Mrs. Bombardier, had died within the last two years, the other within three years.

They went down to the next drawer and found a similar percentage, two red tabs out of eighteen folders. One person had died six months earlier, the other almost two years in the past. Every dead patient's chart listed myocardial infarction as the cause.

"Amazing how many people with weak hearts this particular doctor has encountered," Mitch said.

"Let's see if we can find Uncle Charlie's folder," Al said, after they recorded the three deaths found among the charts in the third drawer. He reinserted the steel rod and slapped on the padlock. Going down the line of file cabinets, Al selected the one he thought might contain the names beginning with "J" and picked that lock, only to find that the files there only went through names starting with "H."

"On to the next," he said, locking that cabinet and opening the next one in line. There he found a red-tabbed folder marked "Jeffrey, Charles A." and pulled it out. The next-to-last sheet described Uncle Charlie's stroke and ended with the hand-written notation, "Patient released from hospital on 14 June at his wife's request and seems to be responding positively to treatment. Still unable to speak."

The last page ended with Uncle Charlie's death at home being noted on 15 June and giving the cause as myocardial infarction.

"Seems to be responding positively to treatment," Al said. "Well, he sure took a negative step the next day."

"Funny how every single one of them died of heart failure, no matter what they were suffering from," Mitch said. "Your Uncle Charlie had a stroke, Mrs. Bombardier did have heart trouble, a couple of people had respiratory ailments, but every damn one of them died of heart failure."

"We need to pass this information on to the doctor friend of your columnist buddy, Granger, so we can get his reaction. This could be enough to blow Doctor Sinfahdi right out of the water."

"The problem will be finding a legal way to get at these charts."

"We'll let the good doctor worry about that. He probably has access to a smart lawyer." Al was turning to slide the steel bar back into place down the front of the cabinet when they heard someone whistling a tune in the corridor outside the room.

The whistling was accompanied by footsteps, which were moving in their direction from the front of the building. Mitch quickly switched off the flashlight and they retreated to the end of the row of cabinets where they flattened themselves tightly against the wall.

The footsteps and the whistling kept coming. The footsteps stopped just outside their door, but the whistling continued while the whistler rattled the doorknob—once, twice. Apparently satisfied that it was locked, the whistler moved on down the corridor where they heard him trying each door in turn. While Al and Mitch listened in the darkness, the whistling went down both side hallways, passed their door again, moved to the reception room and finally was silent.

"Must be a security guy who checks the place," Mitch whispered. "Glad I locked the door behind us."

"Now that he's gone, let's get our butts out of here," Al said. "We've got plenty of ammunition, we don't need to hang around."

"It's going to be fun climbing out that window. I think I'll go feet first." Mitch flicked on the flashlight and they went to the door. They had slipped into the corridor and shut the office door, which locked behind them with a click, before they realized there was a light on in the reception room.

"Is somebody there?" said a man's voice from the lighted area. Mitch looked that way in time to see a chubby, middle-aged man in a khaki security guard uniform, rise from a reception room chair with a sandwich in one hand and a thermos-top cup of coffee in the other.

"Go!" Mitch said in a stage whisper, pushing Al out in front of him. "To the right and out the emergency door on the left at the end of the hallway."

"Hey! Stop! Halt!" yelled the man in the uniform as he started to pursue them.

Mitch, who was bringing up the rear, found himself sincerely hoping that the guy was not carrying a gun.

CHAPTER 18

SEE HOW THEY RUN

Alan Jeffrey and Warren Mitchell raced down the dark hallway toward the glowing red sign above the emergency exit. Behind them, the guard was still shouting for them to stop. He continued to shout as Al banged through the door and an alarm bell began clanging at a hundred and fifty decibels. The two news gatherers found themselves hoping they wouldn't become news items as they raced toward the street and turned toward their car, a block and a half away. They could still hear the alarm clanging when they reached the car, both of them huffing and puffing and drenched with sweat, but the security guard was not within sight or sound.

"We lost the fat little bastard," Al gasped as he pulled open the door on the passenger side.

Mitch kept his mouth shut because he felt very much like throwing up as he slid behind the steering wheel. He concentrated on starting the car and driving away quickly. As they turned south toward the St. Paul city line, they heard a police siren wailing in the distance and Mitch's breathing had normalized to the point where he was able to say, "Of all places for that dumb bastard to eat his lunch!" He slowed down to stay within the speed limit in case any police cruisers were in the immediate vicinity. This was no time to attract the attention of a zealous cop bearing speeding tickets.

"You missed the news," Carol Jeffrey said when her husband dragged himself into the kitchen at a few minutes after eight o'clock in the morning feeling tired, sore and grateful that Wednesday was this week's day off. "Your Uncle Charlie's Doctor Sinfahdi had a break-in at his office last night."

"No kidding?" Al said. "What did they say happened?" He affected a tone of innocent ignorance.

"According to the radio this morning, a security guard told the police that he surprised two huge goons wearing black ski masks over their heads, who knocked him down and ran out the back door."

"Knocked him down?" Al's tone was unguardedly incredulous.

Carol looked at him sharply. "Is that so surprising?"

"Oh, no," Al said quickly. "I was just thinking the guy was lucky he didn't get shot. Sometimes burglars shoot first and ask questions later."

"Anyhow, they got away. The police figure they were looking for drugs, but apparently the guard spooked them before they found anything."

"So, was that it? Anything else?" He was back to sounding sweetly innocent, but trying not to overdo it.

"No. That's all they said on the radio. I imagine the old doctor is kind of shook. You'd think a doctor's office would be harder to break into."

"Yeah, you would. It's kind of amazing that anybody could get in there without setting off an alarm or something. Did the cops say how they did it?"

"Nope, just that they were in there when the guard made his rounds in the wee small hours and they jumped him."

Wearily, Al groped his way through breakfast like a zombie leaving the graveyard. His condition caused Carol to ask if he was sick, but he satisfied her wifely concerns by saying he had stayed up late reading a horror novel and then had trouble getting to sleep.

In addition to being weary from an under-supply of sleep and an over-supply of physical exertion, he had a very tender spot on his left hip where he'd scraped the skin off, squeezing through the ladies' room window. Worst of all was the pain in the muscles on the fronts of his thighs, which he apparently had strained in the sprint for freedom after the guard spotted him and Mitch.

Al finished breakfast and went back upstairs, out of Carol's earshot, and used his cell phone to call Warren Mitchell's home number. When Mitch answered in a death-warmed-over voice, Al asked, "D'ja hear the radio this morning?"

"I woke up with such a headache I didn't turn on anything that made a noise louder than the coffee pot," Mitch said. "What did I miss?"

"It seems that the north suburban office of one Doctor Ravi Sinfahdi was broken into last night and a security guard told the cops that two huge guys wearing black masks jumped him and knocked him down."

"Knocked him down?"

"That's what the radio report said. Either the asshole is making up an excuse for why he didn't catch the burglars or he's looking to collect some kind of insurance claim."

"The insurance company ought to have some local newspaper check up on the little fat-ass bastard."

"Shall I call them and volunteer the services of the Daily Dispatch? I could offer them an expert witness."

"Let 'em witness for themselves. We got more important things to do. I am about to call the famous newspaper columnist, Jerry Granger, at his home and tell him we have some interesting numbers for his doctor friend."

"Don't let me keep you from your work," Al said. "Talk to you later."

Jerry Granger couldn't come to the phone just now and Mitch left a message on the answering machine to call him as soon as possible.

Mitch suffered from a shortage of energy and an abundance of stiff muscles, but he summoned enough strength to spend the morning looking through the names and numbers of Doctor Sinfahdi's dead patients again. He and Al had hardly scratched the surface of the doctor's files and they had upped the body count to twelve in the last year and fourteen within the last two years. "Wish we'd had time to run through all those charts before we had to knock that guard on his ass," he said to Sherlock Holmes. "But it was slow reading through the eye slits on those ski masks."

Mitch hoped Jerry Granger's doctor friend would know how to deal with the legal machinations required to subpoena those charts. He figured the information would be dynamite in court. The numbers would be enough to start an investigation and they also should raise some questions about how many of those people really died of heart failure—or what it was that caused the heart failure. The Daily Dispatch would have a blockbuster of a story and the doctor would be out of the shot-giving business.

In mid-morning, the phone rang at the Jeffreys' house and when Carol answered, a woman's voice asked for Mr. Jeffrey.

"Yes?" said Al.

"Mr. Jeffrey, this is Nurse Darnell at Doctor Sinfahdi's office. Have you heard the awful news about last night's break-in?"

"My wife heard something about it on the radio, and I'm told that the Daily Dispatch's police reporter is working on a story for the afternoon paper," Al said cautiously. "Why do you ask?"

"Mr. Jeffrey, the only thing we found disturbed after the burglars ran away was a file cabinet containing patients' medical records. It had been broken into and left unlocked when the criminals attacked the security guard and fled. It so happens that your uncle's chart was in that cabinet, Mr. Jeffrey, and we're calling to let you know that everything in the chart is still there and is intact. We wanted you to know that so you won't be worried in case the police contact you."

Al swallowed hard and beads of sweat appeared on his forehead. "I'm very glad to hear that nothing is missing or out of place," Al said into the phone after an all too pregnant pause. "It's very thoughtful of you to call."

"Well, we're calling everyone whose charts were in that file cabinet—or their next of kin if the patient happens to be deceased—just to reassure them that everything is safe and in order. You have a good day, Mr. Jeffrey."

Al wiped the sweat from his forehead on his sleeve, but his palms were still clammy as he described the nurse's comments to Carol in as calm and innocent a tone as he could muster.

"Why would somebody break in and go poking around in the doctor's files?" Carol asked.

"Beats hell out of me," Al said. "I'm just glad Uncle Charlie's chart is all okay. You never know when he might need it." Before Carol could pose more questions, he said he needed to get something from his dresser and went back upstairs. Again he grabbed the cell phone and called Mitch.

"Some great sneak thieves we are," Al said. "We left the damn file cabinet unlocked—the one we were in when Whistler's father came tootling down the hall and rattled our cage. Now they're alerted to the fact that somebody has been snooping in their records."

"Wonderful!" said Mitch. "As cat burglars, we've gone to the dogs. First we almost have the whistle blown on us and then we show the doctor why his office was raided. What the hell else can go wrong?"

Before Al could respond, Mitch's call waiting signal buzzed and he put Al on hold to see who was on the line. It was Jerry Granger.

"Hey, Jerry, we've got some very interesting information about Doctor Sinfahdi's patients for you to show to your doctor friend," Mitch said.

"Oh, shit! Haven't you heard?" Granger said. "No, you wouldn't have because you don't know his name."

"What haven't I heard?"

"My doctor friend lost control of his Jaguar last night and plowed into a tree at about seventy miles an hour. He's dead."

Mitch asked Jerry to hold for a minute, switched back to Al and said, "I think I just found out what the hell else can go wrong."

"So-o-o, now what?" Al asked. He had told Carol he had some errands to run and driven directly to Warren Mitchell's apartment for a council of war.

"Don't know," Mitch said. "Granger doesn't know any other doctor well enough to broach a ticklish subject like this to him. Looks like we're back on our own unless he pulls something out of a hat."

They sat in silence, Mitch in his only living room chair and Al on the sofa next to the slumbering Sherlock Holmes. Finally, the photographer said,

"So, who do we know who is acquainted with some doctors that deal with a lot of old farts and fartresses?"

"Nobody that I can think of."

"Think hard, with the emphasis on 'hard,' as in hard-on!"

Mitch looked at him in complete puzzlement, then the light went on. "Jennifer?" he said.

"Bingo! Does Jennifer not work with a number of doctors who treat patients in the various facilities that use her therapeutic services?"

"Yeah, but ..."

"Yeah, but what?"

"I don't think Jen wants to do any more detective work. She's already inquired about death rates with some of them and it sounded like her session with Doctor Sinfahdi and Nurse Whatzername was going to be her last performance as a private eye."

"Why don't you ask her, and, if necessary, try your usual method of persuasion? If nothing else, you'll enjoy using your persuader."

"So what do we actually want her to do?"

"Good question," Al said. "Let's figure out what the options are and pick one, and then you go sweet-talk Jennifer."

Rather quickly they decided that there weren't many options available. The best they could hope for would be for Jennifer to take a guess at which of the doctors she worked with would be the most open to discussing the possible misconduct of a colleague and introduce that doctor to Alan Jeffrey and Warren Mitchell. "Jennifer might have a feel for which doctor would be the most friendly to our numbers," Al said.

"As long as that friendly doctor doesn't have a feel for Jen," said Mitch.

"What? Do you have exclusive feeling rights on Jennifer?"

"I hope to hell I do. I'm not interested in sharing her with anybody."

"Then, by all means, get your butt out to Afton."

"When? You mean tonight?"

"There's no time like the present, dear boy. Every day that goes by puts another of the old doctor's patients at risk. By mounting fair Jennifer's body tonight, you could keep Doctor Sinfahdi's body count from mounting tomorrow."

CHAPTER 19

ALL HOT AND BOTHERED

"You look like you spent the whole night persuading Jennifer," Al said when Mitch dragged himself slowly past the photo desk on Thursday morning.

"I discovered I had some very sore muscles from the previous night's little escapade, but I managed to keep the important muscle functioning," Mitch said. He plopped heavily into his chair, waved a limp hand toward the photo department's coffee pot and said, "I'm too pooped to get up."

Al took the hint, rose and poured the weary reporter a cup of the inky liquid and asked, "Did you persuade her to feel out—for want of a better phrase—the doctors she knows and make us acquainted with anyone who might be helpful?"

"I'm pleased to say that things went a lot better with Jennifer last night and she said this morning that she'll try to find somebody for us to talk to."

"Lucky us. And on the 13th, at that!"

"That's right, it is the 13th, isn't it?"

"Yes, sir," Al said. "As one of the characters in Pogo used to say, Friday the 13th come on Thursday this month."

Mitch spent the time between his morning phone checks organizing the evidence against Doctor Sinfahdi so they could make a clear and concise presentation to any doctor willing to see them. He listed the former patients on a chart by the dates of their deaths and put the stated cause of death—myocardial infarction—behind each name.

"Couldn't be easier to read," Mitch said when he showed Al his work during the noon lunch break.

"Hell of a lot easier than any prescription," said Al.

"This particular prescription could be real bad medicine for our dear Doctor Sinfahdi."

"And be a preventative medication for a hell of a lot of potential myocardial infarctions in the northern suburbs of St. Paul."

In mid-afternoon, Richard Bombardier called to tell Al that a hearing on the disability status of Dennis O'Neal had been scheduled for Monday of the next week. Bombardier's lawyer had told him that the person who took the photographs of Dennis da Menace dancing at Hurley's Hangout should be present in court to verify their authenticity. Al agreed to meet Bombardier and his attorney in the courthouse at 8:30 Monday morning to run through the photos before the nine o'clock hearing.

"Maybe you should wear a disguise," Mitch said. "Dennis da Menace may take a negative view of your photo work."

"I shutter to think of that," Al said. "I'll suggest that he focus on the fact that I caught him in some rather distinctive poses. He might want to consider buying them to use for publicity shots since he'll obviously be needing more income after the judge gets a look at some of the gyrations being performed by a man with a supposedly bad back."

"Just don't expose yourself to any trouble with Dennis or his asshole buddies at Hurley's Hangout."

"Believe me, I won't let anything like that develop."

Mitch spent the next hour interviewing a legislative candidate in the interview room and when he got back to his desk, he found a note to call Jennifer Tilton at a number in Maplewood.

The news was not what he wanted to hear. Jennifer said she had talked to a doctor who treated several of the patients with whom she worked and had struck out cold.

"What happened exactly?" Mitch asked.

"I just sort of talked a little bit about patients dying and asked what a doctor might do if he thought another doctor was losing more patients than seemed normal. He looked at me like I was some sort of a nut and said such a thing would never happen, and then he walked away."

"Doesn't sound like he'd be much help."

"I'm crossing him off the list right now. I hope I don't get all these doctors pissed off at me for talking about patients dying all the time."

"Well, do what you feel you can without getting yourself in trouble with the people you have to work with," Mitch said. "Don't push your luck with anybody who doesn't seem to want to discuss the subject."

"Next thing I know, they'll be watching me to make sure I'm not trying to finish off one of their patients."

"That would be a killer. If you have better luck finding a live one tomorrow, we can talk about it when I come out for the weekend."

"Okay," she said. "Now I'm going home. Talk to you later."

"Are you going to be tying up the phone on the internet tonight?"

"For awhile anyway."

"You've really gotten hooked, haven't you?"

Jennifer's voice took on a dreamy quality as she said, "You wouldn't believe how hooked I am. Bye now."

Mitch shook his head as he hung up. He viewed computers strictly as work tools and couldn't, for the life of him, imagine what fun it was to sit in front of a keyboard staring at a screen for hours on end when it wasn't required. He would much rather read a book or a magazine—anything from James Joyce to *Better Homes and Gardens*—to while away the hours between supper and sleep. Even television occasionally offered something better than words typed on a computer screen.

"Oh, well, different strokes for different folks," Mitch said as he shut down the computer on his desk, put away the notes from the interview with the politician, figuring that writing the story could wait until the next morning, and went out into the afternoon heat. It was ninety-eight again in downtown St. Paul—the eighth day in a row that the mercury had soared above the ninety mark—and the only cloud in the sky was a manmade reddish-brown hydrocarbon haze. He wished he had gotten up and gone jogging early in the morning when it was only seventy-nine. He didn't even want to think about that kind of exercise at this temperature. Anyway, he had heard that the air quality was so unhealthy that it wasn't safe to breathe too heavily outdoors.

As he walked in the back door of his apartment building, he met Martha Todd—wearing running shoes, a T-shirt and the shortest of shorts—on her way out.

"I don't believe you," Mitch said. "You're going running in this heat?"

"Got to keep my girlish figure," Martha said. "Besides, I'm part Cape Verdean; folks like us don't mind the heat."

"You're part soft as a grape if you go out in this weather. You'll wind up in the hospital with heat exhaustion."

"Maybe they'll have better air conditioning there than I've got in my apartment," she said. "You can come visit." He watched as Martha went out the door, enthralled at the rolling movement of that ever-enticing ass, which was barely contained in the snug little shorts.

In his own apartment, Mitch soon understood what Martha meant about the air conditioning. The long unbroken string of ninety-degree days had overwhelmed the small window unit that was supposed to keep his living quarters cool. Even with the blower running full blast, the temperature in the apartment stayed at the approximate level of the third ring of Dante's Inferno until long after Mitch went to bed. As a result, he lay awake sweating naked on top of the sheet for the better part of an hour, during which he tried to sort out his thoughts on the Doctor Sinfahdi story.

He wondered when it would be time to take the statistics he and Al had compiled to some authority—and what authority should that be. The options he could think of were the AMA, the local police or the county attorney. If they were going to claim that some or all of the deaths actually had been induced by Doctor Sinfahdi, they needed to produce some incontrovertible evidence. However, the bodies of every one of the dear-departeds Mitch could think of had been cremated, making it impossible to test the remains for any kind of poison.

Wait a minute, he thought. Mrs. Peterson had said her sister's funeral and burial would be in Askov. Mitch was almost certain this meant that a whole body, not ashes, had been buried.

"Oh, God!" he muttered to the sleeping cat beside him. "I can't imagine asking Mrs. Peterson to dig up her sister and send her body to a lab for testing." He finally fell asleep while trying to compose such a request and he awoke with a start a couple of hours later after a dream in which he was at his desk at the Daily Dispatch, talking to Doctor Sinfahdi's nurse about borrowing the doctor's file cabinets, when a dirt-encrusted coffin rose slowly out of the floor next to his chair. Mitch's sudden movement brought a "meowr" of complaint from Sherlock Holmes, who had been curled up against his feet.

"Sorry, pal," Mitch said. He closed his eyes again and wished he could dream of Martha Todd's lively running shorts instead of Mrs. Peterson's dead sister. Nothing so sweet occurred.

A mile or so away, in the Midway district, Alan Jeffrey had also lain sweaty and awoke in the second-floor bedroom of an old house that, like Warren Mitchell's apartment building, depended on window units for air conditioning. Thoughts of Uncle Charlie, Diana and Doctor Sinfahdi boiled and bubbled through his brain as he tried to find a comfortable position and go to sleep. Next to him, Carol had dozed for awhile, but Al's restless rolling and twitching eventually brought her back to full consciousness.

"Heat keeping you awake?" she asked softly.

"Yeah," he said. "That and the stuff that keeps running through my mind."

"Like what?"

"Like wondering if Uncle Charlie would still be alive with a different doctor."

"You still think Doctor Sinfahdi didn't give him good enough care?"

"Worse than that," Al said. He decided that he might be able to induce sleep by unloading his troubled thoughts, so he launched into a tale of what he and Mitch had been doing and learning, omitting the parts about his erotic encounters with Diana and the after-hours visit to the doctor's office.

"You actually think that Doctor Sinfahdi might be killing his patients?" Carol said when the words stopped tumbling out of Al's mouth.

"The number of dead patients we've turned up by talking to people we know and looking through newspaper obits seems to be way out of proportion to what other geriatric specialists are losing. At least compared with those that Jennifer Tilton questioned," Al said.

"That's horrible. What are you going to do about it?"

"That's the problem; we don't know. We're not sure where we should go or who we should go to with the information we've put together. The one possibility we had is now dead, thanks to his meeting with a tree at seventy miles per hour." He explained to Carol about the suspicions expressed by Jerry Granger's doctor friend and about the friend's untimely demise.

"Have you told Diana about what you're thinking?"

"No. And I don't plan to until we can absolutely prove that Doctor Sinfahdi is responsible for several patients' deaths, including Uncle Charlie's. I just wish she hadn't had Uncle Charlie's body cremated."

They lay in silence for a few minutes until Carol said, "If you're right, there has to be some way to stop this doctor."

"I hope to hell there is. The problem is finding it."

"On the other hand, if you and Mitch accuse him of what amounts to murder and you're wrong, both of you could be looking at a nasty lawsuit."

"I'm well aware of that, sweetheart. The possibility of losing everything we own makes this even harder to deal with."

She rolled toward him and laid a warm hand on his moist cheek. "Let's think about what to do in the morning. You want to try to sleep or do you want to do something else as long as we're all hot and sweaty already?"

"Let's do something else," he said, and their hot, sweaty bodies melted together and grew even hotter and sweatier.

Tracy Tilton, wearing a two-piece, little girl's swimsuit, opened the door for Uncle Mitch when he arrived at the River Hills residence on Saturday evening for his customary overnight visit.

"Mama's doing stuff on her computer," Tracy said after giving Mitch a kiss and a hug. "She won't let Tony and me in her room unless we knock."

"Must be important stuff," Mitch said. "Let's us go knock."

Jennifer's voice responded to Tracy's tap on the door. "Who is it?"

"It's your white knight, come to cure his blues by taking a suntanned damsel to a dinner worth its weight in gold," Mitch said.

"Oh, God!" Jennifer said. "Just a minute; I'll be right out."

"Half a minute, then we're coming in," Mitch said, taking Tracy by the hand.

"No, that's okay," Jennifer said hastily. "I'll be right there." Mitch could hear a rapid clicking of computer keys, then the door opened and Jennifer stepped out of the room wearing a stretchy pink halter and pale gray shorts. Her face was flushed, her forehead was moist with sweat and Mitch felt a slight tremor in her hands as they gripped the back of his neck while they kissed hello.

"Jesus, what were you doing with that machine?" he asked. "Is your chat room so intense it gets you all hot and bothered?"

"It's hot in that room," Jennifer said. "Really hot and muggy. Did I hear you say something about going out for dinner?"

"I thought that might be a good idea to let somebody else do the cooking on such a sweaty summer night. This is, after all, our tenth straight day with temperatures above ninety degrees."

"Great idea," Jennifer said. "Let me freshen up and get the kids' faces washed." She wheeled away from him and walked swiftly into the bathroom, leaving him to wonder how the computer room could be so extremely hot and muggy when the rest of the house was cooled to a comfortable temperature by central air conditioning.

On Monday morning, Alan Jeffrey arrived at the Ramsey County Courthouse promptly at 8:30 and found Richard Bombardier already in the lobby. Together they waited for fifteen minutes until Bombardier's lawyer, a round little man with a bald head and a bristly moustache named Howard Rumble, appeared for their 8:30 appointment. Rumble appeared seconds after. Al told Bombardier, "Lawyers and politicians are always late. They think their time is more valuable than anybody else's."

True to form, Rumble didn't even bother to apologize. "This is a hearing in front of a judge; it isn't a big formal trial. I'll show you these photos and ask you if you took the pictures and when it was that you took them and where you were when you took them," he said to Al. "You just answer the questions and I'll submit them as Exhibit A. This should be enough to hang Dennis's dumb ass."

"Let's hope," said Bombardier.

They went into the courtroom and sat quietly in the back while the judge listened to a pair of lawyers arguing another case. At a couple of minutes before nine, the door behind them opened and in came Dennis O'Neal and his lawyer. They were accompanied by the man who had introduced himself as Derek DelMonico, the owner of Hurley's Hangout, and one of the surly twosome who had escorted Al and Mitch to their car the night Al took the pictures. Dennis was wearing a white, padded, circular brace around his neck and was walking in a slightly stooped position.

"Look at that phony son of a bitch," Richard Bombardier whispered as the quartet passed them and took seats closer to the bench.

"Wait'll he sees these pictures," Howard Rumble said. "These'll straighten him up in a hurry."

At nine-thirteen the other hearing ended and the bailiff announced that the next proceeding would be a hearing on a complaint by Richard Bombardier, proprietor of Bombardier Trucking, that Dennis O'Neal, an employee of said Bombardier Trucking, had been inappropriately collecting worker's compensation payments.

The lawyers presented themselves to Judge Winston Parks and both Richard Bombardier and Dennis O'Neal were identified. Rumble told the judge he had a witness to the fact that Dennis O'Neal was not suffering from a disabling back injury, as claimed, and soon Al was looking at the photos he had taken and answering the questions Rumble was asking.

As he finished, Al glanced at Dennis and his entourage and his eyes were met with glares of anger and hate. Al suppressed the urge to flip them the bird and sat down next to Richard Bombardier.

O'Neal's attorney argued that the photos had been obtained illegally without a warrant and should not be admitted as evidence. Howard Rumble countered his claim with some item of case law that Al couldn't quite follow. O'Neal's lawyer then said his client and two witnesses from the dance club would testify that Mr. O'Neal was in constant pain when he danced and always wore a brace between performances. The judge said their testimony wouldn't be necessary in light of the photos.

"If Mr. O'Neal has the range of motion depicted in these photographs, and is able to perform in this manner despite his pain, I see no reason for him to continue collecting workers' compensation," said the judge. "I hereby order that workers' compensation payments to Dennis O'Neal cease immediately." Then an assistant to the Ramsey County attorney stepped forward and announced that his office would soon be charging Mr. O'Neal with fraud.

Jack Martin, a reporter who covered the courts for the Daily Dispatch, gave Al a wave and a nod of approval as the photographer left the courtroom. Martin, who normally wouldn't have been sitting in on this sort of hearing, was there because he had been alerted to the possibility of an "interesting" news story by Mitch.

"It's always fun to see some asshole get caught stealing money," Martin had said when Mitch told him about the hearing.

The men who had accompanied Dennis O'Neal into the courtroom were less complimentary as they filed out of the room.

"You think you're pretty fuckin' smart, don't you?" said the owner of Hurley's Hangout. "I remember you sitting there fiddling with your little pack of cigarettes and I wondered what the fuck you were up to."

"Just doing my job," Al said.

"Yeah?" said the surly-faced heavy at DelMonico's side. "We'll be doing a job too, one of these nights. We know where you work and we'll find out where you live."

"You'll wish to hell you'd stuck to taking pictures of tea parties and puppy dogs," said Dennis O'Neal, who had removed the neck brace and was walking straight up. "We got ways of dealing with assholes like you."

"I lave a good day," Al said, and he walked out into the oppressive heat and humidity that still gripped downtown St. Paul. He was pleased to see dark clouds in the western sky and he heard the rumble of thunder as he walked toward the Daily Dispatch. Maybe the thermometer wouldn't hit ninety today.

"How'd it go?" Warren Mitchell asked as Al, coffee cup in hand, perched on the corner of the reporter's desk.

"We blew Dennis away," Al said. "But he had a couple of the nasties from the club with him and all three of them said they're going to come looking for me. Of course I'm terrified."

"It wouldn't hurt to watch your back for awhile. Those are the kind of people who might do something stupid."

"I'll stay away from dark alleys. How was your weekend?"

"It was okay," Mitch said. "I have to make some phone checks; talk to you later."

The weekend, like the previous one, had not been entirely okay. At times, Jennifer had seemed to be tense and distracted. Their night-time love making had ended earlier and provided much less satisfaction than usual, with Jennifer not showing her customary hunger and reckless enthusiasm. She also cut their morning maneuvers short on Sunday with the excuse that the kids might come in, a possibility that had never been of great concern on previous visits because

Tracy and Tony had been instructed to wait in the TV room until Mommy and Uncle Mitch got up.

Mitch wanted to ask Jennifer what was happening in her life that was creating this feeling of distance, but he remembered her outburst the previous weekend and was afraid such a question might precipitate a nasty quarrel. He and Al needed Jennifer's help finding a doctor who could provide some assistance in exposing Doctor Sinfahdi, so despite his desire to find out what was troubling her, Mitch decided not to risk fomenting a fight that could widen the crevasse into a canyon.

Instead, he chose a positive approach and suggested they go on a weekend get-away the next time he had both Saturday and Sunday free. "Just the two of us," he said. "We could go up the north shore, spend Saturday night in a fancy hotel, hike in one of the parks for awhile and find a nice restaurant for dinner."

"What about Tony and Tracy?" she said. "I can't leave them for a whole weekend with that teeny-bopper who watches them during the day."

"I'll bet Al and Carol would take them for a weekend if we asked them to."

"Mmm," she said and lapsed back into silence.

"I could call Al right now," Mitch said. "We could get it set up."

"Why the sudden urge to go off on a trip with me?"

"I think it would be good for us to be alone together without having to think about the kids, or cooking dinner or whatever other distractions come up around here."

"I'll think about it," she said. She had been wishing that Mitch would come up with something more romantic than a trip to the zoo with the kids and a roll in the hay in her bedroom. "Let me ask the kids how they feel about staying with Al and Carol before you set anything up."

"That works," Mitch said. He was thinking that a romantic weekend on the north shore might offer the ideal opportunity for him to pop the big question.

When he kissed Jennifer goodbye Monday morning, she promised to question some more doctors and call him with the results. He hoped she would also give him the go-ahead to enlist Al and Carol as babysitters and reserve a north shore hotel room. With luck, he could restore their once cozy companionship without precipitating another blow-up. Mitch had no qualms about asking tough, argumentative questions on the job as a reporter, but he dreaded confrontations in his personal life.

His train of thought was derailed by a shout from the city desk. "Hey,

Mitchell, there's a hell of a thunder storm going on out there. Get on the phone to the weather bureau and see if the hot spell is over."

It was Tuesday afternoon before Mitch heard from Jennifer. The Monday storm had cooled the city and the temperature was only seventy-five when she called to tell him she had broached the subject of excessive patient deaths to two more doctors with negative results.

"They both looked at me like I had two heads," she said. "Either they really don't think any doctor would be screwing up so badly that his patients were dying or they're in denial about the possibility. Anyway, they don't like to hear that kind of question and they have no intention of talking about it."

"Well, thanks for trying anyway," Mitch said. "Do you have any other prospects to question?"

"Only one and I don't expect anything better from her. She's really a cold fish and I can't see her showing any interest."

"When do you see this frosty finny?"

"Thursday. But I think you guys are out there on your own."

"Okay," Mitch said. "Dangle the bait in front of that final fish, cold or not, and meanwhile we'll be looking for some way to get at those records." As he hung up, Mitch thought once again about Mrs. Peterson's sister lying in a grave in Askov. No, he said to himself. There's got to be a better way to get at the doctor than digging up a corpse. But he wondered what it could be.

Al exploded when Mitch told him about his idea.

"You got any better ideas for proving, or for that matter disproving, our theory about Doctor Sinfahdi? Jerry Granger's guy can't help us any more and Jen's getting nowhere with her doctor contacts."

"Who are you planning to dig up?"

"I had Mrs. Peterson's sister in mind."

"You'd ask that nice little old lady to have her sister's body dug up?"

"Well, we can't do much with your Uncle Charlie, can we? And all of the others we know personally were cremated too," Mitch said.

"Do you think Mrs. Peterson will say yes?"

"Not right away. I expect her to be horrified by the idea at first. I just hope I can schmooze her along and eventually talk her into it."

"So what makes you think she'll ever agree to do this?"

"If I can convince her that her sister would still be alive if Doctor Sinfahdi hadn't slipped her something lethal, she might be mad enough to say yes. On the other hand, she might get so pissed at me for suggesting it that I'll have to find a new apartment."

"I'd offer you my garage, but it's full of junk."

"So is my apartment, but in my case it's called furniture."

"So when are you going to beard the aged lioness in her den?"

"Tonight, if I can work up the guts. This is one of those times I wish I still drank booze so I could stoke up on liquid courage before tackling her."

"As I remember your drinking style, you were more likely to become anesthetized than supercharged. It's a good thing you aren't drinking or you'd probably toss your cookies on her shoes when she opened the door."

"You have the nicest way of saying things," Mitch said. "Have you ever thought of going into journalism?"

"I used to think about it, but working at the Daily Dispatch cured me of that."

After work, Mitch decided to put off his visit to Mrs. Peterson as long as possible by eating dinner at the Index Café. His hope was that Martha Todd would be on duty as a waitress and this time; fortune smiled. So did Martha when she approached his table.

"You look awfully serious," she said after they exchanged greetings.

"I've got something awfully serious on my mind," he said.

"Want to tell Doctor Todd about it?"

"Here or on your couch, doctor?"

"Depends on how much time you have. I get off here at eight."

"I'm afraid I can't wait that long. My problem is about something I have to do before then."

"Let Doctor Todd put in your order and she will come back," Martha said. "As you can see, it's pretty slow in here tonight."

Mitch ordered a cheese and bacon burger with fries, which made Martha grimace. "You sure you want all that fat?" she asked.

"I need all the fat I can get for what I'm going to do tonight," he said. "I've got to stoke up for something very unpleasant." The look on Martha's face a few moments later when he told her what he was planning to do, almost made up for the feeling of dread that came over him every time he thought about approaching Mrs. Peterson.

CHAPTER 20

GRAVE CONCERNS

When Alan Jeffrey arrived home after work, he noticed a strange car—a black, compact sedan with some rust spots on the rocker panels and fenders—parked in front of his next-door neighbor's house. All the houses on Hamline Avenue had garages behind them, facing a north/south-running alley that split each block. Nearly all the residents on Al's block used their garages for storage and parked their cars in front of their homes. Everyone knew everyone else's vehicle (or vehicles), so it wasn't hard to spot a non-resident's car when one appeared beside the curb.

"Jacobsons must have company," Al said to himself as he locked up his red Toyota. He thought he had detected movement inside the black car, like someone ducking down as he drove past it so he parked a couple of car lengths ahead of it. But, standing in the street and looking straight on, he decided he must have seen flickering shadows cast by the fluttering of the leaves in the gentle, late afternoon breeze that was blowing down the street.

"Anybody home?" Al asked as he walked through the front door. Carol's voice responded from the kitchen and she met him in the hallway with a hug and warm, welcoming kiss.

"So, what's the joke of the day?" Al asked.

"You will be if your children see that story in the paper," said Carol.

"You mean the one about the sleaze-bag nightclub dancer? What's so funny about that?"

"Can't you just hear Kevin giggling and Kristin asking what her daddy is doing taking pictures in a crazy place like that?"

"Earning money for her college education, that's what he's doing," Al said. "That job actually paid pretty well."

"Well, I'm glad. You couldn't pay me enough to go into that joint."

"If you did, you'd be the only real female in there." Through the open front window Al heard a car start and looked out to see the black compact pulling away from the curb. Al tried to get a look at the driver as the car passed the house, but all he could see was that it was a man wearing a baseball cap.

*   *   *

Warren Mitchell walked slowly along Grand Avenue and dawdled in front of some store windows on the way to his apartment building, so it was almost seven o'clock when he finally rapped on Nellie Peterson's door. He heard her approach and stop to look through the peephole and he was tempted to duck down and walk away before she could see who was there. But he held his ground, mentally reviewing the words he was going to say, and the door opened halfway to reveal Mrs. Peterson wrapped in a faded blue chenille bathrobe and wearing the same floppy koala bear slippers she'd had on the night she told him about her sister dying after being visited by "Doctor Symphony."

"Mr. Mitchell, this is a pleasant surprise," she said.

"You won't think it's so pleasant when you hear what I've got to say," Mitch thought. Aloud he said, "How are you, Mrs. Peterson?"

"Oh, not so bad for an old lady," she said. "What can I do for you?"

"I'd like to talk to you about something very important," Mitch said. "Can I come in for a few minutes?"

"Yah, sure," Mrs. Peterson said, backing in and opening the door all the way. "Have a seat over there in the living room. Can I get you a cup of coffee?"

"That would be nice," Mitch said, not wanting to refuse her hospitality, even though he was saturated with coffee from his after-supper stalling.

"I got some nice peanut butter cookies I baked today to go with it," she said, coming out of the kitchen with a large coffee mug in one hand and a plate piled with cookies in the other. She set the cookies on the table next to the armchair he had chosen and handed him the mug, which was filled with an extremely dark and fragrant brew. Mrs. Peterson's coffee looked and smelled like it would dissolve the enamel on the drinker's teeth.

She sat across from Mitch on a vintage, Victorian-style sofa and said, "Now, what is it you want to talk about, Mr. Mitchell? Is there something wrong in your apartment?"

Mitch took a bite of cookie and chewed and swallowed it before he answered. "This is not an easy thing for me to say, Mrs. Peterson. It has nothing to do with my apartment. I've come to ask if you would consider helping me solve what appears to be a series of very serious crimes."

"What kind of a crime could an old lady like me ever help you solve?"

He primed his tongue with a sip of the powerful coffee and said, "It's a possible series of crimes that involves the doctor who treated your sister before her death."

Mrs. Peterson's eyes opened wide. "You think the doctor is a criminal?" she said.

"As I said, it's possible. A friend of mine, whose uncle also died after being treated by Doctor Sinfahdi, and I, have been doing some checking and we have found an unusually high death rate among the doctor's patients. We think that either Doctor Sinfahdi is not giving his patients the right kind of care or that he might actually be doing something to cause their deaths."

The look on her face was one of disbelief. "You think the doctor might be killing people?" she said.

Mitch took another bite of cookie before replying. "We think it's very possible," he said while he chewed.

"You don't think that Doctor Sinfahdi might have killed my sister do you?"

"That's what I want to talk to you about." He took another sip of coffee and regretted having accepted it because he could feel the four cups he had consumed in the restaurant beginning to arrive in his bladder. He was certain that the tension of the moment was helping to speed the process and he was wishing he had gone to his apartment for a bathroom stop before knocking on Mrs. Peterson's door.

While his thoughts were centered on his bladder, Mitch heard Mrs. Peterson ask, "So, what is it you want me to do?"

He took a deep breath and said, "We'd like you to have your sister's body tested for poison."

"But my sister's body is buried in the ground."

"I know. That's what makes this so hard to ask. It would require what's called an exhumation."

"You mean digging Grace's body up?" The doubtful expression had turned to one of horror.

He took another sip of coffee because his mouth had gone bone-dry. "That's what I mean," he said. "Like I said, it's a very hard thing to ask you to do. I'm only asking because if Doctor Sinfahdi really has been killing his elderly patients, we want to stop him from killing any more."

"Oh, no," she said. "I couldn't do that. You better ask somebody else. What about your friend whose uncle died?"

"His uncle's body was cremated. So were the bodies of the other patients that we've heard about. Your sister is the only one we know of whose body still exists. Otherwise, I never would have asked you to think about this."

"I'm sorry, Mr. Mitchell. I just could not do that to Grace."

"I'm asking you to give it some thought before you say no. The lives of many other potential victims would be saved if it was found that your sister had been poisoned and Doctor Sinfahdi was put in prison."

Mrs. Peterson stood up and folded her arms across her chest. "Grace needs to rest in peace," she said. "I'd like to help save other people, but I can't disturb her final rest. You need to talk to somebody else."

Mitch wanted to make an attempt to soften her resistance, but it was obvious she was showing him the door. What's more, the pressure on his bladder was reaching critical mass. "I won't try to push you into doing something you really don't want to do," he said as he set the coffee cup on a table beside the chair and started toward the door. "But I do wish you would give it some more thought. Think especially about the lives you might be saving."

"My thought is that my sister's grave is sacred and it ain't to be touched," Mrs. Peterson said as she opened the door. "I'm sorry, but that's the way it's got to be. Good night, Mr. Mitchell."

"Good night. And thanks for the coffee and cookies." He exited gracefully, waited for the door to close behind him and then sprinted across the hall to his own apartment, brushed past Sherlock Holmes, despite a welcoming "meow" and raced into the bathroom, hastily unzipping his fly as he went.

"How'd it go with your landlady?" Al asked Mitch on the phone the next morning. Both of them had this day off.

"The good news is she didn't kick me out of my apartment," Mitch said.

"And the bad news?"

"She isn't pulling her sister out of her coffin, either."

"Did you really think she would?" Al asked.

"I thought she might at least consider it, but I guess it was wishful thinking."

"Well, that buries our hopes of testing a body for poison."

"How can you make stupid puns in a grave situation like this?"

"Just thinking about digging up the facts," Al said and he hung up.

After a supper of canned baked beans and a couple of microwaved hot dogs, Mitch punched in Jennifer Tilton's phone number and was pleasantly surprised to hear it ringing on the first attempt. For a change, she wasn't tying up the phone line with a long evening session on the internet.

"Did you see the cold fish doctor today?" Mitch asked after the initial greetings.

"I did," Jennifer said. "With about the expected results."

"About?"

"Well, she did seem more interested than the other doctors I sounded out, but she made it clear that no doctor would get involved in an investigation of another doctor unless the circumstances were really extreme."

"You don't think these circumstances are extreme? We've got fourteen bodies that we know of in a time span that other doctors say they've lost two or three patients."

"I couldn't tell her that. I mean, I did the best I could, but I didn't dare start throwing numbers at her or she'd wonder how I got them. You're the investigative reporter; if you want to talk to her, I'll give you her name and number, but I'm not going to rock the boat. I happen to need this job." Her voice was rising both in volume and pitch with each sentence.

"I understand," he said quickly. "Give me her name and number and I'll call her if I can figure out a way to present the evidence. I'm not trying to get you involved."

"Just a minute," Jennifer said as she put down the phone. She returned a moment later and said the doctor's name was Annette Carpenter and gave Mitch a phone number in Roseville. "Don't tell her you've been talking to me, whatever you do," she said.

"I always protect my sources. And speaking of protection, I'll be out to guard my favorite Afton household right after work tomorrow. I'm taking Saturday off as my Fourth of July holiday."

"Oh, you are?" She paused for a moment, then said, "Umm, why don't you wait till Saturday to come out? I, uh, ... I promised the kids I'd take them to that new Disney movie Friday night."

"We could all go. I can get there in time."

"Oh, um, ... why don't you wait? I'd like to take them out just by myself for once. Okay?"

Her reason didn't ring true with him, but Mitch decided not to press the issue. There already was enough tension between them. "Okay," he said. "Saturday it is. Bright and early?"

"Not too bright and early," she said. "I'd like to sleep in."

"Can't I help?" he said with a leer in his voice.

"I've had a hard week. I need some rest."

"Okay," Mitch said with a sigh. "You sleep in and I'll see you when I see you."

"You're not mad are you?"

"No, Jen, I'm not mad. Just disappointed that I can't see you right away tomorrow."

"I knew you'd understand. We'll have plenty of time together Saturday and Sunday. Bye now."

"Sure we will," Mitch said after he hung up. He turned to Sherlock Holmes and said, "You may not appreciate it, old buddy, but the best thing I ever did for you was to have your nuts cut off so you don't have to be out there chasing pussy."

"Merowr?" said Sherlock, and he rubbed himself around and around against Mitch's ankles until Mitch pulled the big beggar up onto his lap and gave his ears a good scratching.

When Alan Jeffrey arrived home after work, he noticed a small, black sedan parked about fifty feet away, on the opposite side of the street. "Is that the same car that was in front of the Jacobsons' last night?" he wondered. It looked very much like the same rust pattern he had seen marring the black finish. Al was tempted to walk up the block and take a closer look, but decided not to when he saw a couple of neighbors out in their yards on that side of the street. "They'll think I'm either nosy or nuts," Al thought and went in to greet Carol and hear the joke of the day.

"A guy walks into a bar and offers to bet the bartender fifty bucks he can bite his own right eye," Carol said. "The bartender takes the bet and the guy pulls a glass eye out of his right socket and bites it. The bartender is mad, but she pays the fifty bucks and the guy leaves.

"A half-hour later he comes back and says he'll bet fifty bucks he can bite his left eye. The bartender knows he isn't blind, so she takes the bet. This time guy takes out his false teeth and bites his left eye, collects another fifty bucks and leaves.

"Pretty soon he's back again and he says he'll give the bartender a chance to win back her money. He bets her a hundred dollars he can pee in a glass on the bar fifteen feet away. She knows she's got a sure winner, so she puts the glass on the bar and he climbs up on the bar and pees everywhere but in the glass. He's grinning as he pays her the hundred bucks and she's grinning as she takes it, but she asks him why he's so happy when he's lost a hundred dollars.

"The guys says, 'Because I just bet that man over there one thousand dollars that I could pee all over your bar and you'd be happy as hell about it.' "

"That's a real pisser," said Al. "Now, what's for dinner?"

"Pizza. You're taking us out."

"Is that another joke?"

"Ask your children," she said, gesturing toward Kristin and Kevin who had magically appeared.

"Pizza!" they shouted in unison.

"Oh, cheese, talk about crust," Al said, and he turned and walked out to the car. The black car was still parked on the other side of the street, but Al couldn't see anybody inside. As they drove past, he made a mental note of the last three numbers on the license plate: two-four-six. They should be easy to remember.

Mitch didn't sleep well Friday night. He had been looking forward to having Jennifer's soft, sensuous body beside him and over him and under him and wrapped all around him. Alone in his own bed, he tossed and turned for a couple of hours, got up and made a cup of hot chocolate, went back to bed for more tossing and turning, finally fell asleep about three o'clock and woke up at six. Sherlock Holmes gave him a look of reproach as he dragged himself out of bed, leaving the drowsy cat without a warm back to curl up against.

Mitch showered, shaved his chin, trimmed his moustache and decided to go out for breakfast. He polished off an omelet and a pot of coffee at a nearby café and at 7:30 decided to head for Afton. If Jennifer was still in bed when he got there, he might be able to slip in with her for a quickie while the kids were in the rec room watching the Saturday morning cartoons.

It was about quarter after eight when he drove into Jennifer's driveway and was surprised to find a shiny new car parked in front of her garage. "Who the hell is visiting this early?" he wondered as he let himself in the front door.

Tony and Tracy were in the family room, eating sugar-coated dry cereal and watching the cartoons. Mitch greeted them quietly and said, "Where's your mom?"

"Mama's still in bed," said Tracy. "We're supposed to stay out until she gets up."

"I'll see if she's awake," Mitch said softly. "You guys watch your programs."

Still wondering about the car he had seen in the yard, Mitch walked down the hall to Jennifer's bedroom, opened the door and went in. He was silently closing the door when he became aware that there were two heads resting on the pink-slipped pillows. And one of those heads had short hair and a beard.

CHAPTER 21

ALL BOTHERED AND HOT

When Alan Jeffrey awoke at eight o'clock Saturday morning, he performed his usual ritual, which ended with a trip to the front porch for the newspaper. Sometimes it was lying on the top step just outside the porch door, and sometimes, when the paper boy's aim was not so good, it was on one of the lower steps, the concrete walk that began at the bottom of the steps or the front lawn. On this particular morning, he saw the paper lying on the walk, several yards beyond the porch door.

Al went down the steps, let the door slam shut behind him, retrieved the paper and turned back toward the house. He stopped in mid-stride when he saw the porch door. Spray painted on the white door in three-foot-high, sloppy black upper-case letters, was the word PIG.

He stared, unbelieving, for a minute, wondering who would have done such a piece of dirty work. Then a thought struck him and he looked up the street for the black car, which still had been parked there when the Jeffrey family returned from their pizza run the night before. The car was not there. Nor could he see it anywhere else on the block on either side of the street.

Al looked at the vandal's work again, then walked slowly into the porch and summoned Carol with a shout. She looked stunned when she saw the mess.

"Who would do this?" Carol asked.

"In court Monday, after the judge nailed Dennis O'Neal for fraud, Dennis and his butt-hole buddies from Hurley's Hangout said they'd get even with me for taking the photos. And they said they'd find out where I lived."

"I'm calling the police," Carol said, starting toward the house. There was a sick feeling in Al's stomach as he followed her in past the ugly artwork on the front of his home. "Two-four-six," he muttered. "We'll see if those plate numbers lead to anybody we know."

The sheet was pulled down far enough on Jennifer's side of the bed to reveal one bare shoulder and one bare breast—one of the suntanned, silky-smooth breasts Mitch loved to kiss and caress. He suppressed the urge to walk over and grab the pinkish-brown nipple and give it a good twist. Instead, he said, "Good morning, lady and gentleman!" in a Marine drill sergeant's voice. Both pairs of eyes opened. The man's mouth fell open also and the color drained from Jennifer Tilton's deeply-tanned face.

"What are you doing here?" she said.

"I have a date for the weekend, beginning on Saturday morning, remember?" Mitch said. "Well, this is Saturday morning."

Jennifer looked at the digital alarm clock on her bedside table. "It's not even quarter to nine," she said. "You weren't coming this early."

"I couldn't sleep. I was awake most of the night and obviously so were you."

Jennifer's face turned red and she pulled the sheet up to cover her naked breast. The man beside her managed to close his mouth but his eyes looked frightened. "You weren't coming this early," Jennifer said again.

"You might introduce me," Mitch said, with a cold, threatening look at the wide-eyed, bearded face on the pillow next to Jennifer.

"This is Adam," she said weakly. "He's from my high school class in New Jersey."

The man finally found the power of speech. "Jen and I got reacquainted at the class reunion this spring," he said. "We used to date in high school. We even went steady our senior year."

"I'd say you got very reacquainted," Mitch said. "Were you two screwing all the time Jennifer was out there?"

"We didn't do anything out there," Jennifer said. "Except talk. But we've been doing it on the internet since I got back."

"Doing what?" Mitch said.

"We've been having cyber sex," Adam said.

"What the hell is cyber sex?" Mitch asked.

"Cyber sex is fucking long distance by computer, stupid," Jennifer said. "You remember the night you kept trying to call me and I said the line was tied up so long because I couldn't get off? Well, I really meant 'I couldn't get off.' You know; I couldn't come."

Mitch felt his knees begin to wobble. His legs felt so buttery weak he wished he could sit down, but he didn't want to lose his commanding position at the foot of the bed. His head felt ultra-light, as if it would float off his shoulders, his stomach was churning like cake batter in a mixing bowl and he hoped he wasn't going to lose the omelet on Jennifer's bedroom floor.

"You two have been having sex on the internet?" he managed to say.

"Almost every night," Jennifer said.

"It's really great," said Adam. "But it's a whole lot better this way. But I guess you know that because you've had a turn. But don't worry, I ain't the jealous type."

Mitch could not believe what he was hearing. "And when did you arrive on the scene?" he asked.

"He got in last night," Jennifer said.

"Yes, it's pretty obvious he 'got in' last night."

"That's not what I meant, you asshole!" The drowsiness and embarrassment were gone from her voice and her eyes were flashing with anger. "He flew into the Twin Cities last night. He rented a car and was here at the house when I got home from work."

"So what were your plans for this weekend?" Mitch said. His knees were beginning to steady themselves and several deep breaths had relieved the queasiness in his stomach.

"Adam was going to be gone by the time you got here and I was going to tell you about him before you and I went to bed together. I told you not to come out here so goddamn early!"

"Well, pardon me all to hell for messing up your schedule, Mrs. Tilton," Mitch said. "Would you like me to go out and come back at the proper time?"

"No! I just want you to get the hell out of here!"

"No sooner said than done," Mitch said. He turned and started out the bedroom door, then looked back and said, "Nice to meet you, Adam. Glad you aren't the jealous type. And I'm so very happy that you don't have to jack off in front of your computer anymore. You can really fuck up a keyboard that way."

He slammed the bedroom door behind him, waved goodbye to Tony and Tracy as he passed the den and barreled out the front door. On his way past Adam's shiny rental car, he pushed the outside mirror out of line and gave the left front door a kick that left a burning pain in his big toe and a satisfying dent in the thin metal.

"So, you think you might know who done this?" the investigating officer asked Alan Jeffrey as they looked together at the spray-painted word PIG.

"I have a notion," Al said. "I was threatened by an individual and there has been a strange car hanging around the neighborhood."

"And what individual made this threat?"

"There were several men, actually, but one name I'm sure of is Dennis O'Neal. You might check his vehicle registration to see if he owns a black compact sedan with a license number that ends with two-four-six."

"Why would this O'Neal person threaten you?"

"I took a batch of photos that were used in court to deprive him of his workers' compensation, which he had been drawing for a fake on-the-job injury. He did not take kindly to the loss of income."

"Most cheaters don't," said the officer. "I'll have O'Neal's plates checked when I get back to the station. We're going to take some pictures here ourselves, and then you can call your insurance company. Your homeowner's should pay for the cleanup, or part of it. It depends on your deductible."

Al stood back while the police photographer did his work, then said goodbye to the officers and went into the house.

"They're going to check on Dennis O'Neal's registration," he said to Carol.

"What if it turns out it wasn't him?" she asked.

"Then we have a mystery, because I don't know who else could be that pissed off at me." He paused for a moment, then said, "Oh, Jesus!"

"What?"

"If it was them, they might have gone after Richard Bombardier, too." He ran upstairs, grabbed his pocket phonebook off the dresser, found Richard Bombardier's number, went back down and called him on the kitchen phone. Al told the trucking company owner what had happened on Hamline Avenue and asked if anything had occurred at the Bombardier residence.

"No, nobody did nothing here," Bombardier said.

Al had another thought. "How about at your truck garage?" he said.

"I don't know about that; we been closed this week for vacations."

"Maybe you ought to take a run out there and see if you've had visitors."

"Yeah, maybe I should. If that little prick spray-painted your house he might have done something to me, too. I'll take a look and call you back."

If you had asked Warren Mitchell about the drive home from Afton that morning, he would not have been able to describe the traffic conditions, the weather or any of the roadside scenery. His mind and heart were embroiled in such turmoil, that he was lucky to find Grand Avenue, his alley and the parking lot behind his apartment building. Once there, he sat in the car for a long time with thoughts of Jennifer Tilton's smiling face and voluptuous body running through his mind. He thought of her voice and her laughter and her perfume. He found that the memories of the many nights he had spent wrapped in the rapture of the sweet-faced brunette's welcoming arms and legs were interrupted by periodic bursts of hatred for the man called Adam, the state of New Jersey and the entire computer industry.

"Fuck it!" he said at last and dragged himself out of the car. Maybe if he went for a walk, or better yet, a jog, he could clear his mind of the picture of Jennifer and Adam lying side-by-side and obviously naked in Jennifer's pink bed. "Fuck'em both!" he said as he opened his apartment door and brushed past Sherlock Holmes. He automatically looked at his telephone answering machine and saw that the message light was blinking. He pressed the play button and heard Jennifer's voice saying, "Mitch, honey, I know you're pissed off at me and you have every right to be, but please call me when you get home so I know you're okay. I didn't mean to hurt you like this."

"Fuck you!" Mitch shouted in the general direction of the answering machine and went to change into jogging clothes.

A few minutes, later he roared out of the apartment, slamming the door behind him, and practically ran out the back door. In the parking lot, Martha Todd was getting out of her car and she looked surprised to see Mitch wearing a sweat suit.

"This is a tough time of day to go jogging," Martha said with a smile. "Don't you know only mad dogs and Englishmen go out in the noonday sun?"

"I'm not an Englishman," Mitch said brusquely and he took off at a brisk pace down the alley without even bothering to stretch out.

"Well, excuse me," Martha muttered as she locked her car door.

Al had just finished arguing with a woman at the insurance company, when Richard Bombardier called back. The woman had wanted to wait until Monday to send an adjuster out to assess the damage and Al had insisted that she dispatch someone today so he could get rid of the offensive graffiti right away. After saying twice that such a thing was impossible on a Saturday, the woman yielded to Al's growing fervor and said she would try to get someone out there this afternoon.

The tone of Richard Bombardier's greeting removed any doubt as to whether his truck garage had been vandalized. He told Al that the phantom painter apparently had exhausted the contents of several spray cans covering doors, walls and even windows with an assortment of insults, obscenities and symbols of hatred.

"I've got the cops coming over right now," Bombardier said. "I'm going to put that little fucker in jail if I don't kill him first."

"He's pretty damn stupid to hit both of us at the same time," Al said. "Didn't he see how obvious it would be?"

"Nobody ever said the little shit had any brains. Believe me, this wagon is a couple of bales short of a full load of hay. Look how easy we caught him cheating on his workers' comp, for Christ's sake!"

"You're right. Hey, if the cops can find out where he lives, they can probably grab him right out of his bed today. Between messing up my place and yours, he must have been up all night."

"I've got the little bastard's home address right here. If the cops won't pay him a visit today, you can damn well bet that I will."

"I'd go with you, but I'm hoping to see an insurance adjuster here this afternoon," Al said. "Let me know what happens."

"Goddamn right I will. Oh, here come the cops. So long."

He had been jogging—no, running—for about ten minutes when it registered on Warren Mitchell's brain that his body was extremely hot. Sweat was pouring down his face, his sweat suit was turning dark from the product of his pores and his feet were almost sloshing inside his running shoes. He slowed his pace to a normal jog and looked at his wristwatch. It was almost quarter to twelve.

"What did that bitch in the parking lot say about the noonday sun?" he asked himself. He tried to remember her exact words and suddenly realized that the bitch in question was Martha Todd. "Jesus, what did I say to her?" he wondered. "I'll bet it was rude, whatever it was."

Mitch's legs felt rubbery and he slowed to a walk. The temperature had risen back into the high eighties, it had been five hours since he had eaten and he had endured an enormous emotional shock. He felt a little dizzy, so he stopped, bent forward and let his head hang below knee level. The world around him stopped spinning, but the wet-noodle weakness in his legs stayed with him. He looked for a place to sit down to rest and saw a bus stop shelter at the end of the block. It seemed to take forever to cover the distance and he was weaving and panting when he finally plopped down beside a pair of middle-aged women who promptly stood up and walked away. The whirling sensation had returned to his brain and he put his head down between his knees. In this prayerful posture, he heard one of the women say something about "drunk at this hour of the day."

"What a wonderful idea," he thought. "Oh, God, if I only had a bottle with me right now!"

A bus stopped and the women got on. Slowly, Mitch's dizziness went away and his breathing returned to normal. The sweat continued to flow all over his body, but his face was not dripping any more as he sat up and leaned against the back of the bench.

"Drunk," he said to no one in particular. "Drunk would be good." What had two years of sobriety and AA meetings brought him, anyway? A swift kick in the balls from the woman to whom he had seriously considered proposing marriage. He would go into the first bar he could find, knock down a couple of shots of straight whisky and abolish the pain from his brain. Or, even better, he could find a liquor store and buy a whole bottle and render himself unconscious in the peace and quiet of his apartment.

A major roadblock stood between Mitch and the immediate achievement of his mind-numbing goal. He was carrying no money and no credit cards, either. He had stormed out of his apartment in his sweats without putting his billfold into a pocket. In order to buy booze, he would have to go home and get some money.

Gingerly, Mitch stood up. His legs felt better; he was pleased to find that they were supporting him again. They might even have been strong enough to jog, but he decided that discretion was the better part of valor and started for home at a walk. He was soon glad he hadn't tried to jog because by the time he reached his apartment door, his mouth was as dry as last winter's fireplace ashes, his face and body were once again swimming in sweat and the rubbery feeling was returning to his legs.

Standing in front of his apartment door, he became aware that his billfold wasn't the only thing he had neglected to take along. All his pockets were empty. The key to his apartment was on the dresser in his bedroom.

Mitch leaned his head against the door and tried to think rationally. Mrs. Peterson had a master key. Shaking, he walked across the hall to her door and knocked. He waited. No footsteps approached the door. He knocked again. Still there was silence and the door did not open.

"Nobody home. Now what?" he said aloud. His legs were barely supporting him, his tongue felt like sandpaper inside his wood-lined mouth and he was shivering even though rivers of sweat were rolling down his nose.

He looked down the hallway toward the front of the building. Supporting himself by putting his left hand against the wall, he walked the length of that hall on wobbly knees and propped himself against the frame beside the door of the front apartment. He tried to make a fist with his free hand, but his fingers wouldn't curl. Frustrated, he thumped weakly on the door with the heel of his hand three times. Miraculously, the door opened and he saw Martha Todd standing in the doorway wearing a yellow T-shirt and the blue jeans that always turned him on. Martha's eyes went wide open and she put her hand over her mouth when she saw him.

"Will you help me?" Mitch asked. "I need a drink."

By four o'clock Saturday afternoon, no insurance adjuster had appeared at the Jeffrey home on Hamline Avenue. Frustrated, Al called the insurance company again and was rewarded with a recording stating the firm's office hours: eight to five, Monday through Friday and eight until noon on Saturday.

"Shit!" he said, causing eleven-year-old Kristin to look up quickly from her task of spreading peanut butter on a slice of bread. "Daddy!" she said.

"Oops, sorry," Al said. Then he punched in the police department's non-emergency number and asked for the officer who had investigated the vandalism that morning. He was told that Officer Ridley was out but was expected back and would be instructed to return Al's call.

Carol was setting the table for dinner when the phone rang and Al answered. "This is Officer Ridley," said the voice. "What can I do for you?"

"You can tell me what's going on," Al said. "Did anybody pay a call on Dennis O'Neal?"

"I just got back from there, Mr. Jeffrey. The registration check showed that Mr. O'Neal owns a black Dodge Neon, license plate IPS-246, so we went to his apartment and found nobody at home. We got a key from the landlady and went in but it looks like Mr. O'Neal has packed up and moved out. All we found was a lot of trash , a couple of pieces of dirty laundry and a pile of porno magazines."

"Thanks," Al said. "I know that my friend who owns Bomb's Away Trucking also got hit. Are you involved in that investigation, too?"

"Yes, sir," said Officer Ridley. "I was there before we went over to Mr. O'Neal's apartment. Mr. Bombardier really has a mess to clean up. He's pretty upset."

"I don't blame him. I'll give him a call later to see how he's doing. Thanks again, officer." Al hung up, tried Bomb's Away Trucking and got a recording listing the firm's business hours. At Richard Bombardier's home, he got the answering machine and left a message saying he had called.

"I wonder where Bombardier is now?" Al said to Carol, who had signaled that supper was ready while he was listening to the answering machine. "I hope he didn't do something stupid, like going over to Hurley's Hangout looking for trouble."

CHAPTER 22

TIME TO COOL OFF

"My God, do you ever need a drink!" Martha Todd said as she put an arm around Mitch and half carried him into her living room. She eased him down into a rose-colored arm chair, said, "I'll be right back," and hurried to the kitchen. She returned with a glass of clear liquid and said, "Drink this slowly; don't gulp it but drink it all."

Mitch took a swallow and said, "It's water!"

"Of course it's water," Martha said. "You're as dehydrated as an Egyptian mummy. Now drink that nice and slow and I'll get you some more."

He obeyed and handed her the empty glass. "I was looking for something stronger," he said as she went to the kitchen for a refill.

"Like what?" she said, handing him the glass again. "You told me that you don't drink booze."

He drank half the water and said, "Today I would."

"What's so special about today?"

"I went out to Afton this morning and found Jennifer entertaining a former high school classmate."

"Is that bad?"

"The classmate is male and she was entertaining him in her bed."

"That's bad."

"It's horse shit," Mitch said. "Have you ever heard of cyber sex?"

"Yes, I have. As I understand it, people somehow get off by talking dirty to each other on the internet."

"Well, that's what Jennifer and this old high school boyfriend Adam have been doing ever since she was back and saw him at their class reunion. Now they've decided to eliminate the middle man, or the middle computer."

He emptied the water glass and Martha took it from him. "More?"

"Maybe one more," Mitch said. "I'm still kind of dry. Then I'm going out for a bottle of the real stuff."

She handed him the third glass of water and perched on the arm of the chair while he slowly drained it. His head hurt, but the whirlybird feeling had gone away and he wasn't sweating any more.

"How long have you been off booze?" Martha asked.

"A couple of years. Why?"

"I just wondered. Seems like you've worked awfully hard to clean up your act. Do you really want to go back to drinking because somebody else did you dirt?"

"That somebody else is a woman I almost proposed to."

"Almost. But you didn't?"

"No. I didn't."

"So there wasn't any kind of agreement, verbal or otherwise, that you and she were each other's exclusive property?"

"Well, no; but I thought we had an understanding."

"Maybe she didn't think that."

Mitch glared at her. "You're taking her side?"

"I'm just trying to show you the world from her perspective," Martha said. "You say she went to school with this Adam person?"

"Adam said they dated in high school. Went steady for awhile."

"Okay, look at it this way: Jennifer meets an old flame at her class reunion, the sparks are still there and she comes home to a guy she likes very much but who hasn't made any commitment to her. The old flame starts lighting her fire on the internet and she still sees no move toward commitment from the man who has been—how shall I put this?—her weekend lover, for what? Six or seven months?"

"Ten months. Well, nine at the time she started this cyber sex crap."

"As a friend, I'm sorry for you," Martha said. "But as an almost lawyer, I don't think you've got a case."

"I don't need a lawyer, almost or otherwise. The case I need is full of beer or something stronger."

"That did you a lot of good the last time you tried it, didn't it?" She got up off the chair arm and took his empty glass back to the kitchen.

"That's a low blow," Mitch said.

She returned and stood in front of him. "If it takes a low blow to keep you from making a huge mistake, consider yourself socked solidly south of the belt line."

"You don't understand the pain I'm in."

"I don't?" Martha said. "Meet a woman who was married to a man who screwed everything in skirts and then came home and punched his wife in the gut when she complained about it."

She turned and walked back out into the kitchen and Mitch realized he must be feeling better because, for the first time since she had dragged him through the door, he was appreciating the view of her backside undulating inside those wonderful blue jeans as she retreated. He also found himself appreciating the fact that he was not the only person in the world who had suffered at the hands of the opposite sex.

"I didn't know your marriage was like that," he said. "I'm sorry."

"Doesn't matter," Martha said. "It's over and done with."

"How did you handle it?"

"I cried a lot, which I guess men aren't allowed to do, then I decided to get on with my life. Since then, I've kept my distance from any and all men. That's probably not healthy, but it's safe."

"So you think I should have kept my distance from Jen?"

"Either that or gone all the way and made a commitment when you felt the urge to propose. She may have decided you were just coming around for the sex and nothing else was ever going to happen."

"That's all Adam is coming around for."

"How do you know? If they're old high school sweethearts he might have something more permanent in mind. New Jersey to Minnesota is a long way to travel just to get laid."

"I never thought about that," Mitch said. "That's kind of scary."

"You'd go back to her if Adam went back to New Jersey?"

"Oh, Christ, I don't know. I might try to go back and pick up the pieces. Right now my brain is all fucked—sorry—all screwed up."

"I've heard that word before," she said with a smile. "Tell me, don't you think it would be smart to stay sober while you try to unscrew your brain?"

"You really are an almost lawyer, aren't you?" Mitch said. "Always arguing your case. Well, I'm not sure what I'm going to do about that, either."

"At least I've introduced a reasonable doubt."

"True. But the jury still has to deliberate."

"Let me know the verdict, will you please? Before you pronounce a stiff sentence on yourself."

Mitch laughed and hauled himself out of the armchair. For a woman who said she was keeping her distance from all men, it seemed to him that she was unusually concerned about his future.

"Thanks for the water and the consultation," he said as he walked to the door on legs that no longer felt like rubber bands. "But would you tell me one thing?"

"It depends on what that one thing is," she said.

"Why is it you've always been available to talk to me? You've never seemed to be keeping yourself all that distant."

"You wouldn't say that if you'd ever seen me get really close to you," said Martha. "But seriously, I've always felt safe around you because I thought you were firmly committed to another woman."

"And what now that you know I'm not and may never be?"

"I may never speak to you again." She smiled when she said it.

"If that happens, I will definitely go back to drinking," he said.

Mitch started through the door, but she caught his shoulder with her hand and stopped him. "Remember, you promised not to go shopping for booze without consulting your almost lawyer," she said.

"Yes, counselor, it's a deal," he said and he kissed her lightly on the cheek. He was pleased to find that she did not flinch and when he reached the door of his apartment, he looked back and discovered that she was still watching from her doorway.

She waved and ducked back in and shut the door while Mitch was fumbling in his pocket for the key. Then he remembered where it was and went across the hall to see if the building manager had come home while he was being re-hydrated. As he rapped on Mrs. Peterson's door again, he wondered what seeing Martha Todd get "really close" would be like.

It was after supper before Al heard from Richard Bombardier again. "I just wanted you to know I appreciate your calling me this morning," Bombardier said. "I managed to snag an insurance adjuster this afternoon and I've been at the garage all day cleaning up the mess. Now I'm on my way out to Golden Pond to check on my grandfather. Right after your message on my answering machine there was one from the head nurse saying Grandpa was having trouble breathing. I'll talk to you later about catching up with that little bastard O'Neal, okay?"

"Yeah, sure," Al said. "I hope everything is okay with your grandfather."

"They said they'd have the doctor look at him. So long."

"How the hell did he get an adjuster so damn quick?" Al wondered as he put down the phone.

Nellie Peterson returned home in mid-afternoon to find Warren Mitchell sitting on the hall floor with his back against her apartment door.

"I went out jogging without my key," he said in response to her surprised and quizzical expression. "I need to borrow your master key."

"I hope you ain't been waiting too long," she said. "I just went to pick up a few groceries and I was walking pretty slow because of the heat. I can't imagine you going out there and running, as hot as it is."

"You know the old saying about mad dogs and Englishmen." It was obvious that she didn't, but he didn't offer to explain as she handed him the master key. It was the first time they had spoken to each other since Mitch had asked Mrs. Peterson to have her sister's body exhumed and the elderly building manager did not seem as pleased to see him as she usually did.

The long wait for Mrs. Peterson had given Mitch time think about what his next step should be. After ranging emotionally from rage to self-pity, he had decided that he must clear the air with Jennifer as soon as he could. He had to find out if her relationship with Adam went beyond mere orgasmic excitement. If it did, Warren Mitchell's role in Jennifer's life would be over, like a child expelled from school. On the other hand, if the sexual dalliance with former flame Adam was merely a fling for old time's sake, life would become more complicated. Then Mitch would have to decide whether to forgive the fling or to forget Jennifer and return to the life of a celibate widower.

Mitch decided that, in either case, getting drunk really wouldn't help solve the problem. Martha was right; he had worked too damn hard to clean up his act just to piss it all away because of something that was beyond his control. His next move would be to make the dreaded phone call to Jennifer.

As he toweled off, he decided not to rush it. Tomorrow would be soon enough to cross that bridge. In the meantime, he was faced with the unusual proposition of spending a Saturday evening all by himself, an evening that he hoped to get through without losing his resolve to stay away from alcohol.

"How'm I going to do it?" he asked Sherlock Holmes. The cat opened his yellow-green eyes, blinked twice and went back to sleep.

"You're sure a lot of help," Mitch said. He was pulling on a pair of khaki walking shorts when the phone rang.

The telephone at Alan Jeffrey's house rang shortly after breakfast on Sunday morning. "It's that Bombardier guy and he sounds very upset," Carol said as she handed the phone to Al.

"What's happening?" Al asked.

"Just one shitty thing after another," said Richard Bombardier in a voice that cracked as if he was holding back tears.

"What now?"

"I went out to Golden Pond to see Grandpa last night and found out he'd had a stroke after they called me about his breathing problem."

"Oh, no! So, how was he?"

"When I got there, he was asleep. The nurse said that the stroke had left him only able to move the arm and leg on one side and that he was having a tough time trying to talk. She said the doctor had just left and that Grandpa was resting comfortably and she thought it looked like he was going to make it okay."

"That sounds hopeful."

"That ain't the end of it. The nurse said the regular on-call doctor was away on vacation so they called in his back-up to take care of Grandpa. I asked her who the back-up was and she said it was that Doctor Sinfahdi."

"Oh, Jesus!" Al said. "How's your grandfather doing today?"

"The head nurse called me early this morning. She said Grandpa died in his sleep last night."

The phone call Mitch received Saturday night was from Martha Todd, who introduced herself as his "almost lawyer" and invited him to join her for dinner in her apartment.

"I've rented a couple of movies for my usual wild Saturday night entertainment," she said. "You could help me watch them."

"What are they?" he asked. "Nothing romantic or sad, I hope."

"They're both comedies. Actually, Mitch, I was thinking of you when I picked them out."

"I'm that funny?"

"That's not what I meant and you know it. Will you join me?"

Mitch could think of no better way to be distracted from his troubles. Martha's motive was transparent. It was obvious that she was doing this to keep him from going out to a bar or a liquor store, but he felt grateful for her concern. "What time?" he asked.

"Give me half an hour," she said.

When Martha opened the door thirty minutes later, Mitch saw that she had changed from the tantalizing jeans to some dressier—and looser fitting—khaki slacks and had replaced the T-shirt with a white blouse that was not nearly as snug across the bust line. She steered the dinner table conversation miles away from any mention of Jennifer or male-female relationships.

When it came time to watch the movies, Martha motioned Mitch toward a chair, rather than the sofa. She sat a few feet away in another chair with the remote control in her lap. Martha was taking care of him like a mother hen and he was sure that there wouldn't be any "really close" action on this particular night. At the end of the second movie, she stayed strategically out of cheek-kissing range as she escorted him to the door.

He slept fitfully, twice disturbing Sherlock Holmes during the night, and awoke early Sunday morning, knowing that he would have to bite the bullet and call Jennifer Tilton sometime during the day. He managed to put it off until mid-afternoon by reading the Sunday paper from front to back, including some of the ads he never, ever looked at. Finally, he said, "All right, Mitch, it's time to screw your courage to the sticking point," picked up the phone and punched in the number in Afton.

"I'm so glad you finally called," Jennifer said when she heard his voice. "I've been worried about you."

"I've been fine," he lied.

"It must have been an awful shock for you yesterday morning. I'm really sorry you found out about Adam the way you did."

"I need to find out more about Adam. Is he still there?"

"He's leaving in a couple of hours. He has to go back to work tomorrow."

"That was a short and sweet visit."

"It's something he had to do and he couldn't get time off right now."

"There's something I have to do too, and that's see you," Mitch said. "Can I come out tonight after dinner?" He dared not suggest an earlier hour.

"Are you going to beat me up?" she asked. "You looked like you were ready to sock me yesterday."

"Don't be silly; I'd never beat you up. But I do need to talk to you."

"I guess you're right about that. Come on out and we can talk after the kids have had their supper."

As he hung up, Mitch wondered if this evening's conversation would be his last with Jennifer Tilton. His eyes began to burn and he thought about Martha's comment that men aren't allowed to cry.

"This is one more thing I can thank that little prick O'Neal for," Richard Bombardier said to Al. "If I hadn't been out cleaning up the mess he made at the garage, I would have been home when the nurse called and I would have gone out to Golden Pond right then, before he had the stroke. Believe me, that quack Sinfahdi wouldn't have got within ten feet of my Grandpa if I'd have been there when he needed help."

"I believe you," Al said. "And I'm really sorry for your loss."

"He's the only relative I had left around here," Bombardier said. "My parents got killed in a car crash four years ago and my only living uncles and aunts are way out in California."

"So, I suppose that leaves it pretty much up to you to make the arrangements for your grandfather's funeral."

"I'm stuck with it, just like I was with Grandma's arrangements when she died. Grandpa wasn't much help with that."

An idea was forming in Al's mind, but he wasn't sure how to express it tactfully to the grieving grandson. It was not an easy thing to ask and it might be even more difficult for Bombardier to handle. Al decided to stick his neck out and make the request. "I'm going to ask you to do something that you may not find very appealing, but I want you to give it serious thought, okay?"

"Yeah, I suppose," Bombardier said. "What is it?"

"I would like you to have an autopsy performed on your grandfather."

"What? Cut him up? No way in hell!"

"It could provide some very important information," Al said. "Information that could save some other people's lives."

"What information? Grandpa died of a stroke. What more information could you possibly need?"

"Richard, it may not have been the stroke that killed him."

"What the hell else could it have been?"

"Well, here's the deal. My reporter friend Warren Mitchell and I have been tracking Doctor Sinfahdi's record and we're starting to think that—I'm not sure how to put this—that the doctor is worse than a quack."

"What do you mean by that?"

"This is a tough thing to discuss on the phone," Al said. "Could I come over to your house and talk to you in person?"

"Yeah, sure, come on over," Bombardier said. "But you ain't going to talk me into having Grandpa cut up for no autopsy. I had the home call the crematorium to pick up the body and that's where it's at right now."

"Oh, God, Richard, don't let them burn it up until I talk to you! Please, promise me that. It's really, really important." Al was shouting into the phone so loud and with such passion, that Carol came running into the kitchen to see what was wrong.

Al's fervor impressed Richard Bombardier as well. "Okay, okay," he said. "I'll call and try to make sure they don't do nothing, if they ain't already done it. But you ain't going to change my mind."

"You just might change it when you hear what I've got to say," Al said. "I'll be at your house in fifteen minutes."

"Whatever," said Bombardier, and he hung up.

"So what was that all about?" Carol asked when Al put down the phone. He explained that Bombardier's grandfather had died after a visit from Doctor Sinfahdi and reminded her of all the evidence of possible foul play that he and Mitch had gathered. She still looked skeptical as he talked about the possibility of the death of Richard Bombardier's grandfather having been caused by something other than the natural failure of a stroke-weakened heart.

When Al finished, Carol said, "I've been thinking about this since the other night when you told me that you and Mitch were suspicious of Doctor Sinfahdi and I still have a hard time believing that any doctor could actually be doing something to kill off his patients."

"We've totaled up fourteen deaths—fifteen now, with Bombardier's grandfather—during a period of time when most geriatric specialists seem to be losing only two or three patients," Al said. "Doesn't that seem strange to you?"

"What seems strange is for you guys to be playing cops and robbers with a highly-respected doctor. I still don't understand what got you started on all this. Where is all this going?"

"It's all going to the cops if we can come up with some evidence of wrongdoing. It started when Mitch and I talked to several people whose elderly relatives had died right after being treated by Doctor Sinfahdi. There's no way to check on what Doctor Sinfahdi said caused their deaths because all of those people's bodies were cremated. That's why I want Bombardier to agree to have an autopsy performed on his grandfather's body."

"What do you expect to find?"

"I don't know. Poison maybe?"

"Give me a break!" Carol said. "Again I ask you: Why would a doctor—a very nice doctor, I might add—be poisoning his elderly patients?"

"I don't know anything about why he would do it. I'm just looking at numbers and circumstances that suggest he might be doing it and I want to find out for sure, one way or the other. This is our chance, before Grandpa Bombardier gets cremated."

"Well, good luck talking your friend into doing an autopsy, but I think you and Mitch are headed for serious trouble if you start making criminal accusations against Doctor Sinfahdi."

"That's why we need evidence," Al said. "I'm going over to see Bombardier right now. I'm just hoping that the crew at the crematorium doesn't fire up the furnace on Sunday."

CHAPTER 23

HOT AND HEAVY

The Minnesota July air matched Warren Mitchell's mood—damp and dreary—as he drove toward Afton after sharing a take-out pepperoni pizza with Sherlock Holmes for dinner. The evening sky was leaden, the heat was oppressive and the humidity was so high that a gray layer of water vapor hung over the St. Croix Valley.

As usual, the sight of Jennifer raised both Mitch's blood pressure and amorous desire when she opened the front door. The fluffy brown curls that framed her pixie face were arranged to perfection, as were the various parts of her female anatomy inside the stretchy knit top and form-fitting black shorts that she wore. He wanted to pull her to him and hold her as he usually did upon arrival, but he wasn't sure if he should.

Jennifer solved the problem for him by grabbing his hands, pulling him into the cool comfort of the air-conditioned house, encircling him with her arms, pressing her breasts and belly tight against him and kissing him softly, but briefly, on the lips.

"Let's talk in the kitchen," she said. "The kids are playing cards in the family room." She took him by the hand and led him down the hallway.

Back in St. Paul, Alan Jeffrey had held a different kind of conversation with Richard Bombardier that afternoon. During the short drive to Bombardier's house in St. Anthony Park, Al tried to compose an argument that would sway the man without revealing all the details of the investigation to date. Al thought it unwise to mention the late-night perusal of the doctor's files, but decided it was okay to say that Mitch had phoned survivors listed in obits and quizzed them about who their dear departeds' doctor had been.

With the temperature and the relative humidity both in the mid-nineties, Al wasn't sure whether he was sweating because of his twanging nerves, the stifling weather or both. Thus he was gratified to see that Bombardier's unshaven face also was shiny with perspiration and to feel that his handshake was damp. Bombardier ushered Al into the living room and motioned him toward an over-stuffed, leather-upholstered chair. The leather was unpleasantly warm, adding to Al's discomfort. If the house had air conditioning, Richard Bombardier had not bothered to turn it on. He also had neglected to open the blinds, leaving the room dark and the air oppressive.

"I called the crematorium and they won't do nothing with Grandpa's body until I call again," Bombardier said as he lowered himself onto a straight-back chair facing Al. "Now, what's the story on this Doctor Sinfahdi?"

Carefully, Al explained how he and Mitch had been compiling numbers and comparing stories with survivors, and how a pattern of death after injection had emerged. Bombardier listened but looked doubtful.

"You guys think that Doctor Sinfahdi is putting something in those shots that makes the patients die?" he asked.

"The number of deaths combined with the similarity in how they occurred has pointed us in that direction," Al said. "But we don't dare bring this to anyone's attention unless we have some real solid evidence. That's why I'm asking you to have an autopsy done on your grandfather."

"What do you expect to find?"

It was the same question Carol had asked and Al was no better prepared to answer. "Well, probably either some kind of drug overdose or something equally poisonous," he said. "All these people are dying of heart failure after the doctor gives them a shot that is supposed to help them get well."

"What if they do the autopsy and they don't find nothing like that?"

"Then we forget about Doctor Sinfahdi and go about our business."

"And Grandpa's body will have been chopped up for nothing."

"No, not for nothing. If there's nothing toxic in his body, it will end our suspicions. If something is found, it will give us real evidence to take to the authorities. It's a win-win situation."

"Except for Grandpa," Bombardier said.

"He won't know anything about it," said Al. "And he could be contributing something to save the lives of others."

Bombardier leaned forward and buried is face in his hands for a couple of minutes. Finally he sat up and broke the silence. "I'm sorry. I just can't do it."

"Please give it some more thought before you make up your mind for certain," Al said. "Remember, if the doctor is causing his patients to die, he has murdered both your grandmother and your grandfather."

Bombardier winced at the word "murdered."

"Let me think about it some more. Let me talk to my aunt in California. It's her father, you know."

"Okay, talk it over with her; but be sure you give her all the facts. Remember, we know of fifteen people who all died in similar fashion after a visit from Doctor Sinfahdi just in the last couple of years."

"I don't think she'll go for it, no matter what," Bombardier said. "I'll either call you tonight or tomorrow at the paper when I've made up my mind for sure."

"That's all I can ask," Al said as he rose and started toward the door. He felt relieved to get back out into the daylight, even though the suffocating afternoon air still hung like a steaming blanket over the city. He wondered what he would do if it was his grandfather's body on the slab. Or his Uncle Charlie's.

When Al got home, he reported on his conversation with Bombardier to Carol and then thought it would be prudent to bring Mitch up to speed. He was about to make a phone call to Mitch's apartment when the thought struck him that this was the weekend and Mitch would be spending it in Afton, rolling around in the sack with Jennifer Tilton. Al considered calling him there, decided the news could wait and put down the phone without punching in the number.

They sat facing each other across Jennifer Tilton's oval, walnut-finished kitchen table. She broke the awkward silence by offering to pour Mitch a glass of iced tea and he declined. Another minute ticked by as each waited for the other to speak.

"I guess I should apologize again for the way you learned about Adam," Jennifer said finally. "It was awful for you—for all of us."

"It wasn't the most pleasant surprise," Mitch said.

"I'm glad you're not the violent type. Some guys might have gone wild and started smacking people around."

"My first thought when I saw you laying there beside Adam with one bare boob showing was to twist your nipple off and stuff it down your throat. But I'm too fond of that nipple, I guess."

Jennifer stiffened and said, "Lucky me. What was your next thought?"

"That you were a sneaky, rotten slut."

"Do you still think that?"

"I don't know what to think. Suppose you tell me about what's going on with you and Adam."

"Well, like I said, we went steady in high school. We were hot and heavy all through our senior year and into the summer after that. In fact, he was the guy who broke my cherry."

"Why did you break up with him?"

"We didn't really break up, we just sort of drifted away from each other.

He went off to college in Connecticut and I went off to college in Minnesota. He met a girl at Yale and I met Timothy Tilton at Carleton. We both came home from our freshman year engaged to marry somebody else."

"Lucky that both of you found somebody. Usually one person gets the shaft."

"It did make it easier to split up. We both graduated, got married and went our separate ways until this year's class reunion."

"You're divorced and your ex-husband is dead. What about Adam's wife?"

"She divorced him and married a hotshot computer millionaire she met where she worked. They didn't have any kids."

"Adam is not such a hotshot?"

"He does okay. He sells insurance for a company in Hartford."

"It figures," Mitch said. "I never cared for insurance salesmen."

"Sorry," she said. "Anyway, we ran into each other at the reunion, we talked, we danced, we had a good time. We also exchanged e-mail addresses and when I got back here, Adam wrote to me and I answered and things got more personal until we sort of slid into the cyber sex thing. Then last week he said he was coming to see me because he had something very important to say that he couldn't say on the internet."

"And what was that?"

"When he got here, he asked me to marry him." The words sent a chill along Mitch's spine and he felt the hair on his neck stand up as straight as troops at inspection.

"Did he propose before or after you went to bed?" Mitch asked.

"Don't be an asshole," Jennifer said. "As a matter of fact, he proposed right in this room while we were both standing upright and fully clothed."

"Sorry. Are you going to tell me what your answer was?"

"There's no question in my heart that I still love the guy." Her hands were on the table, with the right one resting on top of the left. She moved the top hand to reveal a huge diamond ring sparkling on the third finger of the hand below and said, "My answer was yes."

Somehow Mitch knew it was coming, but her announcement still hit him like a big rock slamming into his gut at the speed of a major league fastball. He felt the semi-digested pizza rising in his throat, swallowed as hard as he could and took a couple of deep breaths.

"You don't look so good," Jennifer said. "Can I get you something?"

"No," he said. "I'm just having trouble digesting this, along with what I had for supper."

"I'm sorry, Mitch. I really like you very, very much and we've had some great times together, but Adam is my first love and I guess you could actually call him the love of my life."

"Answer one more question?"

"Depends on what it is."

"If I had asked you to marry me on the Fourth of July, would you have said yes?"

She thought for a moment before she replied. "I can't really answer that," she said. "It would have been a really tough choice right then. Now if you had asked me on the fourth of June ..." Her voice trailed off and Mitch felt the stinging in his eyes again. He would tell Martha that her theory about men not being allowed to cry was bullshit.

To Jennifer, he said, "Like I said, usually one person gets the shaft."

"I've got some news you won't believe," Alan Jeffrey said as he perched on the corner of Warren Mitchell's desk Monday morning.

"So have I," Mitch said in a voice that lacked enthusiasm.

"Okay, you go first."

"My news is that Jennifer is selling her house in Afton, moving to Hartford, Connecticut and marrying her high school sweetheart."

"Right! And I'm running off to Reno with my Aunt Diana for a quickie divorce and remarriage."

"I'm not shittin' you, Al. Jennifer's 'first love,' as she calls him, showed up here this weekend and gave her a diamond as big as the Rock of Gibraltar."

"Holy shit! No wonder you look like death warmed over this morning."

"I didn't get much sleep last night. If it hadn't been Sunday, I'd have probably gone into the first bar I came to and gotten as drunk as a sailor swimming in beer."

"Don't even think about getting drunk. I don't want to have to run you up to Hazelden again," Al said.

"Don't sweat it. I'm past the wanting to get drunk stage. Like Martha said, it's not worth throwing away two years of sobriety because of somebody else's action."

"Martha?"

"You know, the woman whose grandmother we borrowed to scope out Doctor Sinfahdi's office. She rescued me Saturday when I ran myself into heat exhaustion after walking in on Jennifer and her future husband naked in the sack together."

"Jesus, what a weekend you had! Why didn't you call me?"

"I was too fucked up to talk to anybody," Mitch said. "Anyway, now you've heard my wonderful news. What's yours?"

"Nothing that compares with that," said Al. "But it might turn out to be more productive." He went on to describe the weekend events involving the vandalism at his house and Bomb's Away Trucking and the subsequent death of Richard Bombardier's grandfather after a visit from Doctor Sinfahdi.

"So what are the odds that he'll okay an autopsy?" Mitch asked.

"Well, I was afraid they were zilch until I used the word murder," Al said. "That seemed to shake him up a little, but I'm still not betting on it, especially if the aunt in California says no."

"Damn it, we can't let this chance get away."

"I don't know that we've much choice if I can't persuade Bombardier to ask for an autopsy before the crematorium does its thing."

"What the hell difference does it make to him whether the body is intact or has a few cuts on it when it goes into the goddamn furnace?"

"I don't know, Mitch. People are funny about bodies. Somehow a little-bitty scalpel makes them more squeamish than a great big fire."

"It's nuts. Well, here comes Don with an assignment, so I guess it's time to go to work. Let me know when Bombardier calls."

The assignment took Mitch out of the office to cover a press conference on the University of Minnesota's St. Paul campus. When he got back to his desk after lunch, he found a note from Al that said, "RB called at noon and said he hadn't been able to reach his aunt, but that he had decided against the autopsy. I tried to get him to hold off, but the cremation is on for this afternoon. Guess we're screwed."

"Maybe not," Mitch said to himself as he punched in the number of a private line at the St. Paul police station. The voice that answered said, "Homicide, Brown," in a monotone that ran the two words into one.

"Brownie, this is Mitch at the paper. How are you?"

"I'm good. What's with you? You covering the Murphy case?" A 13-year-old girl named Angela Murphy had been raped and strangled and her nude body had been stuffed into a dumpster sometime Saturday night. The story about a homeless trash-picker finding the corpse on Sunday morning had been at the top of page one in this morning's paper.

"No, Bob Larson is working on that one. I just have a hypothetical question I want to ask you."

"You've never asked a hypothetical question in your life, you sneaky son of a bitch. What is it you want to know?" the chief of the city's Homicide

Department said.

"Suppose, hypothetically, that you thought a person had been murdered by an injection of poison and you wanted to have the body autopsied? Is there a way for your department to do that without the family's consent?"

"What the hell are you working on?"

"Answer the question and maybe I'll tell you."

"Well, there is, providing somebody presents enough evidence to convince a judge that there's probable cause, in which case he could issue an arrest warrant for the suspect and an order for an autopsy. But it's a damn messy business without the family's consent and it could turn into one hell of a long legal wrangle between the family, the accused and the department. Now will you tell me what you've got?"

"I've got maybe enough evidence and maybe not. I need to talk it over with somebody before I jump into anything."

"Well, don't jump off the deep end, Mitch, or the guy you're accusing could sue your ass for every penny you've got."

"That isn't much, Brownie."

"Neither is your case if you don't have enough hard evidence to convince a judge that there's probable cause."

"Thanks, Brownie. I'll let you know what I decide to do." Mitch hung up and asked himself if fifteen deaths under similar circumstances would be enough to convince a judge that there was probable cause. Was it worth it for him and Al to take the leap? Would it be wise to try to talk to that woman doctor Jennifer had quizzed? What if they accused Doctor Sinfahdi and the judge said there was no probable cause. Or what if the autopsy proved the doctor hadn't injected anything poisonous into Richard Bombardier's grandfather? Mitch's eagerness to get at the facts was tempered by the knowledge that Al had a hell of a lot more to lose than he did in a slander suit.

Mitch's thoughts kept churning. Why the hell couldn't Richard Bombardier see the need to learn the real cause of his grandfather's death? Why the hell did Adam from Hartford have to turn up with an engagement ring? Why the hell wasn't Mrs. Peterson upset enough about Doctor Sinfahdi to have her sister's body exhumed and autopsied? Why the hell hadn't he proposed to Jennifer Tilton before she went to her class reunion? At the moment, Warren Mitchell's life was proving the accuracy of that old saying: "The hour is always darkest just before everything goes totally black."

CHAPTER 24

HOT SHOTS

Al's mood was as grim as a graveside farewell and his mind was so distracted that he forgot to load his camera before walking from the parking lot to the beach at Lake Phalen to look for some hot weather shots. He was all set up to photograph a trio of nubile, nearly nude young women in string bikinis who were baking in the sun on the beach, when he had to excuse himself and go back to the car for film.

As he loaded the camera, his thoughts remained on Richard Bombardier's refusal to have an autopsy performed on his grandfather's body. It was a crushing blow. Al had no lingering doubts about Doctor Ravi Sinfahdi being responsible for Uncle Charlie's untimely demise and he desperately wanted to secure the evidence that would put the doctor away.

"Are you sure that's a real camera?" asked one of the bikini-clad cuties when Al returned. "I think you're just one of those voyageurs that likes to stare at girls without much clothes on."

Al resisted the temptation to tell her the word she wanted was "voyeurs" and said the proof would be in tomorrow's paper.

"Will I make the front page?" she asked, leaning back and pushing her generous breasts out as far they would go. Al guessed her age at about nineteen and her bust measurement at double that number.

"Hold it right there while I get my wide-angle lens," Al said, smiling for the first time since Bombardier's phone call.

"Hurry up and shoot before my boobs pop out of my top," she said.

"That would make the front page," Al said. "But not in our paper." He took several shots and lowered the camera. "If I ever need a model for a Playboy feature, I'll give you a call," he said in parting.

"Yeah, look me up," she said. "Look up my friends here, too."

Looking up all three of you would be a great pleasure, Al thought. He resisted the temptation to say it out loud. People who talked about "voyageurs" staring at naked women probably wouldn't catch his double entendre anyway.

When he returned to the office at four o'clock, he found a message to call Richard Bombardier at Bombs Away Trucking. "Probably wants to tell me that his Grandpa is now a pile of ashes," Al muttered as he punched in the number.

"Well, I got some news for you, Mr. Photographer," Bombardier said. "My aunt called back and she's pissed as hell at the idea that her mother and father might have been murdered by a doctor. She said she absolutely wants an autopsy done on Grandpa."

"Can you stop the cremation in time?" Al asked.

"I already did. Got 'em just before they were going to shove the casket into the furnace."

"That's great!"

"So, now what do I do?"

"You call the county medical examiner's office and tell them you want an autopsy. They'll take care of the details."

"Won't they ask why I want it?"

"Tell them your aunt needs it for closure. Or tell them it's for the life insurance; tell them the company requires it before they'll pay off."

"Maybe there is a God after all," Al said to nobody in particular after he hung up. He looked around the newsroom. Now, where the hell was Mitch when he wanted to give him some good news for a change?

Mitch's mind wandered in and out of the room during the long press conference at which three speakers discussed every excruciating detail of the university's development of a new hybrid wheat variety they hoped would alleviate world hunger for all time. He took sporadic notes between doodling elaborate variations of Jennifer Tilton's initials and anatomy in his notebook and staring out the window thinking about how good it had felt to have her bare body pressed tightly against his. It didn't seem possible that he would never nibble at those delectable breasts again and never have the pleasure of feeling himself sliding ... "Oh, stop it!" he said to himself. "It's over and done with, for Christ's sake!"

He drove straight home and took some small solace in being greeted with enthusiasm by Sherlock Holmes. "At least you haven't dumped me yet," Mitch said as the cat rubbed against his ankles and rolled onto his back to invite a tummy tickle.

"All I have to do is feed you and scratch your belly and you'll never run away with a slick-talking cyber-sexer," Mitch said as he provided the desired rubbing motion. "If only women were that easy to understand."

There was a message on the answering machine. It was Al, requesting a call at home any time after 5:30. Well, it could wait until after supper. Probably confirmation that the flame-reduced remains of Grandpa Bombardier were now in a little square cardboard box.

Maybe eating out would improve his mood, he thought. He wondered if Martha Todd was on duty at the Index Café. Only one way to find out, he decided. He gave Sherlock a farewell pat and walked up Grand Avenue. On the way to the Index Café, he passed a bar and a liquor store and was pleased to discover that he didn't feel compelled to enter either one. "Guess those self-flagellating AA meetings have done something good, after all," he said to himself. Or was it the tender ministrations of Martha Todd at a key moment?

Mitch walked into the Index, was ushered to a table by the hostess and watched the waitresses as they emerged from the kitchen. One approached his table and introduced herself as Sandy.

"Is Martha working tonight?" Mitch asked in as casual a tone as he could muster.

"No, she's not," Sandy said. "I heard she's taking some time off to go somewhere out of town."

"Oh, thanks," he said aloud. To himself he said, "With my luck she's gone off to marry her high school sweetheart and live someplace far away."

"Welcome home," said Carol Jeffrey as Al walked in the door. "What happened to you today? You look like the cat that swallowed the cream."

"It's Doctor Sinfahdi who is going to get creamed," Al said, wrapping his arms around her and planting a long kiss on her lips. "Our buddy, Richard Bombardier, is requesting an autopsy on orders from his aunt, whose heart is not filled with the milk of human kindness after the loss of both parents. It seems that she isn't as cowed by the thought of an autopsy as our Bombs-away boy is."

"I guess that's good news," she said, with an expression that said otherwise. "What happens if the coroner finds something?"

"Then we're off and running with a real case against that cheesy doctor. But tell me, while I'm in such a good 'mooed,' what is today's internet joke?"

"Your Auntie Diana wants you to call her."

"My 'Auntie' Diana?"

"That's how she's introducing herself now. 'This is Al's Auntie Diana,' she said when I answered the phone. You two seem to be getting pretty chummy after all these years of not speaking to each other."

"I'd hardly call it chummy," Al said truthfully. He thought it best not to describe Diana's actions, which went well beyond chumminess, during his recent visits. "Did she say what this is about?"

"It seems she's found some more of Uncle Charlie's stuff that she wants you to take, so give her a call and tell her when you can pick it up. I'm going to start working on dinner while you do that."

When Diana answered the phone, Al introduced himself as her "little nephew Alan" and asked what was up.

"You would be if you had phone-a-vision," she said. "I just got out of the shower after a dip in the pool and I'm standing here all dripping wet and naked."

"My loss," he said. "If you want to hold that pose for a couple of hours I'll come over right after supper and get whatever it is that you want to give me."

"Auntie Diana will give her little nephew anything he wants," she said in her most teasing tone. "What I originally had in mind was a couple of shelves full of numismatic books and auction catalogs, but if you have other desires ..."

"I'll settle for getting the books and catalogs, thank you. How about tomorrow afternoon—late?"

"Oh, little nephew, I can't stand here naked all that time."

"Again, my loss. I'll have to settle for whatever you're wearing at four o'clock or so tomorrow, if that time's okay with you."

"I don't see anything on my busy social calendar. I'll pencil you in at four. If you want to take a dip in the pool, I can give you a towel to dry off with."

"Thanks, but I'm not sure where my swim suit is."

"Who needs a suit? There's a fence around the pool and nobody here but me to see what you've got."

"Thanks, but I'll still settle for the books and catalogs. See you then."

"You're a naughty nephew." Again the teasing tone was heavy. "It's not nice to get Auntie all worked up and then chicken out."

"I think it was Auntie who got herself all worked up. Maybe Auntie should take another shower—a cold one. Bye, bye."

It was dark in Herby's Grand Avenue Bar, and the air was thick with cigarette and cigar smoke. That's a smell you don't get much anymore, Mitch thought, what with all the anti-smoking laws and no-smoking policies in effect at restaurants, public buildings and workplaces. Indeed, the smell took him back to his days as a hopeless, floundering drunk and reminded him that he had stopped in to absorb the atmosphere and cool his throat with a tall drink of something non-alcoholic. He ordered a ginger ale on the rocks and soon he was sipping from a glass filled with ice and the fizzy soft drink, nibbling from a bowl of popcorn on the bar and savoring the smoke and the darkness and the general hubbub of bar patrons' conversations.

As he sipped, Mitch's mind wandered from its preoccupation with Jennifer to curiosity about Martha Todd. He wondered where she had gone and how long she would be away. He asked himself why he always felt better after talking with her. He wished she had not chosen this particular time to take a vacation.

Mitch's reverie was broken by the bartender, who saw him staring into a glass of half-melted crushed ice and asked, "Another one, sir?"

"Huh?" Mitch said. "Oh, no, I guess not. I should get going."

"Yes, sir. Good night." The bartender walked away and drew a foamy stein of tap beer for a customer at the end of the bar. God, that looks good, Mitch said to himself. I guess I really should get going.

He forced himself off the barstool and went out. When he hit the clean, albeit muggy, night air, he noticed that his clothes reeked of cigarette smoke. When he got home, Sherlock Holmes noticed it, too, and stalked away in disgust after one circuit of Mitch's ankles. "Jeez, now you're giving me the brush off, too," Mitch said. "Okay, I'll throw these smoky clothes in the hamper and put on something more compatible with your highness's delicate smeller."

While he was stripping, Mitch remembered the message on his answering machine. He wrapped himself in a light summer bathrobe and, with some trepidation, made the call to Al. A moment later, Mitch found himself listening in jubilation to the first good news he had heard since he woke Jennifer and Adam from their post-coital slumber Saturday morning.

"You mean we're really going to have an answer about our Doctor Sinfahdi?" Mitch said.

"It looks that way," Al said. "Bombardier's aunt apparently went bullshit over the possibility that her parents were prematurely shuffled off this mortal coil by the dear doctor from India."

"I'm glad somebody went bullshit. I can't believe that guy Bombardier not wanting to let Grandpa have a little minor surgery before making an ash of him."

"Well, Richard may not have thought an autopsy before cremation was such a hot idea, but Grandpa's girl on the west coast is going to help us cook Doctor Sinfahdi's goose. Now we need to think about what we'll do if the coroner does find something toxic in the body."

"Right now I'm having trouble thinking about anything but what an ash Jennifer made of me."

"Well, take a cold shower and try to get a night's sleep. We need to have some ideas in mind about what we do next if the medical examiner says Grandpa Bombardier died of something other than natural causes."

"Then it automatically becomes the cops' problem, right?"

"Yeah, I suppose they could arrest Doctor Sinfahdi on the basis of the coroner's report. But what do we do with the evidence we've put together? Is it enough to nail Doctor Sinfahdi for Grandpa Bombardier's death or do we need to go after him for some of the others? How involved do we want to get all these other families in a police investigation? Do I bring up Uncle Charlie's death or don't I, seeing as how the evidence went through the oven at the crematorium? What do I tell Diana?"

"You've got my head spinning like a dirty dancer at Hurley's Hangout. Let's talk about it tomorrow at lunch time, okay?"

"If I'm not off somewhere shooting hot weather shots again. I'm picking up Uncle Charlie's numismatic library after work tomorrow and I'd like to say something to Diana, but what?"

"Why say anything? I'm sure as hell not going to say anything to Mrs. Peterson or Martha Todd until Bombardier gets his report."

"But they're not your uncle's wife. And they didn't invite Doctor Sinfahdi to make a house call on their loved one."

"You don't think Diana is somehow involved in Uncle Charlie's death do you?"

"I don't know what to think about Diana. She says she loved Uncle Charlie but his dying left her with a house probably worth $400,000 that's all paid for and a nice big life insurance check."

"You are one suspicious son of a bitch. Is she acting at all strange?"

"I don't know her well enough to know if she's acting strange or not," Al said. He decided this was not the time to go into detail about his erotic encounters with his uncle's horny widow. "Let's talk about it tomorrow."

Al's head was still churning with questions when he went to bed that night. He asked himself what he should say to Diana if his suspicions about Doctor Sinfahdi were proven to be correct. And he wondered what Diana would say to him tomorrow when he picked up Uncle Charlie's books. He was afraid she might be planning another surprise.

CHAPTER 25

HEAVENLY BODIES

There was no opportunity for a strategy session at lunch or any other time on Tuesday. Al was out shooting photos all morning and Mitch was sent to the police station to cover for the regular police reporter.

Al dropped off the day's last roll of film at about 3:45, was told there was no reason to hang around the office and, uncertain of what to his wondering eyes would appear, rang the doorbell at Uncle Charlie's house twenty-five minutes later. His question was answered in a matter of seconds. The door opened and there was Diana, looking tanned and tantalizing, and wearing both halves of the yellow string bikini.

"You said you'd be here at four, you naughty boy," she said, with her generous lips puckered in a pretended pout. "I've been counting the seconds waiting for you."

"I'm sure it was the longest ten minutes of your life," said Al. "Are the books packed up or should I have brought some boxes?"

"Aren't you even going to say 'how are you?' to your auntie?"

"Sorry. How are you?"

"Thank you for asking," she said in a tone that dripped with sarcasm. "Actually, I'm fine. Do I look fine to you?"

"You look like you just stepped out of the pages of Playboy. I'm glad you're doing okay."

"I'm wearing much too much clothing for Playboy. Would you like to see a real Playboy pose?" Her right hand went behind her back to the bow knot that held the bikini top together.

"Not necessary. I have a monumental memory of your mammaries from a previous exhibition. Now, I think you said you had some books for me."

"You certainly are all business today," she said, letting go of the string she had been prepared to pull. "But then, you've always hated me, haven't you?"

"I thought we had called a truce on our little feud. I don't hate you, and I don't mean to be rude, but you keep flashing that gorgeous body at me and you know I'm not into playing those kind of games."

"That's right; you're the steadfast, loyal husband who never fools around. Lucky Carol. Okay, forget the Playboy shot. How about sitting by the pool with a cold drink and telling me what more you've found out about Charlie's doctor?"

Al was only too happy to change the subject to something less personal. "There's not a lot to tell, but I will sit down with a cold drink. These ninety-degree days are beginning to wear me out."

Diana led him through the house to the pool, gestured to a chair, brought him a tall, icy brandy and soda and settled herself in a semi-reclining position on a full-length lounge with a glass of white wine in hand. She was facing Al, and as she stretched out her legs, she spread them just far enough apart to give him an unobstructed view of the narrow strip of yellow cloth that ran through her crotch.

Al tried to look elsewhere as he told Diana about some of the families Mitch had talked to. She smiled and nodded and gave him the feeling that she was enjoying his discomfort at her pubic display.

Finally he decided to tell her about Richard Bombardier's grandfather. He managed to shift his gaze to her face and watched very carefully for a reaction as he told her of the impending autopsy, and what it would mean if the coroner found something other than natural causes.

Her eyebrows went up a fraction of an inch as she asked, "Would that prove that Doctor Sinfahdi did something bad to Charlie?"

"It would sure as hell convince me that he did," Al said. "Of course we couldn't really prove it in court because Uncle Charlie's body was cremated."

Diana sat up straight, pulled her knees up to her chin and hugged them with both arms. "So, there wouldn't be any big, long investigation and nothing would really change," she said.

"No, there wouldn't be any major investigation of Charlie's death and nothing would change officially. But it will sure as hell make me feel better to find out one way or another whether the doctor is doing in his patients."

"It'll make me feel weird if the autopsy proves Doctor Sinfahdi poisoned your friend's grandfather. I mean, that doctor was in this house. He gave Charlie a shot of something right here in our bedroom."

"The thought of that upsets you?"

"Of course it does. What do you think, that I wanted to lose Charlie that way?"

"Of course not." He was afraid he didn't sound convincing.

Apparently he didn't. "You still don't think I loved Charlie, do you?" she said.

"I'm taking you at your word, Diana. I really didn't mean to start this conversation again."

"Bullshit!" she said, swinging onto her feet. "It's time for you to take your books and run home to your precious wife. The stuff is all in a couple of boxes in the den." She pointed toward the house and Al went in, stacked one heavy box filled with numismatic reference works and auction catalogs atop the other and hoisted them in his arms. He had lugged them as far as the front door, and was trying to turn the knob with two fingers without putting the boxes down, when he heard Diana's voice behind him, calling his name.

He turned to face her and she was standing not much more than an arm's length away. "I was going to offer you the stars, the sun and the moon," she said. "But now it's just the moon."

At that she turned her back, pulled down the bikini bottom and bent way over at the waist, startling him with a moon shot only four feet from his face. Then she dropped the strip of yellow cloth to the floor, stepped out of it and turned to face him, spreading her legs until her feet were wide apart. Al couldn't help staring at the obvious place and he found himself wondering how much of the jet-black triangle between her legs had been shaved in order to accommodate the tiny, low-slung bikini. He felt his face and his groin grow warm as the blood flowed into both areas, and he almost dropped the heavy boxes on his feet.

"See anything you like, nephew dear?" Diana asked.

Al knew his eyes must be popping half out of his head as he tried to form the words to answer his Auntie Diana's question. Finally, he managed to say, "With a showcase like that, how could I miss seeing something I like?"

"Well, too damn bad, little nephew," Diana said, letting her fingers lightly touch the area upon which Al's eyes were fixated. "You could have had this any time you wanted it but now the offer is closed, and so are Auntie Diana's legs. Now take the damn books and get the hell out of my house." She slid her feet together, turned and walked back toward the pool, removing the bikini top and giving Al one last look at the rolling motion of her sun-tanned bottom as she went.

He felt an overwhelming urge to follow the lure of those bewitching buns, pull Diana down with feverish passion onto the poolside lounge and spend the next couple of hours apologizing in the proper manner. Carefully, bending at the knees so as not to strain his back, he set the boxes down on the floor.

CHAPTER 26

OF BODIES, LIVING AND DEAD

In his mind's eye, Al could see himself making love to Diana in a dozen different positions. He had never been treated to a nude display of a more lush and enticing body. Carol's curves were symmetrically trim and slim, but Diana's dimensions truly were worthy of the centerfold in any magazine for men.

Ah, yes, Carol. Along with his fantasy of sexual satiation in Diana's smoldering arms, Alan Jeffrey had an accompanying vision of what Diana might do the next time she got mad at him. He could imagine her describing their afternoon tryst by the pool to Carol, or, worse yet, telling Carol that Al had forced himself on her against her will.

"You gotta be out of your mind," Al said, deciding it was a risk not worth taking. If Diana was waiting naked by the pool for him, she would have a long, long wait. He opened the door, picked up the boxes, let himself out, pushed the door shut with his heel, loaded the books into the Toyota and headed for the safe haven on Hamline Avenue.

Later that evening, Mitch and Al talked briefly about what they would do after the autopsy, which was being conducted the next afternoon. They decided that all they could do until the results were announced was tend to their jobs and wait for a call from Richard Bombardier. However, when the call finally came to Al at the photo desk three days later, he was not prepared for what Bombardier had to say.

"I need your help," the trucking company owner said.

"What kind of help?" Al asked.

"I'm in jail," was the surprising reply.

"What the hell for?"

"A couple of my Teamster's Union drivers and me went over to Hurley's Hangout last night to see if that little prick O'Neal was there. The management was not glad to see us."

"They threw you out?"

"They tried to."

"Do I want to know what happened?"

"We beat the shit out of Dennis and the manager and one of his goons and busted up some furniture, but the cops came before we could get out of there, and they didn't go along with our reason for being pissed off."

"So you're in jail in Minneapolis?"

"Right. And the autopsy report on Grandpa is due to come out this afternoon."

"I don't have any money to bail you out."

"I ain't asking for that kind of help. My lawyer's working on getting us out of here, but we're due in court at one and it don't look like I can be at the medical examiner's office when he's ready to give me his report."

"So what can I do?"

"Take my place. Tell the medical examiner I had an emergency, and you're designated to pick up the report."

"I'm not sure the M.E. will go along with that."

"I'll call him and tell him I'm not going to make it, and I want him to give you the report. Can you be there at two o'clock?"

"You couldn't keep me away with a team of elephants," Al said. "I'll make some excuse to my boss so I don't get sent out somewhere on a shoot. You call the M.E. and tell him I'm your man. He knows me from some photo jobs so that will help, but call me back if he says he won't give me the report."

"Sure thing. And thanks. I really appreciate your doing this. Should I call you at your office when I get home?"

"Okay. If I'm out, talk to my reporter friend Mitch." Al hung up and walked over to where Warren Mitchell was composing a story about this being the hottest July 28th in St. Paul in twenty-seven years. Mitch looked up as Al said, "You ain't gonna believe this."

The Ramsey County medical examiner did his work in the bowels of a building that faced University Avenue near Regions Hospital. Al had always thought this was quite a handy arrangement. For a patient who died in Regions, it was just a hop, skip and a jump to the ME's table.

Al told the photo editor that he had a two-o'clock dental appointment and, as he approached the medical examiner's office, he found himself thinking that a trip to the dentist might be more pleasant than this. He was sincerely hoping that he wouldn't have to go into the area where the bodies were kept and the autopsies performed. He had been in that room on a photo assignment and had no desire to experience the chill, the smell and the general dank atmosphere again.

He was relieved to find the medical examiner, Doctor Albert Simmons, seated behind a desk in the front office. Doctor Simmons, a short, balding, round-bellied man in his early fifties, was expecting Al and rose to greet him. "So you're standing in for Mr. Bombardier?" the doctor said.

"Yes, he's tied up this afternoon and didn't want to delay getting the report on his grandfather," Al said.

"I understand he has to appear in court this afternoon, but he didn't tell me why. Some traffic matter, I suppose."

Al decided he wouldn't provide the medical examiner with any specific information, either. "I guess so," he said. "Mr. Bombardier didn't elaborate on the details with me either."

"Well, here's my report," Doctor Simmons said, handing Al a sealed manila envelope. "I think you should tell him before he opens it that the findings are quite surprising, and he might also find them to be quite disturbing."

"What do you mean by that?"

"I can't really discuss it with you. But when you deliver the report, please warn Mr. Bombardier before he reads it. He may be quite upset if he doesn't have knowledge of the situation."

"Situation?"

"Please, I can only discuss my findings with members of the deceased's family. I think it would be wise for Mr. Bombardier to call me after he has had a chance to review the report and talk with his aunt in California."

Al took the envelope, thanked the coroner and left the office. Out on the street, he found himself fighting the temptation to tear open the envelope and pull out the report. "I can't do that," he told himself. "Bombardier should be the one to open it and read it first. I sure as hell hope he's done with court and out of jail."

Back at the office, Al checked his messages and found none from Bombardier. Then he looked for Mitch and was told that he was out on an assignment and probably wouldn't be back until morning.

"Hey Al, can you catch a quick shot at City Hall?" asked Solly Greenstein, the photo editor.

"Sure," Al said. "What have you got?"

Half an hour later, Al returned from the City Hall shoot and found no message from Richard Bombardier. Al had tucked the manila envelope into a desk drawer and was again battling temptation when Bombardier finally called at almost quarter to five. "You know how the damn courts are," he said. "They tell you the arraignment is at one o'clock and keep you sitting on your ass until after three. Did you get the report?"

"Yes. Did you get your charges settled?" Al asked.

"My lawyer entered a not-guilty plea and the judge set a preliminary hearing date. I guess it's up to the D.A. whether they want to prosecute or not. What's in the report?"

"He wouldn't tell me anything, except that I should warn you that the findings are surprising and possibly disturbing. Can I bring it to your house right now?"

"Yeah, bring it over. Is that all the guy said?"

"Just that he can only discuss it with members of the family, and that you should call him after you've read it. I'm on my way."

Al checked out with Solly, saw that Mitch's chair was still unoccupied and went to his car with the manila envelope clutched tightly in his hand. Twenty minutes later, he was ringing Richard Bombardier's doorbell.

Bombardier's appearance set Al back a step. The burly man's left eye was ringed in several spectacular shades of purple and green, and the lid was swollen so badly that the eye was nearly closed. On the other side of his face, the upper lip was puffy and bore a large scab where it had been cut open. Bombardier noted Al's reaction and said, "The assholes at Hurley's got in a few punches, but they look a hell of a lot worse than we do."

"My God, are they in traction?" Al said.

"I wish they was. We should of broke their knee caps."

He took the envelope that Al held out to him, led Al into the house, handed him a cold beer and invited him to sit down. "You might have to help me read this," Bombardier said. "I only got one eye."

"I'll be glad to help if you need it."

Bombardier tore open the envelope, pulled out a sheet of paper and began to read, his lips moving slightly as he did. After a moment he took a deep breath and looked up at Al with his good left eye. "The medical examiner wasn't kidding about this being a real pisser!" he said. "Just listen to this."

CHAPTER 27

COMES THE DAWN

It had been another boring afternoon for Warren Mitchell, who had been sent out with a photographer to do a "man-on-the-street" series of interviews asking pedestrians in downtown St. Paul what they were doing to combat the heat and humidity that had permeated the Twin Cities for more than a month.

He wanted to find some sort of diversion before preparing this night's dinner, which he had decided would be potato chips and micro-waved hot dogs, and he considered a return visit to Herby's. It was cool in there, but the thought of subjecting his lungs to that much cigarette smoke turned him off and he went home to discuss the state of the world with Sherlock Holmes.

Sherlock was licking up the crumbs from the bottom of the potato chip bag when the doorbell rang. Mitch opened the door to find Alan Jeffrey and Richard Bombardier standing before him. There was a manila envelope in Richard's hand and a gleam of triumph in Al's eyes.

"We got the autopsy report," Al said. "Take a look."

Bombardier offered the envelope and Mitch took it, waving them toward chairs at the kitchen table. Mitch opened the report and scanned it quickly until he hit the key line.

"Morphine?" he said. "Heroin?"

"That's what the man says," Al said. "The medical examiner found morphine, which most likely came from an overdose of heroin, in Grandpa Bombardier's system. Enough morphine, in fact, to stop the heart of a healthy young man, much less an old man who'd just suffered a stroke."

"I take it your grandfather wasn't a user?" Mitch said to Richard.

"No way," Bombardier said. "Grandpa took a glass of wine or a nip of bourbon now and then but he always said that drugs, even marijuana, were stepping stones on the path to hell."

"Besides, how could a man who was partially paralyzed by a stroke give himself a shot of heroin?" Al asked. "I do believe that we've got Doctor Sinfahdi right by the short hairs on this one."

"Maybe," said Mitch. "And maybe not. You'd have to prove that the heroin came from the shot Doctor Sinfahdi gave him, and you can bet that he's long since ditched the needle."

"I also can bet that the nursing staff at Golden Pond will testify that nobody else gave the man any kind of medication," Al said. "I think we can put the bastard in jail."

Suddenly Mitch felt cheated. "You know what pisses me off?" he said. "We did all the legwork on this story and it should be ours to break. But as soon as the cops get this report and open an official investigation, it will be public record and the Minneapolis papers and every TV station in the Twin Cities will be on it like a hawk swooping down on a three-legged field mouse."

"You're right," Al said. "I'd also like to have a talk with Doctor Sinfahdi about Uncle Charlie's sudden death before the cops put that son of a bitch away. But what can we do about it?"

"I don't know. I just know I'd like to get it first." Mitch looked at Richard Bombardier. "When are you going to contact the medical examiner about what's in this report?"

"I figured first thing in the morning."

"Could you maybe hold off a few hours—until after lunch, maybe?"

"What are you thinking about?" Al asked.

"I'm thinking about us meeting at Doctor Sinfahdi's office first thing in the morning and confronting him with the evidence. Story and pictures in the afternoon edition." Again Mitch looked at Bombardier. "What do you say? Will you wait?"

"Hey, you guys have been good to me all the way," Richard said. "I'll hold off calling if you want me to."

"That's great," Al said. "But Doc Simmons seemed pretty upset by what he found. He might call you."

"Okay, I'll stay away from my office in case he calls," Richard said. "I can take a truck out somewhere and be gone until you guys are done."

They decided that Al would be waiting at the door when Doctor Sinfahdi's office opened the next morning and that Mitch, after calling the city desk to tell Don O'Rourke that they had a red-hot story, would come in while Al was demanding to see the doctor. Al would then insist that Mitch sit in on the interview. Mitch would be carrying the list of names of dead patients compiled through his interviews and the nocturnal visit the pair had made to the office files. With this in hand, he and Al would grill Doctor Sinfahdi.

When Al and Mitch were finished, Mitch would return to the newspaper office with his notes and Al's film while Al stayed with the doctor to prevent him from destroying evidence or running away. Mitch would phone Bombardier at his beeper number and let him know when it was time to call the medical examiner and the police. If everything went as planned, the story of the doctor turned serial killer would break in the Daily Dispatch that afternoon and all the rival news organizations would see it printed there first.

"What if the doctor won't talk to you?" Bombardier asked.

"He'll talk to me," Al said. "He won't get out of the building alive without seeing me." To Mitch, he said, "Call Doctor Sinfahdi's office right now and see what time they open. This is the first time I've ever looked forward to going to see the doctor."

"Just be patient while I call," Mitch said.

The doctor's recorded message had said office hours were from 8:00 a.m. to 5:00 p.m., so Alan Jeffrey was in front of the door when the woman who sat behind the registration desk unlocked it. He pushed past her into the waiting room and announced he was here to see Doctor Sinfahdi.

"Do you have an appointment?" she asked.

"No, but it's very important. My uncle was a patient of his and I need to talk to the doctor right away this morning."

"Doctor is making hospital rounds," the woman said. "He always does that before he comes in."

"What time do you expect him?"

"We never know for sure." She walked around behind the counter and looked at the appointment book on the desk. "Doctor's first appointment today is at nine o'clock, so he should be here by then."

"That late?" Al didn't want to sit there cooling his heels for a whole hour.

"I'm sorry," the woman said. "Can someone else help you?"

"No, I'm afraid not." Then he had a thought. Maybe he could glean some more information and enlist some additional help before the doctor arrived. "Maybe I could speak to Nurse Darnell, if she's in." Surely, the nurse would be shocked to hear that one of the doctor's patients had died of an overdose of heroin.

"Oh, yes, Nurse Darnell is here. I'll buzz her."

A moment later, Nurse Emily Darnell, looking crisp and businesslike as always in her white uniform, appeared in the doorway that led to the offices and examining rooms. "Good morning, Mr. Jeffrey," she said in an even but pleasant tone. "Can I help you?"

"I think maybe you can," Al said. "I have some very important issues to discuss with Doctor Sinfahdi and, as his chief assistant, I think you should be told about what's been going on. You may want to give me some very valuable help when you hear what I know about the doctor."

The nurse's precisely-plucked eyebrows rose a scant fraction of an inch, but otherwise her expression did not change. "Really?" she said dryly. "Why don't we go back to a less public place and talk about whatever it is that you know?"

"Sounds good to me."

"Follow me, please." She turned to lead him down the hall and as he passed the registration desk he said softly to the woman, "A friend of mine will be joining me in a few minutes. When he gets here, bring him on back."

The emotional roller coaster on which Warren Mitchell had been riding kept him either fully or half awake until almost sunup, when he finally slid into a deep slumber. The alarm clock rang, he became semi-conscious long enough to hit the snooze button and then sat bolt upright five minutes later when the clock buzzed again. "I've got to get my ass out to Doctor Sinfahdi's office," he said over his shoulder to Sherlock Holmes on the way to the shower.

When he was dressed, he called Don O'Rourke at the city desk and told him that an investigative story he and Al had been working on was coming to a head this morning, and that if all went well they would have something exciting for the afternoon edition.

"It's about murder—several murders, in fact. Guaranteed to make your hair stand on end. I gotta go, Don. See ya." Mitch could imagine Don shaking his head, which was hairless except for a one-inch fringe just above the ears, as he put down the phone.

Mitch dumped some cat food into Sherlock's dish, filled his water bowl and walked quickly out to his car. As he backed out of his parking space into the alley, he found it very difficult to turn the steering wheel.

"Don't tell me," Mitch said. He put on the handbrake, walked around the car and discovered that the right front tire was flat. The only thing between the rim and the asphalt surface of the parking lot were two folds of collapsed rubber.

"Great timing!" Mitch said as he dragged out the jack and the lug wrench. "Well, Al baby, you're going to have to deal with Doctor Sinfahdi all by yourself for awhile."

Nurse Emily Darnell led Al into a large examining room furnished with chairs that looked much more comfortable than the straight-backed models one usually sees in a room filled with medical paraphernalia. She closed the door and motioned for him to sit. Seeing a quizzical look on his face as he sank into a high-backed upholstered armchair, she said, "This is a room where we examine and talk to some of our oldest and most difficult patients, and we want them to be comfortable while they're here."

"Very nice," Al said.

Nurse Darnell sat facing him in the other chair. She smiled ever so slightly, crossed her legs, which, Al noticed, were muscular but well-proportioned, and said, "Now, Mr. Jeffrey, just what is it that you know about Doctor Sinfahdi?"

He asked if she remembered a patient named Leonard Bombardier, who died in the Golden Pond home over the weekend. Still smiling, Nurse Darnell said she did recall Doctor Sinfahdi being summoned to Golden Pond to see a gentleman with that name. "Mr. Bombardier had suffered a stroke, as I recall," she said.

"Do you recall the gentleman dying?" Al asked.

"Yes, I do remember that he passed away. But please get to the point, Mr. Jeffrey. It's not unusual for elderly patients to succumb to serious ailments."

"That is my point. It's altogether too 'not unusual' for Doctor Sinfahdi's elderly patients to, as you say, succumb."

Her lips straightened to a hard line and her blue eyes turned icy. "Just what do you mean by that, Mr. Jeffrey?"

"I'll tell you what's happened and you can see for yourself. Mr. Bombardier's grandson, Richard, was the only relative living nearby, so he took charge of the body and the making of funeral arrangements. When he told his aunt in California that her father had died—apparently of heart failure—after being seen by Doctor Sinfahdi, she demanded that an autopsy be performed to determine the exact cause of death. ..."

The nurse cut him off with a sharp question, "Why would she do that?"

Al decided to fudge a little on the answer and omit the part about how he and Mitch had urged Richard Bombardier to request an autopsy. "She was upset because her mother also died immediately after being treated by Doctor Sinfahdi several months ago, also supposedly of heart failure," he said. "She wasn't comfortable with his diagnosis."

"I don't understand why the cause of death was so important to her. What does it matter, now that he's dead?"

"It turns out that it matters a great deal." Al decided it was necessary to share more information about his role in the matter. "You see, I've been concerned about my Uncle Charlie's death for quite some time because I have been meeting people like Richard Bombardier whose elderly relatives died of heart failure shortly after being treated by Doctor Sinfahdi, just like Uncle Charlie did. It seemed strange to me that they all died the same way within hours of the doctor's visit, but there was no way to double-check the cause of death because the bodies had all been cremated. So, when I saw that Mr. Bombardier and his aunt were quite upset after losing both relatives in basically the same way, I suggested an autopsy."

Nurse Darnell uncrossed her legs and leaned toward him. "And has this autopsy been performed?"

"Yes, it has." He looked at his watch, saw it was 8:15 and wondered why Mitch hadn't appeared. The reporter should be hearing this conversation.

She stood up, took a step back and said, "And you have the results?"

"That's what I came to talk to Doctor Sinfahdi about. I'm afraid those results will be a shock to you."

The nurse walked over to a supply cabinet attached to the wall on Al's right, turned around to face him and leaned back, resting her buns comfortably against the counter under the cabinet. "I'm not easily shocked, Mr. Jeffrey. What did the medical examiner tell your friend?"

"He told Richard that his grandfather apparently had died of an overdose of heroin. That the old man had enough morphine in his system to stop the heart of a much younger and healthier man."

Her voice was level and cool as she said, "Is it your feeling, then, that Doctor Sinfahdi had something to do with the administration of this heroin?" She half-turned away and opened the cabinet door. Al saw her take something out but her body blocked his view so he couldn't determine what it was.

Again Al looked at his watch. Where the hell was Mitch?

"I don't see any other possibility," he said. "Doctor Sinfahdi gave Grandpa Bombardier a shot and nobody else did anything except try to make him comfortable."

"You don't think it's possible that your friend provided his grandfather with a dose of heroin in order to make him, as you say, comfortable?" She had a package in her hand and was opening it while she spoke.

The nurse's calm demeanor in response to this information was beginning to worry Al. He remembered that Nurse Darnell had given some inaccurate patient death numbers to Jennifer Tilton. The thought occurred to him that he might be telling the nurse something that she already knew. It is possible, he thought, that she has been covering up for the doctor's crimes.

"I don't think so," Al said in response to her question about Richard Bombardier providing the heroin. "When Richard heard that his grandfather wasn't feeling well, he couldn't go out to Golden Pond right away because his business place had been vandalized and he was needed there. He didn't get out to Golden Pond until after his grandfather had the stroke, had been given an injection by Doctor Sinfahdi and was sleeping the sleep that turned out to be his last."

Her back was to him and she was doing something on the counter. "What about the nurses at the home? Why don't you suspect them?"

"Because my reporter friend and I have been doing some research and we have found that the death rate of Doctor Sinfahdi's patients far exceeds that of any other geriatric specialist in the area." Wondering what her reaction would be, he added, "I'm sorry to say this, Nurse Darnell, but it looks like your Doctor Sinfahdi has been systematically killing his patients before it was time for them to die of natural causes."

She laid the object in her hand on the counter and turned to face him. "How do you know it wasn't time for them to die? These people were very old and sick, Mr. Jeffrey. Maybe they were ready to move on to a better place." Her tone was still serenely calm and cool.

"And then again, maybe not. My Uncle Charlie seemed to be bouncing back from his stroke. Then, all of a sudden, he's dead of a so-called myocardial infarction."

"Sometimes it's best for these patients to pass on painlessly," the nurse said in a tone as soothing as a slow-running stream. "Think of the pain and suffering they are spared and the expenses that the families don't have to face. Prolonging life is not always best for people who are old and sick, Mr. Jeffrey."

Al sat up straight as the meaning of her words registered. "Then you know what Doctor Sinfahdi has been doing."

Nurse Darnell reached behind her and picked the object she had been working with off the counter. Al saw that it was a liquid-filled syringe capped with a long, thin needle. Her mouth and eyes formed a smile that sent a chill through Al's bones and he rose from the chair.

"Oh, my God!" Al said. "It isn't Doctor Sinfahdi who's been killing them. It's you!"

CHAPTER 28

GETTING TO THE POINT

In the parking area behind the apartment building on Grand Avenue, things were going from bad to worse for Warren Mitchell. He had jacked up the car, won the battle with some rusted-on lug nuts in order to remove the flat tire and had replaced it with the doughnut spare from the trunk. Then, when he let the car down off the jack, the doughnut collapsed almost all the way to the ground for want of air.

Uttering a string of expletives, Mitch jacked the car up again, removed the doughnut, carried it down the alley and walked up Grand Avenue for several blocks until he came to a service station with an air pump. "Al is going to be really pissed," Mitch thought as he rolled the inflated spare like a nine-teenth-century children's hoop back toward the apartment building. "He'll be getting a whole line of excuses and bullshit from Doctor Sinfahdi and I'm not there to write them down."

The syringe, with its slender, silvery needle, glistened in Nurse Darnell's right hand as she continued to lean comfortably back against the counter.

"Of course it was you," Al said. "You're the one who loads the syringes he uses for the shots he gives his patients."

The predatory smile faded from her face. "Doctor Sinfahdi is a kindly old man who has a deep concern for his patients," she said. "Sometimes he is blind to the reality of their need for release from the rigors of this life."

"But Nurse Darnell knows what's best for them?"

"And for all of us," she said in a soft, dreamy tone. "An injection of heroin, which is really just a much more potent derivation of the pain-killer commonly known as morphine, provides a smooth and quiet road to a better world for those who are no longer of any use in this one. When these people become so ill and so feeble that they are no longer able to care for themselves and are a burden to everyone around them, including the doctor, why should they not be allowed to pass away peacefully in their sleep?"

"What if they would just as soon hang around for awhile? What if their families don't mind taking care of them until nature takes its course?"

"That's really what is happening, Mr. Jeffrey. Nature is taking its course. The medication we're providing is merely assisting nature in the process and quite possibly freeing these patients from a much more painful demise. Don't you understand?" Her voice was close to a purr.

"I'm afraid I don't understand," Al said. "Some of these people might have several months or even years of life left if they were given the proper kind of medication."

"But how pleasant and productive would those months and years be? Think how frustrating it must be for an active person like your Uncle Charles to lie in bed half-paralyzed with people waiting on him hand and foot for who knows how long?"

"Think how those of us who loved Uncle Charlie miss him and would have liked to have had him around to talk to and play cribbage with for a few months or a year or so longer." In his mind, Al again was wondering why in the hell Mitch had not been brought to this room by now. Did the woman at the desk have orders from Nurse Darnell to detain him?

"You'd have soon gotten tired of it," she said, standing up straight and cradling the syringe in her left hand. "I've seen how long-term care of bedridden patients affects family members. Believe me, Mr. Jeffrey, what we have been doing here is a service both to our patients and to their families."

"You're saying 'we.' What is Doctor Sinfahdi's part in all this? Does he or does he not know what is going on?"

"I used the word 'we' in the editorial sense, Mr. Jeffrey. As a newspaperman, you should understand that. Doctor Sinfahdi is a kindly and somewhat forgetful old man who would never for one minute suspect that he was providing nature with a means of accelerating its final course."

"But he examined all these bodies and said they died of heart failure."

"They did die of heart failure. Heroin will stop the heart and so will potassium chloride, and they don't leave any external signs. Doctor Sinfahdi determined that the hearts of these extremely frail people had failed and he saw no need to look further for a cause of death. If you look at the records, you will find that all of them had previous symptoms of a heart condition. Until now, none of the families has been rude enough to ask for an autopsy. Some have even made contributions to our clinic in gratitude for the care Doctor Sinfahdi had been providing. Most people are grateful, not angry and suspicious like you and the Bombardiers."

"You can tell that story to a judge. When I leave this office, I'm going directly to the police."

"I don't think so," she said in almost a whisper. Her eyes were like pale blue chips of ice. "Younger men, even some in their middle thirties, also have been known to die of an unexpected failure of the heart."

She took a step toward him and Al, seeing that the needle in her hand was pointing straight at him, took a quick step toward the door.

"That won't do you any good," she said in a louder, matter-of-fact voice. "We often have patients who will wander away if they are left alone too long, so the lock on the door of this room can only be opened with a key." She reached into the pocket of her skirt and held up a ring from which dangled a half-dozen keys. "You need one of these to get out." The keys went back into her pocket and she took another step toward him.

Al saw no place to go. The only two chairs in the room were too heavy to pick up and use as shields and there was no other loose furniture. He could play tag around one of the chairs for awhile but eventually she would catch up and he would have to wrestle her for the needle.

Maybe he could scare her off. "I have a partner joining me here in a few minutes," Al said. "He should actually be here by now. He'll know damn well that you're responsible if he finds me dead."

"Victoria's messenger riding comes," Nurse Darnell said. "That's from my favorite musical, 'Threepenny Opera.' Do you know it?" Another step on her part sent Al stepping quickly back behind the chair.

"I do. And I also know that Victoria's messenger does arrive in time to save Mack the Knife from the hangman's noose."

"That was fiction, Mr. Jeffrey. And this is fact. First of all, I don't believe you. Second, even if your friend does come, he will find us feverishly trying to revive the victim of a tragic heart attack. Unsuccessfully, I might add." The smile returned to her lips but the eyes remained frozen.

"I guarantee you there will be an autopsy if my partner finds me dead when he gets here. He has been involved in the research on Doctor Sinfahdi's dying patients from the beginning and he knows things aren't right here."

"In that case, I suppose Nurse Emily Darnell will have to move on to bigger and better things in some distant place with no forwarding address before the autopsy is conducted." She moved toward him, brandishing the syringe as she spoke, and they began a slow circle dance around the chair as he desperately tried to stay beyond the reach of the needle's tip. "Come on, Mr. Jeffrey, it's time we take our medicine," she said in her most soothing nurse's bedside voice.

CHAPTER 29

CLOSING THE CIRCLE

Al's hands were wet and slippery with sweat as he gripped the shoulder-high chair back. He discovered that by tilting the big chair onto its back legs he was able to pivot it around on the slick linoleum floor so that the full depth of the chair was between him and Nurse Emily Darnell. The tip of the gleaming needle was only inches from his hands as she stretched out her arm in an effort to drive the point into his flesh. Her smile broadened and her eyes gleamed with excitement as she feinted first left and then right and then leaped and jabbed at him with the syringe.

Al pulled away from the thrust, dropping the chair as he drew back and Nurse Darnell quickly slipped around behind it so that she could control the fulcrum, chasing him to the front of the chair with her strategic move. He heard himself shouting for help as she gripped the back of the chair with her left hand and planned her next move. Her chin was just above the tall chair back, and he could see the satisfied smile on her lips and the heady look of the huntress in her eyes.

"You might as well save your breath for your next try at playing dodge ball," Nurse Darnell said. "We also made this room virtually soundproof so that screaming Alzheimer's patients wouldn't disturb the rest of the clinic."

He yelled for help again, anyway, hoping that someone might be passing close enough to hear him. He saw that the nurse was clearly enjoying his performance. She was actually resting her forearms on the back of the chair and grinning at him. She waggled the syringe in her right hand and said, "Give it up, Mr. Jeffrey, and come get your nice little fix of heroin."

Al had a desperate thought. If he suddenly pushed the chair into her, he might throw her off balance long enough to get a grip on the hand that held the syringe. In fact, if he pushed hard enough he might even shove Nurse Darnell all the way to the wall, which was only about three feet behind her. If he could pin her there ... And then what? How long could he hold her? Could he grab her hand before she stuck him and pushed the plunger? It was worth a shot.

Al grabbed the front of the chair arms and slammed all his weight against them, moving the chair quickly toward the nurse's body. But he had waited a split-second too long. She had already raised up and was moving to her right as the chair came at her. Her momentum allowed her to squeeze out from behind the chair before it hit the wall with a thud. Now she was free and the protective back of the chair was jammed tight against the wall.

"Looks like we've lost our little shield, Mr. Jeffrey," Nurse Darnell said. "Why don't we just sit down and take our medicine like a good boy?"

Gesturing toward the seat, she came toward him again. Al, who had jumped quickly to the side opposite Nurse Darnell, tried to twist the chair so he could get behind it but he realized that he would then be pinned against the wall and she could come right over the chair and stab him. He wanted at least to have a shot at wrestling the syringe out of her hand so he stepped away from the chair, leaving nothing between them but six feet of open floor.

The nurse crouched like a cougar stalking its prey and took another step toward him. Al's hands were up in a defensive position, ready to grab at her arm if she lunged, as he took another step back—a move that brought him one step closer to the wall at his back. "Where in hell is that goddamn reporter?" he asked himself as he stared into the glistening blue eyes of the woman who was preparing to strike him dead.

The goddamn reporter was cursing his luck as he sat in a long line of motionless vehicles waiting to be waved through an accident scene. Some idiot in an SUV had been following too closely and had rear-ended the car in front of him when the driver made the mistake of stopping for a yellow light. The car had been pushed partly to the left, so that both northbound lanes were blocked and a police officer was funneling traffic around the damaged vehicles at what seemed to Mitch to be a snail's pace.

"I'm missing all the fun," Mitch said, fuming at the officer's lack of urgency. The officer let six cars ahead of Mitch pass through the intersection, then called a halt, leaving Mitch's car the second one in line. "Damn it, why couldn't you have waved two more of us through?" Mitch muttered.

Again he sat and waited and fumed.

"By now Al will have Doctor Sinfahdi pinned against the wall, begging for mercy," Mitch mused. "He'll have the little bastard all wrapped up and ready to be hauled off to jail before I get there. Come on, cop, let us go!"

In reality, it was Alan Jeffrey who was pinned against the wall, but he knew it would be useless to beg for mercy. He had retreated as far as he could go and was trying to decide whether it would be better to make a move toward Nurse Darnell or wait until she attacked and try to parry her thrust. He felt a chill and realized that his clothes were soaked with sweat and rivulets of water were running down his face.

"I'm really very good at giving shots, Mr. Jeffrey," she said, again using the bedside voice. "This won't hurt a bit. And when it's over, you can just sit down in that chair you like so much and drift off into a nice, peaceful sleep."

"Sorry, I'm not sleepy," Al said. "In fact, I'd just as soon stay awake for another fifty years or so."

"Isn't it a shame your heart isn't strong enough for that? Just look how you're perspiring. It's obvious that a severe cardiac event is about to occur."

Al's gaze was fixed on the needle that was aiming straight at his torso. He decided to go on the offensive and was gathering himself for a decisive counter-attack when they heard the locked doorknob rattle.

The sound distracted them both, delaying Al's rush and taking Nurse Darnell's unwavering gaze off him for a split second. The nurse looked back in time to see him start moving toward her and she sprang backwards across the room just as the door swung open. Standing in the doorway with a key ring in his hand was Doctor Ravi Sinfahdi.

At last Warren Mitchell was past the accident scene, through the clogged intersection and on his way to Doctor Sinfahdi's office. "What else can go wrong this morning?" he wondered. "Flat tires. Accidents. I sure as hell hope Al made it to the clinic in time to catch the doctor before he went off to give somebody else a going away shot this morning."

Mitch's attention wandered briefly to the sound on the radio. They were playing Bobby Darrin's recording of "Mack the Knife." Mitch hit the button and changed the station. "Never did like that version," he said to himself. He preferred to hear songs from the "The Threepenny Opera" performed the way they were written.

"Damn, I hope I haven't missed all the fun," Mitch said as he finally turned into the strip mall and parked in front of Doctor Sinfahdi's clinic. "The way things have been going for me, Al could have finished with the doctor and called Bombardier and the cops. They could have him on the way to jail by now."

A quizzical expression came over the little doctor's wrinkled bronze face as he looked around the room, first at the nurse, then at Al and then back to Emily Darnell, who stood frozen with the syringe still in her hand. The look of excitement and triumph that had been on her face as she stalked Alan Jeffrey had changed to what Al later described as "the proverbial deer in the headlights."

"Nurse Darnell, I'm sorry," Doctor Sinfahdi said. "The door was locked. I had no idea that anyone was in here."

"That's okay, Doctor," she said in a half-whisper. "No problem."

"What are you doing?" the doctor asked, the look of confusion and curiosity still in his eyes as he focused on the syringe in her right hand.

A mask of calm came over Nurse Darnell's face as she replied: "I was talking with Mr. Jeffrey about a wound I had sustained from a rusty nail and I was just about to give myself a tetanus shot." With that, she slipped the needle smoothly into the soft flesh on the inside of her forearm.

"No!" Al screamed, leaping across the room to grab her. But he was too late. She had pushed the plunger all the way down, sending the deadly fluid gushing into her arm.

Al was grasping her upper arms with both hands, and she looked into his eyes with their faces only inches apart and smiled serenely. "Like I told you, Nurse Emily Darnell will be going to some distant place with no forwarding address," she said.

She pulled against his grip and he let her go, standing in horrified silence while she calmly deposited the syringe in the proper receptacle under the counter, walked to the other chair and sat down, still smiling. "I will admit this wasn't quite the place I had in mind," she said.

Al finally regained the power of speech. Turning to Doctor Sinfahdi, he yelled, "You've got to save her, Doctor. She's just poisoned herself!"

Those were the first words Warren Mitchell heard as he entered the room running at almost full speed, with the startled receptionist in pursuit a half-dozen steps behind.

CHAPTER 30

SUCH SWEET SORROW

Doctor Ravi Sinfahdi's face showed complete incomprehension as he said, "I don't understand, Mr. Jeffrey. She's given herself a tetanus shot."

"That tetanus shot was a load of heroin," Al said. "You need to give her some kind of antidote."

"You must be mistaken," the doctor said. "We have no heroin here."

"I told you he had no clue," Nurse Darnell said from the chair. Al saw triumph in her smile and noted that her face had become slightly flushed.

"What the hell is going on?" Warren Mitchell asked from the doorway.

"That needle was loaded with heroin," Al said, his face inches from Doctor Sinfahdi's. "She's trying to kill herself and you need to give her something to stop it."

"There is no heroin in this office," Doctor Sinfahdi said again. "Are you all right, Nurse Darnell?"

"I'm fine, Doctor" she said with a reassuring smile.

"She's confessed to me that she's been killing your patients with heroin and now she's killing herself, you idiot," Al shouted into the doctor's face. "Do something for her, for Christ's sake!"

"Please calm down, Mr. Jeffrey," Doctor Sinfahdi said, backing away. "I don't know what you're talking about."

Al heaved a sigh of despair, turned to Mitch and said, "Go out front and call 911 and tell them we've got a woman heavily OD'd on heroin. Quick!"

"They'll never make it in time," said Nurse Darnell. "You might as well save them the trip." She was sliding down in the chair with her limbs flopping loosely like a rag doll as she spoke.

"You're not getting off that easy," Al said. "I want you alive so you can face the families of all those people you killed." He grabbed her arms up near her shoulders, jerked her toward him, peered into her face and saw that the pupils in her ice-blue eyes had become mere pin pricks.

"Sorry, but I'm on my way to facing somebody—or something—else," she said in a dreamy whisper. She closed her eyes and Al sensed that she was barely breathing.

He let go of her arms and she sank back against the chair. He watched in horror as the muscles throughout her body tightened and contorted while she went through a brief series of convulsions. Desperately, he ran back to Doctor Sinfahdi, who had turned away to question the receptionist about the identity of these visitors, spun the little man around by the shoulder and shouted in his face, "Jesus, Doctor, don't you have anything to counteract heroin in this office?"

"We have no need for anything of that sort, Mr. Jeffrey," the doctor said. "We don't treat drug addicts here." He looked again toward the nurse and asked, "Nurse Darnell, are you sure you're all right?"

This time there was no answer from the limp form lying in the chair.

The ambulance arrived five minutes later while Al was trying to explain what had happened to a still-uncomprehending Doctor Sinfahdi and an astonished Warren Mitchell.

"Pulse is faint and irregular," they heard one EMT say as the rescue crew wheeled the gurney bearing the unconscious nurse out of the room. "B.P. is ..." and they were gone out of earshot.

"I'm afraid I still don't understand what is going on," Doctor Sinfahdi said when the room was quiet.

"Sit down, doctor, and we'll go over this from the very beginning," Al said. "Then I'm sure the police will want to talk to you about what has happened to quite a number of your patients. You might want to call your lawyer to have him sit in with you when they come."

"First, run through your session with the nurse real quick; I can still phone in a story for the afternoon edition," Mitch said.

"Guess what," Al said. "I didn't even get any pix of the killer."

City Editor Don O'Rourke was stunned by Mitch's tale of multiple murders—at least fifteen and probably many more—and an attempt on the life of a Daily Dispatch photographer. Mitch composed the story in his head and dictated the words to a rewrite man who kept interrupting with interjections of incredulity.

Mitch finally said, "Just shut up and take what I'm giving you, okay? I know this stuff is hard to believe, but we're on a goddamn deadline." When he finished, he apologized and told the rewrite man to have someone call Regions Hospital to check on Nurse Emily Darnell's condition. "Find out if she's still alive and get that in the story," he said. "We'll be in after we clean up things out here."

Cleaning up things in Doctor Sinfahdi's office took the rest of the morning and part of the afternoon as detectives, lawyers from the D.A.'s office, the doctor's attorney and the bewildered doctor himself peppered Al and Mitch with questions. Carefully skirting any mention of their uninvited nocturnal perusal of the doctor's files, the pair described how they "put two and two together" and came up with the "four-gone" conclusion that Doctor Sinfahdi had been systematically killing his patients.

"Then, when I told Nurse Darnell that we were going to go to the police with the evidence we had gathered, she made it quite plain that it wasn't the doctor who was loading up the needles," Al said. "In fact, she gave me a demonstration that I'll remember for as long as I live."

Al and Mitch parked their cars side by side in the ramp in Lowertown, hiked through the skyway and walked into the office together shortly after two o'clock. They were immediately surrounded by excited colleagues clamoring for more details and offering congratulations for a great story. Even Don O'Rourke, who normally went home at 1:30 because he started work at five in the morning, was still in the office, awaiting their arrival.

When the hubbub subsided, Al asked the question that had been on both their minds as they drove in from Doctor Sinfahdi's office: "What's the word on Nurse Darnell?"

"She didn't make it," said Don O'Rourke. "Her heart stopped on the way in to the hospital."

"Shit!" said Al.

"I talked to one of the EMTs who took her to the hospital," Don said. "He said if she was shooting pure heroin that she had enough in that syringe to croak a goddamn horse."

"Well, she won't have to face the families of her victims or go to court either, but I hope she's in front of an even tougher judge than she'd have stood before here on earth," said Al.

"So, what happens next?" asked Don.

"Next, the homicide detectives, with Doctor Sinfahdi's help, comb through the records and try to figure out exactly how many people that nutty nurse sent to an early grave," Mitch said.

"Then, after the families are told and the lawsuits roll in, I suspect Doctor Sinfahdi's practice will be as dead as all those patients," said Al.

Al arrived home at about 3:30 and found Carol swabbing the kitchen floor with a wet mop.

"Hi, gorgeous," he said. "What's the joke of the day?"

"Wow! You're home early," Carol said, leaning the mop against the kitchen counter and giving Al a hug. "How was your day?"

"Here," he said, handing her the afternoon edition with Mitch's story at the top of page one. "Read all about it."

He went to the phone in the kitchen to call Richard Bombardier while she was unfolding the paper. Bombardier was just saying "hello," when Al heard Carol shriek, "Oh, my God!"

Nobody welcomed Warren Mitchell with a hug when he arrived at his home on Grand Avenue. Sherlock Holmes gave him the usual feline felicitations but Mitch really wanted a human forum where he could unload his story and vent his pent-up emotions.

Mitch wondered if Martha Todd had returned from wherever it was she had gone. He was sure that she would want to hear how they had discovered the truth about her Grandpa Mendes's death. Down the hall he went, but he got no response when he knocked on Martha's door.

"Damn!" said Mitch. Maybe Mrs. Peterson was home. He really should warn her that the homicide squad would be calling on her to discuss her sister's death at the hands of Nurse Emily Darnell.

Mrs. Peterson did answer his knock. "Oh, Mr. Mitchell," she said. "What can I do for you?"

"It's what I can do for you," he said. "I have some news about Doctor Sinfahdi and your sister. Have you got a minute?"

Her tone was cautious. "Yah, I guess so."

"I'm not going to ask you again to exhume your sister's body. There's no need for that anymore."

"In that case, come in and sit down." She steered him toward a chair, gave him some peanut butter cookies and a cup of coffee from the pot that always seemed to be on and listened in fascination and horror as he described the morning's events. He ended by telling her to expect a visit from the homicide detectives who would most likely be contacting all the families involved.

"They won't want me to dig up my sister's body, will they?" Mrs. Peterson asked.

"I can't imagine that they would. They'll probably just want to discuss the circumstances surrounding her death with you."

"How many others were killed by that crazy nurse?"

"Al and I are pretty sure of at least fifteen, and I'm betting the police will turn up quite a few more. I'm going to stay on the story so I'll let you know what they find out."

"Or I could read it in the paper, huh?"

"I hope you will."

She thanked Mitch for the information and he went back to his apartment. The coffee and cookies had been good but he wanted something cold to drink. As usual, the refrigerator was empty.

"Damn!" he said again. He thought a moment, then went out the door and headed up the street for Herby's to get a ginger ale with ice and a bowl of popcorn.

Carol was practically hysterical by the time Al finished briefing Richard Bombardier on the morning's discovery. He kept the phone conversation short by omitting the details of the deadly game of tag he had played with Nurse Darnell.

Most of those details were in the story Carol was reading. "She came after you with a needle full of poison?" she said the second Al hung up.

"Yeah, but I didn't get the point," he said.

"Oh, stop with the stupid puns. You could be dead!"

"If her arms were two inches longer I probably would be. Lucky for me she wasn't six feet tall."

Carol wrapped the length of her arms around him and hugged him so tight his breath whooshed out. "What were you thinking of, going there all by yourself?"

"I didn't plan to be all by myself. Mitch was supposed to meet me there but he had a flat tire and then got hung up in traffic."

"You idiot, you have a wife and two children who love you and want you around for awhile."

"I know, I know. I wanted Uncle Charlie to be around for awhile, too. Which reminds me, I should call Diana and tell her what happened before she sees the story in the paper or on the TV news."

He punched in the number and heard it ring again and again. After ten rings he hung up. "That's strange," he said. "There doesn't seem to be anybody home and the answering machine isn't picking up. Why would she turn it off?"

CHAPTER 31

HOME SWEET HOME

Mitch found the atmosphere in Herby's to be exactly what he needed for the process of unwinding, even with a drink that contained no relaxant. He even struck up a brief conversation with the man on the adjacent barstool about this summer's two major items of distress: the unbearably muggy weather and the unbelievably inept Minnesota Twins.

He was feeling quite relaxed when he got home just in time to turn on the five o'clock news. Everyone in the Twin Cities was on the story by now, of course, and the Channel Five newscast led with the fatal confrontation between Nurse Emily Darnell and Daily Dispatch photographer Alan Jeffrey. The reporter was shown "live in Roseville," standing in the parking lot outside Doctor Ravi Sinfahdi's office, as she summarized the day's exciting events.

A minute later the phone rang and it was Jennifer Tilton.

"I can't believe what I just saw on the news," she said.

"You can believe it," said Mitch. "From what Al said, if that nurse was a little taller we'd be planning his funeral right now."

"At least I was right about Doctor Sinfahdi. I never thought he was the kind of man who would go around killing people."

"No, he had a silent partner that even he didn't know about. It's just too bad she won't be around to face the consequences."

"I'm glad Al is all right. And that you are, too."

"Yeah, the action was all over by the time I got there, thanks to a flat tire and an accident caused by some damn fool SUV driver."

"I'll bet Al was glad to see you, no matter what time you got there."

"He'd have been a hell of a lot gladder several minutes earlier. God knows what would have happened if Doctor Sinfahdi hadn't opened the door when he did."

"Kind of weird, isn't it? You guys have spent all summer chasing after Doctor Sinfahdi, and accusing him of murdering all kinds of people, and then he comes along and maybe saves Al's life."

"Yeah, it's been frustrating, but when Nurse Darnell killed off Richard Bombardier's grandfather, that was the straw that broke the camel's back— or, in this case, the corpse that broke the camel's back. She finally provided us with a chance to get an autopsy."

After an awkward moment of silence, Jennifer said, "So ... um ... how have you been doing?"

"Fine. And you?"

"I've been real busy. I'm trying to clean up the house so the real estate guy can start showing it to buyers at the same time I'm packing up to move."

"When are you leaving?" Mitch asked.

"Pretty soon. I want to get the kids settled in the new place before school starts at the end of August."

"That's right, it's almost August already, isn't it? I've kind of lost track of what month—or even what day—it is."

"You're not drinking again, are you?" He was pleased to hear genuine concern in her voice.

"Yes, I am. I've become addicted to ginger ale," he said. "After my poorly-timed visit to your bedroom, I went to a neighborhood bar with every intention of getting drunk, but I chickened out at the last minute."

"I've thought about you a lot. I knew you were really pissed off and I was worried that you might do something foolish."

"Nice of you to worry," he said in the most sarcastic tone he could muster.

"Mitch, I really do care about you. You helped save my children from God knows what and you're the sweetest man I've ever met."

"Then why are you marrying Adam?"

"For one thing, he asked me. And, more than that, he was and always will be my first love. But that doesn't mean I don't feel bad about leaving you. We had some really great times together."

"I won't argue that. I just wish I had been smart enough to propose to you before Adam did."

"It's probably good that you didn't. What if we had been engaged when I went out to New Jersey and fell in love with Adam again? That would have been really rough on both of us."

"Maybe it wouldn't have happened."

"I'm afraid it would have. One look at him and I melted like an ice cream cone on one of these awful hot days."

"Then it probably is a good thing that I didn't have the balls to propose."

"You have wonderful balls. I'll never forget them."

"They won't forget you, either, believe me."

After another awkward moment of silence, she said, "Maybe we'd better not talk about that any more."

"No, I guess we'd better think about something more appropriate, now that we won't be seeing that much of each other any more."

"Yes. Oh, that reminds me, the kids would like to say goodbye to Uncle Mitch before we move. Can you come out for a little while some day?"

He felt a stinging in his eyes as the tears formed. "Sure," he said. "Just give me a call when you want me to come."

The next morning was spent talking to investigators from the police departments of St. Paul, Roseville and Maplewood and both the sheriff's office and the district attorney's office of Ramsey County. These were mutual quiz sessions, with Al and Mitch both asking and answering questions as everyone sought to unravel the stories told by Doctor Sinfahdi's medical records.

The doctor, who was in a state of shock that rendered him almost robotic, was helping as best he could. Already a perusal of Nurse Darnell's computer had told investigators that she had fabricated medical histories for many of the patients for whom she had prepared lethal injections, so that anyone looking at the records would find a history of pre-existing heart problems.

Al was allowed to look at Uncle Charlie's chart and found that it contained two examinations involving complaints of chest pains and shortness of breath, which the doctor supposedly had diagnosed as a weakness in the 75-year-old man's heart muscle.

"Are these real?" Al asked Doctor Sinfahdi.

The doctor studied the chart for several minutes before he answered, "My memory is not perfect, Mr. Jeffrey, but I do not remember ever treating your uncle for anything involving his heart. As far as I can recall, the myocardial infarction that occurred after he was weakened by his stroke was the first incidence of heart disease."

"So the information in this chart is false?"

"I believe so, yes. You might double-check with his wife. As I said, my memory is not perfect and I am extremely upset today."

"Good idea. I'll talk to his wife later today and see if she remembers him being treated for any chest pains or shortness of breath."

Back at the office, Mitch wrote a follow-up story and Al turned in photos of the doctor being questioned and the investigative team looking at patients' records. Mitch had given them his list of possible victims—minus the names gleaned from the late-night invasion of the doctor's office—and had called some of the families he had talked with previously. Most had seen the story in the paper or on television and all were horrified.

By late afternoon, the only family Mitch hadn't been able to contact was Martha Todd's. He left a message on Martha's answering machine and told Al there was no way he was going to be the one to call and break the news to Gramma Mendes if she hadn't already heard about it.

Mitch's last call of the day was to Doctor Sinfahdi's clinic, where he spoke to the man from the DA's office.

"Any idea what the total number of deaths will be?" Mitch asked.

"We're up to twenty-five and still counting," said the attorney. "We could be looking at something like forty or fifty. This woman has been killing off the doctor's patients for years."

"Why the hell would she do that?"

"Who knows? Maybe in her delusion she really thought she was doing them a favor. More likely, she was just a fiendish psychopath. The receptionist told us that Nurse Darnell was a control freak—that she ran the office and Doctor Sinfahdi was like a puppet on a string. Unfortunately, the nurse is not around to tell us what was really in her mind. What we're going to do is interview everybody we can find who knew Nurse Darnell and see if we can figure out whether she had any motive beyond a psychopathic need for control over other people's lives—and deaths."

"How's Doctor Sinfahdi holding up?"

"Oh, haven't you heard? We shipped him off to Regions Hospital a couple of hours ago because he was having chest pains and difficulty breathing. Kind of ironic, wouldn't you say?"

"Will he be okay?"

"Probably. Lucky for him he won't be getting an injection prepared by his most trusted assistant, Nurse Emily Darnell."

At home thirty minutes later, Mitch was discussing supper options with Sherlock Holmes. Should he go to the Index Café, stopping at Herby's for an icy ginger ale on the way, or should he open the last box of macaroni and cheese in the cupboard? Sherlock was being noncommittal when Mitch heard a knock at the door. When he opened it, he was pleased to find that Martha Todd had returned to Grand Avenue.

Alan Jeffrey could not explain the sense of foreboding he felt in his gut as he walked up to the front door of his Uncle Charlie's house. He had attempted to call Diana about his uncle's medical history and again the phone had not been picked up, either by her or the answering machine. Frustrated, he had decided to pay a visit in person after work to see if he could catch Diana at home. He still could not fathom why she would turn off the answering machine when she went out.

It was so quiet that the house seemed almost asleep. Al was about to ring the bell when he saw a manila envelope taped to the wooden door inside the screen door. He opened the screen door for a closer look and saw his name printed on the envelope in large black letters.

He sat down on the doorstep and opened the envelope. Inside were some legal-looking papers and a note written in Diana's free-flowing feminine hand, with large looping letters and a little circle dotting every "i." It said:

> *Dear Nephew Al,*
>
> *Enclosed is the deed to this house, which I have signed over to you in the presence of a notary pending your acceptance of the transaction in front of same. It might be a little complicated without me being there at the same time, but I want you to have the property as I no longer have any use for it.*
>
> *You were right about one thing: I did marry your Uncle Charlie for his money. What I hadn't counted on was that I actually fell in love with the sweet old fart after living with him for awhile. What I need to do now is move on and find a rich guy my own age so I can have both money and a real marriage, maybe even with a kid. That isn't going to happen around here.*
>
> *Don't bother trying to find me because I'm not even telling my parents where I'm going until sometime in the future.*
>
> *As ever,*
> *Your Auntie Diana*
>
> *P.S.—There's just one little item involving the house. I borrowed $200,000 against it before I signed it over to you. That and the money from Charlie's life insurance policy should take care of me until I find the millionaire of my dreams. I'm sure you won't mind paying off my little home equity loan. Where else can you get a nice house with a pool and an acre of land in the suburbs for a measly two-hundred grand?*
>
> *P.S. No. 2.—I'm sorry you're such a wimp about cheating on your wife. I'd have loved to have screwed you that way, too.*

Al read the note again in disbelief. Then he pulled out the rest of the papers from the envelope and gave everything a shake. His generous Auntie Diana had neglected to include one small item: a key to any of the doors.

"I got your message but I'd already read it in the paper this morning in Chicago," Martha Todd said as Mitch ushered her into his apartment. "There's nothing like being in an airport 400 miles from home and reading about your grampa's doctor and his serial killer nurse."

"Yeah, the body count was up to twenty-five this afternoon, and the D.A. said they're expecting it to run into the forties or fifties before they're done. The woman was an unbelievable monster."

"Do they have any idea why she did it?"

"They think it most likely was just a power trip. They're going to talk to everybody who knew her to see if there was any kind of hint that the woman was a silent psychopath. I think that part of the story will be keeping me busy for quite awhile."

"Will it be keeping you busy over this coming weekend?" she asked. "On Sunday afternoon, to be specific."

Mitch had a feeling that Jennifer Tilton would be asking him to come and say goodbye to Tony and Tracy Sunday afternoon, but he decided that the kids could wait, an adult bird in the hand being worth two babies in the Afton bush. "I'm not doing anything on Sunday," he said. "What's up?"

"You remember those Twins' tickets we talked about way back before you knew you were chasing a serial killer?"

"Sure, I remember."

"I just acquired two for Sunday's game with the Yankees. Are you interested?"

"Is the pope Catholic? I'd love to go."

"It's a date, then," Martha said, starting toward the door.

"Have you had dinner?" he asked before she turned the knob.

"No, I haven't. I got home, changed out of my travel clothes, listened to your message, phoned Gramma and came over here."

"Why don't we go someplace where you can get something vegetarian and we can talk about your trip? Or were you off in Chicago seeing an old boyfriend that I don't want to hear about?" He wanted to bite right through his tongue one nanosecond after blurting out that question.

She smiled. "Poor Mitch," she said. "No, I don't have any old boyfriends in Chicago, whether you want to hear about them or not. And I do know a great place for vegetarian goodies right on Grand Avenue."

He had noticed something different about her and decided to speak up. "You're letting your hair grow out," he said. "I like it." Indeed, the black strands had increased in length until they looked more like a grown-out crew cut than her usual close shave.

"Thank you," she said. "I decided it was time. I shaved it in the first place because my ex-husband used to drag me around the kitchen floor by it after he knocked me down and kicked me."

"Jesus! That won't happen again."

"Damn right it won't. Give me a minute to grab my purse and we can head out for that restaurant."

She actually trusts me, Mitch thought as he watched Martha walk down the hall to her apartment at the other end of the building. With a feeling of pride, he said softly, "You can bet your sweet ass that this guy will never put a bruise on that body."

In the house on Hamline Avenue, Alan Jeffrey was reading Diana's note—all except the P.S. No. 2—to Carol. He had sent the children "out to play" before his oration so that he would have fewer questions to answer.

"So what are you going to do?" Carol asked when he finished.

"I have no clue," Al said. "What do you think I, or we, should do?"

"Obviously we either have to move into Uncle Charlie's house or sell it fast."

"I've figured out that much. Either way, we're going to be selling a house. The question is, which one?"

"Uncle Charlie's has two bathrooms—and a swimming pool."

"It also has acquired a new mortgage that could put us in over our heads."

"Only if we go off the deep end on other expenditures."

"My God, now you're spouting puns!"

"It's the wave of the future. And you'll be all washed up if I have to tell your children that you sold a house with a swimming pool, a bathroom they could have all to themselves and a backyard as big as a park."

"I can't swim against the tide," he said. "I'm going under." Maybe he should be feeling an afterglow from the figurative screwing that Diana had given him, he thought. If nothing else, Carol seemed to be looking forward to the climax.

The End